The *Ganzfield* Series

Minder
Adversary
Legacy
Accused (August 2011)

Praise for *Minder* and *Adversary*

"A Blkosiner's "Top Ten Authors" Pick"
"5/5...*Minder* grabbed my attention and did not let go!"
"5/5...*Adversary* did not disappoint...the action starts quickly and doesn't let go...Kate writes with beauty and fluidity. Her characters are real to me, and the way she writes them, I laugh with them, mourn with them, and am joyful with them."
— Blkosiner's Book Blog

A Reading Teen "What to Read This Summer" Pick for 2010: *Minder*
Minder: "Absolutely flawless!"
Adversary: "6 out of 6...I loved this book! Even better than *Minder*! It was exciting, surprising, and *completely* exceeded my expectations!"
— Reading Teen

A Missy's Reads and Reviews Featured Series: *Ganzfield*
"5 Stars: I thought I was smart by trying to guess throughout the book what was going to happen next...and found myself completely wrong every single time!"
— Missy's Reads and Reviews

"5/5: Amazing. Kate Kaynak's world is both incredibly original and believable at the same time. The characters are fun, passionate and completely unforgettable...*Adversary* had me on the edge of my seat for the entire ride...I am beginning to believe Kate Kaynak is a G-Positive as her storytelling "superpower" will leave the reader breathless—and wanting more...Kate's done it again...put everything down so you can read this in one sitting...If you haven't already, pick this series up now. You won't be disappointed!"
— Books Complete Me

"*Minder* is dynamic, original, thoughtful, and entrancing...nothing short of brilliant. Both *Minder* as well as *Adversary* leave you holding your breath while laughing out loud. With its original concepts, dynamic and flawless writing, *Adversary* is a book I am thrilled to have on my shelves."
— Book Crazy

"5 out of 5 Stars: I don't know if it was the author's style of writing, the story line, the characters, or what - but this book had me hooked! I laughed out loud on the subway! People looked at me like I was crazy - but I didn't care. It's been a while since a book made me smile and laugh out loud."
— Good Choice Reading

"I LOVED it!! I was totally caught up in the story and couldn't wait to see what would happen next...*Minder* is a terrific read for both teens and adults."
— Sidhe Vicious Reviews

"I was blown away by the first chapter...the writing was flawless...The romance in this book is ah-mazing...This book was PHENOM and I loved it. The ending was effing epic and showed how awesome Maddie really is. I give this book an A+."
— Books and Wits

"*Minder* is an exciting debut, and a wonderful start to a series...The story really is addictive...I could barely get enough of it."
— YA Book Queen

"A fun and intriguing read that pulled me in immediately."
— Candace's Book Blog

"It. Some books have *it*, some don't. *It* is simply what makes you keep reading, what pulls you forward, what keeps a book niggling in your mind until you simply have to reread it...or pick up the sequel. *Minder* has *it*."
Adversary: "Wow. Just...Wow. I can't even begin to tell you how impressed I was by this book...a story that I just *could not put down*."
— Elephants on Trapezes

"This is a must read. Kaynak brings plenty of action, unique story telling, and lots of romance...be prepared for lots of swooning. "
— Cari's Book Blog

"Minder is an engaging psychological thriller with a streak of science fiction for good measure. The world Kate Kaynak creates is dark and twisted, full of intense young adult issues as well as looming supernatural threats and a mesmerizing and heart-pounding race against time. "
— The Bookish Type

"Five stars. *Minder* is fast-paced, edgy, highly powerful and thrilling. It will give you that adrenaline rush and make you grit your teeth in anticipation. Read, enjoy and indulge—this is one ride you will not forget."
— Fantasy for Eva

"I gave this book five coffee cups...Absolutely amazing! I love this book!"
— Elena's Book Café

"WOW! That's the first thought that came to mind when I finished reading *Minder*. I had such an overwhelming feeling of sweet reward and satisfaction from reading this book! I had a silly grin on my face. This book pulled me out of my reading slump...Word to the wise: don't make any plans once you pick up *Minder;* you won't be able to put it down once you start reading!"
"Brilliant! Absolutely brilliant! The author's knack for storytelling is beyond fascinating. Fans of *Harry Potter* and *Fantastic Four* will enjoy this series."
— The Book Vixen

"5-stars...I loved this book...The author did it again! *Adversary* had taken hold of me and didn't let go, even after the book was closed. If I was asked, *"What Young Adult series would I recommend?"*, The Ganzfield Novels would be it."
— Escape Between the Pages

"Clever and creative...this book sucked me in and would not let me go—not that I would have wanted it to."
— Escape Between The Pages

"A fast moving and compelling read."
— Eating Y.A. Books

"Plenty of action and love to swoon over...a compelling, exciting new series to keep your eye out for!"
— Girl In Between

Minder: "I will not only give this book 5 stars, I will be giving it an extra star for 'I could read this again right this minute.'"
Adversary: "5-stars...Intense and fascinating...refreshing and fun!"
— Reading, Writing, Raisin' Boys

"I don't think I've read such an intense opening to a novel...ever. It was nail biting."
— Confessions of a Book Addict

"*Minder* is fast paced, unique, and is addicting...Kaynak surprised me! She created a great plot (full of suspense and mystery) and characters that kept me hooked...I wish for more books like *Minder*."
— Ramblings of a Teenage Bookworm

"This book snatches your attention from the first paragraph and doesn't let go."
— Critique this WIP

"Suspenseful, enchanting, and romantic, *Minder* is a great start to an exciting new series."
— Ellz Readz

"*Minder* is a fun, perfect read for anyone who looks for love, excitement, and a great plot."
— If You Give a Girl a Pen

"Fantastic. *Minder* is an engaging read with unique characters and a steamy romance that sizzles off the page. The ending had me begging for more."
— Wicked Awesome Books

"The plot and premise are unlike anything I've ever seen before. After reading *Minder,* I was left wondering *Damn, wish there were a real Ganzfield around here*...I definitely recommend it!"
— Words on Paper

A great YA paranormal that borders sci-fi...*Minder* is a compelling start to a new series that is sure to be loved by many. It's fun, action-packed and well-thought-out; it's a YA novel that's relevant to this day and age. I honestly cannot wait to see what happens next."
— Erika Breathes Books

"Holy Heck! You know that feeling you get when you bite into some treat sample that is absolutely scrumptious and leaves you wanting MORE? That's what I was feeling when I finished *Minder*. I got started reading I was completely SUCKED into the story. It pained me to put this book down to do everyday things."
— For the Love of YA

"*Minder* is an amazing read. It is truly fantastic. I started reading *Minder* and I just couldn't stop. There was something about it that just drew me in...there were serious elements, and then there were elements that made me laugh out loud. Kate Kaynak has created a great story with *Minder* and I devoured the entire thing in no time, because it really is amazing. I cannot wait to read the next book in the series."
— Everything To Do With Books

"I loved this book! I thought it was amazing! Well written and intriguingly suspenseful, with an incredible romance thrown in...a MUST READ. In a few words: Incredible! Creative! Original! Well thought-out! Great new series! Characters you will LOVE!"
— The Wormhole

"*Adversary* had everything I expected and more. If you enjoyed *Minder*, you should definitely check out its sequel. And if you haven't tried *Minder* yet... what are you waiting for?"
— The Wolf's Den

Spencer Hill Press

Please visit our website at spencerhillpress.com

First Edition January 2011.

Kaynak, Kate, 1971—
Legacy : a novel / by Kate Kaynak – 1st edition
p. cm.
Summary:
Telepathic teenager Maddie Dunn has been left wounded from her encounters with Isaiah. The people of Ganzfield now have to figure out how to stop him before he destroys them all.

Cover design by K. Kaynak

The quotation from Ernest Hemingway's *A Farewell to Arms* in this work adheres to the fair use principles of Section 107 of the Copyright Act.

The author acknowledges the trademarked status and trademark owners of the following wordmarks mentioned in this fiction:
Cool Ranch, Dunkin' Donuts, Fedex,
Friendly's, iPod, Morton Buildings,
Post-its, Purell, Pyreflect, Q-tips, Star Wars,
Thermos, and YouTube.

The charity "Connect"is a real organization for people with aphasia.

ISBN 978-0-9845311-4-1 (paperback)
ISBN 978-0-9845311-5-8 (e-book)

Printed in the United States of America

LEGACY

THE THIRD GANZFIELD NOVEL BY

KATE

KAYNAK

For Alex.

Kate Kaynak

SPENCER HILL PRESS

Dear Reader,

Legacy is the third book in the Ganzfield series and, unless you put down *Adversary* yesterday, you might need a few reminders. I love reading book series, but often the first chapters in the later books are either slowed by the constant intrusion of reminders or confusing because there aren't enough of them. I know there's a fine line between, "I know all this already!" and "Who's *that* guy, and how did he set that thing on fire?" I hope this refresher gives you what you need.

Previously, at Ganzfield...

GANZFIELD

Ganzfield is a secret training facility near North Conway, New Hampshire. A few months ago, an attack killed about half of the people living there, and the second book ended as a group was heading back to re-open it. Williamson's office is in the main building, along with the dining hall and the library. Across the way, Blake House holds a bunch of classrooms, girls' dorm rooms, and the infirmary. Maddie and Trevor live in the old church that sits back in the woods. The sparks sleep in a cluster of fireproof cottages at the edge of the lake. Other houses and cabins dot the property, as well.

MINDERS

Minders are telepaths; they hear other people's thoughts when they are in range. Some can shield their thoughts from other telepaths, and a few can project words, images, emotions, sensations, and dreams to others. But only two have the ability to overload and kill people with blasts of energy.

Seventeen-year-old Maddie Dunn can do all of these things. She came to Ganzfield last October after killing three guys who tried to attack her. In *Adversary*, she got into a mental duel with Isaiah Lerner, the other telepath who can kill with his thoughts. They burned out the speech centers of each others' brains, so Maddie can't talk aloud anymore.

Maddie and her way-more-than-boyfriend, Trevor, connect as pure energy, something they call "soulmating." It turns out this special connection has some interesting side-effects. They now can borrow each other's abilities when they're together, including shielding their minds from other telepaths so they can only be heard by each other, and Trevor can hear Maddie's thoughts when she's in range—unless she shields from him. The two of them also share dreams.

Dr. Jon Williamson is the head honcho at Ganzfield. He funds the place through a little inside-the-head trading in the stock market. He taught Maddie how to do it, too, but a mistake with stock options made her an accidental millionaire. Back in the 1990s, Williamson was one of the first people with the G-positive genetic marker to have his ability enhanced with the synthetic neurotransmitter, dodecamine. Williamson can hear, project, and shield thoughts. His niece, Ann, was a minder who stopped taking dodecamine and left Ganzfield shortly after Maddie arrived.

Seth Black has the largest range of any minder, although this doesn't make things easy for him. His extreme sensitivity makes people's thoughts—especially those of other minders—much louder to him, so Seth spends a lot of time alone in his cabin on the far side of the lake at Ganzfield. He can't project thoughts to non-telepaths or shield his thoughts from other minders but, because of his huge range, he experienced the massacre from *within* the minds of the victims.

Isaiah Lerner isn't part of Ganzfield, although he is telepathic. He learned about this ability back when he was a U.S. Congressman and Project Star Gate was still a secret government program. He has a huge mental range and can send killing blasts of energy into people's heads, but he can't shield. He forced Matilda Taylor to use her healing ability to enhance his brain structure, giving him the additional abilities of a charm and an RV. The charm part is now useless, though—Maddie burned out his speech center and he can't talk anymore—but he *can* RV people over great distances. Isaiah views other G-positives as threats, so he kills them whenever he finds them. He used to run the Sons of Adam—a fringe group who think G-positives are dangerous—but nearly all of his followers were at the gathering in Peapack. He ordered them to freeze and then got tossed through a plate glass window. The Sons of Adam members remained frozen for days until Cecelia released them and charmed their "extracurricular activities" in new directions. Without his voice, Isaiah has no way to charm new people to do his dirty work, so now he's on his own.

TELEKINETICS

Trevor Laurence is the only person at Ganzfield who can move things with his mind. He sleeps in a large, open space—the sanctuary of an old church—since his ability doesn't shut down when he dreams. His two mental hands extend about fifteen feet from his body and he can widen and flatten them like a shield, or shrink them to do tiny work such as picking locks. They can lift several hundred pounds, reach through solid matter, and even stop bullets. Because his special connection with Maddie allows them to share abilities, she's also telekinetic when they have physical contact.

SPARKS

Sparks, like Drew McFee, control fire—make it flare up, die back, and even move things telekinetically when they're on fire. The sparks at Ganzfield all come from two families—the McFees and the Underwoods. Since the helicopter attack this past February, which killed most of the charms and RVs, this is the most common ability at Ganzfield.

CHARMS

Charms can compel obedience with their words. Nearly all of the charms at Ganzfield died in the attack—their killers used earpieces to block out the sounds of the charms' voices.

Cecelia Mitchell survived because she'd just left Ganzfield to start classes at the University of New Hampshire. She uses her ability to keep the other charms from abusing theirs and has also been exploring how charm commands can help people with emotional problems like posttraumatic stress.

Nick Coleman is a corporate lawyer in New York City. Being a charm makes him *very* persuasive both in and out of the courtroom. Coleman takes care of financial and legal issues for Williamson and the rest of Ganzfield.

Zack Greyson is also a charm, although he has an extra gift—he naturally shields his thoughts from minders. Since hearing thoughts is what gives telepaths immunity from charm commands, this shielding *may* allow him to use his ability on minders.

HEALERS

Healers instantly mend cuts, burns, broken bones, internal bleeding, and other physical damage by revving up and controlling the person's natural healing mechanisms. Matilda and Morris Taylor—siblings originally from Liberia—do most of the healing work at Ganzfield.

Hannah Washington is their only current student and she's been training as part of Maddie's team. Heather McFee, the only healer in a family of sparks, studied with the Taylors before she left for medical school and her internship at Dartmouth-Hitchcock Medical Center. In *Adversary*, she snuck some Ganzfield people into that facility for medical tests.

REMOTE VIEWERS (RVs)

RVs can see distant people, places, or things. Some—like Rachel Fontaine—have a nearly limitless range for familiar objects, while others—like Claire Ross—can only view things that are within a range of a few dozen miles. RVs find things uniquely—the visual representation varies from mind to mind. Charlie Fontaine—Rachel's uncle—could locate other G-positives. Isaiah had him studied in a horrible vivisection and then based his own RV ability on the findings.

And now, *Legacy*…

Kate Kaynak
New Hampshire, April 2010

For Mom and Olin

CHAPTER 1

Trevor and I had wanted to wait until dark to steal the car, but that would've been too late. As soon as the last of the dinner stragglers cleared the area around the old barn, Trevor telekinetically opened the large, double doors. We both winced as the old hinges creaked loudly.

Did anyone hear that?

I stopped breathing and listened telepathically for an endless moment. The late-May, New Hampshire evening suddenly felt too warm, and the pinkish-gold cast of the protracted sunset made everything look like it'd been dipped in honey. The sun stayed up until nine at this time of year, so it was later than it felt. Wiping my palm against my jeans, I tried to slow my heartbeat.

I cast a quick mental glance into the main building. Williamson was up on the third floor, his head filled with financial forecasts. I couldn't feel Seth, but that meant nothing—his telepathic range was so large, he'd sense me long before I'd feel him. And the newest minder at Ganzfield was the *last* person I wanted to explain myself to tonight.

Trevor grabbed the keys for the grey sedan from the rack by the door. I slid across the driver's seat to the passenger side, never letting go of his hand. In the three months since we'd returned to Ganzfield, we'd practiced this shared mental shield frequently. It'd saved our lives when Isaiah Lerner had tracked us to my mom's place in New Jersey.

Trevor eased the car out of the barn. The long driveway looped in front of the main building and wound through the trees to the front gate. He turned on the headlights once we entered the gloom beyond the treeline.

Where do you think you're going?

Crap. Seth.

Trevor gave my hand a quick squeeze as a figure moved across the driveway in front of us. I focused on the shield, knowing that even Seth couldn't get through it.

Of all the lousy luck.

I'd hoped he'd be at the power station or the back gate, out of range. If anyone else had been on duty tonight, we could've bluffed our way out with a mention of "minder business."

Trevor rolled the car to a stop. The headlights illuminated Seth as he stood in the middle of the gravel drive, blocking our way. I glanced at Trevor, meeting his warm, chocolate-brown eyes. He gave my hand another reassuring squeeze as I bit my lip. *Maddie, I'll talk to him. It'll be okay.*

Trevor slid the window down as Seth stepped into the shadowed space between the headlights. Shielding, I couldn't broadcast thoughts to anyone other than Trevor. We'd have to talk aloud to Seth, just like normal people.

Actually, since I could no longer talk, Trevor would have to speak for both of us.

Seth's annoyance came through to me loudly—rust-pink

and grating. Nothing kept out other people's thoughts—except distance. I always heard what other people thought around me, even when I didn't want to.

Seth's appearance still didn't match his mental presence to me. I'd never pictured him with this mane of red-gold hair. He kept it pulled back in a ponytail because he hadn't had it cut in years—having people in physical contact made them excruciatingly loud to him. It'd actually hurt Seth to get a haircut.

"Hey, Seth." Trevor spoke as though everything was normal.

Seth's thoughts flashed through all the things wrong with this situation. *Why are they taking a car without permission and sneaking out? They KNOW Isaiah's killing every G-positive he can find! And Maddie's probably at the top of his killing "to-do" list.*

"Rachel said he was down near Atlanta this afternoon." Trevor knew that Seth would understand who *he* was. "It's safe."

Rachel could track Isaiah better than the other RVs could. We'd figured a way for me to share my memories of him to strengthen her remote viewing ability. Once she knew a person or object, she could locate it anywhere on the planet. I sometimes wondered how far into outer space she might be able to find things.

"Isaiah's not the only problem out there. The Sons of Adam—"

"You know I'd never let anyone hurt Maddie, right? We need to do this. It's important."

"What's so important?"

Trevor and I both flushed and I pulled the shield tighter. "Can't tell you. We'll be back soon."

"Let me ask Williamson…"

Tell Seth to get out of the way right now, I told Trevor, *or I'm dropping the shield.* We were busted, but we could still do what we needed to before dealing with Williamson.

"Seth, she's going to drop the shield if you don't stand back." Trevor's voice held a you-know-what-she's-like tone. He didn't enjoy being in the middle of our bickering, but Seth annoyed me like the older brother I'd never had—or wanted.

Seth's shock splashed over me, tinged with annoyance and several really bad words. Dropping the shield wouldn't physically injure him, but my minder-loud thoughts would hurt as though hell itself had set up shop between his ears. He quickly backed out of the car's way. His accusatory mental presence followed us as we drove away and dark-yellow guilt seeped through me.

Crap.

Seth had enough pain in his head without me adding to it. Sensing everyone's final, terrified thoughts as they'd died in the massacre a few months ago had traumatized him.

We keyed in the code to open the front gate. It only took a few minutes to drive out to North Conway. I kept a constant mental scan of the area—alert for ambushes, people who hated us, or traces of Isaiah's mental presence. Once we entered town, the mental babble increased and I flitted from mind to mind, listening for those who wanted to harm us.

—think he's cheating on me—

—more ketchup!

—sick of hearing about her boyfriend problems. She should just dump him and—

—kid whines one more time about the damn ketchup, I'm feeding him to the damn wolverines—

—this dress make me look fat? I feel—

—want to get home and have a beer—

—she looks kinda heavy in that dress—

Paranoid behavior? I wish. It's not paranoia if people really *do* want to kill you.

We found the Rite-Aid, relieved that it was still open. Trevor wrapped invisible arms around me as I slid out of the driver's door behind him. Someone might shoot at us from beyond my mental range so we had to be careful. The anxiety made our muscles hum with a twitchy, nervous energy as we walked together to the front door of the store.

At least we could do that now—my limp was finally gone. One of the strokes Isaiah had caused had damaged my motor cortex so I'd been through painfully boring physical therapy to re-train my brain to control my left leg. Williamson had paid the physical therapist double her rate and had told Cecelia to charm her to forget anything strange that she'd seen—particularly my less-than-traditional way of talking into people's heads. We didn't want other people to find out about all of the unusual stuff up at Ganzfield. If word got out that a bunch of teenagers with super-powers were training up here, it would be bad.

Witch-hunt bad.

I felt Trevor's hand on my shoulder, warm and reassuring, as we stepped into the overly-bright fluorescent light and scanned the signs at the ends of the aisles. The Rite-Aid was nearly empty. It was almost 9 p.m. and they'd be closing soon.

We found the right aisle: Family Planning. I looked at the various products, totally unsure which one we needed. Trevor had even less of a clue than I did. I finally grabbed a purple and white box and we headed up to the checkout.

The blue-aproned woman behind the counter was probably in her sixties—grandmotherly and stern with short, salt-and-pepper hair and narrow-lensed glasses. She looked at Trevor and me, two clearly-anxious teenagers, and then down at the sole item we were purchasing.

A home pregnancy test.

Her mind filled with the obvious conclusion and I felt my whole face flush crimson. She took the cash from my hand. I now had a credit card tied to my ridiculous new bank account, but I didn't want a paper trail for this particular purchase.

The cashier looked critically at Trevor, internally debated whether or not to say something, and then let it out. "I hope you plan to marry her."

I closed my eyes and counted to ten slowly, trying to ignore this stranger's unspoken assumptions. This was *so* not her business.

Trevor's face was serious. "Absolutely." In a different situation, I know he would've laughed.

I held the little plastic shopping bag close as we headed to the car, checking again for people trying to kill us. Driving back, I felt a twitchy tension, like little wild birds under my skin. My hands opened and closed on the box under the thin skin of plastic. The gate closed behind us.

You are SO busted.

I dropped my shield to yell at Seth, annoyed that he'd prudently gotten far enough away that my thoughts wouldn't hurt him. *You are such a JERK! You know we wouldn't leave Ganzfield if it wasn't important!*

What did you think was so impor—

I still had the pregnancy test in my hands, and now Seth could hear my thoughts.

WHAT? HOLY—

Just SHUT UP! It's not what you think. I pushed up the shield again, feeling a painful sinking in my gut. There really was only one thing he didn't know now, but protecting that last secret was important.

Crap.

Seth would narc about this, too. Although Williamson would

know even if Seth didn't actively tell him. Since Seth couldn't shield, his thoughts were open to all the other minders. Which meant...

Crap, crap, crap.

Trevor drove the car back to the barn as the last of the day's light faded. I didn't feel Williamson's mind as we rolled past the main building. No light came from his office windows—he must've gone to bed early. Would he come to the church as soon as Seth blabbed or wait until morning?

Ugh.

Trevor closed and latched the barn doors. I quickly checked the minds inside Blake House. In the infirmary, Morris's thoughts felt cool and untroubled as he considered a new, experimental method to subtly adjust the shape of the human eye with his healing ability. If it worked, none of us would need glasses or contact lenses anymore. Cool, but unimportant right now.

I listened for two specific minds. I couldn't sense Rachel's, but she tended to go to sleep early these days. As for my mom—I *really* had to make sure I didn't attract her notice in the next few minutes.

At the locked door, I tried to remember someone else's code for the new security system. I'd picked up several telepathically, but I was too stressed to recall any of them at the moment. I just used my own, which meant the other minders would know I'd been here tonight. Hopefully, they wouldn't put the pieces together immediately.

I stepped lightly, trying to keep the old stairs from creaking. Trevor stayed by the door, visualizing heavyset people doing the dance moves to "YMCA." I suppressed a snort. Yeah, that'd keep the other minders from focusing into his thoughts. I wished I could block that particular image, as well.

Several people watched TV up in the attic common room, and an air conditioner hummed annoyingly at the top of the stairs. I tiptoed past my mom's door, hearing her inside as she silently read a neurology book. I paused at the room I'd once shared with Rachel and Hannah. Hannah now had her own room down the hall. Even with the new arrivals in the past few months, more than a few empty beds remained in Blake House.

Whether Rachel was really asleep or just not here didn't matter. I opened the door, holding the weight up by the knob—I had experience keeping this particular door from creaking. Rachel lay curled in bed, her arms around her pillow.

I quietly set the pregnancy test box on her bedside table, and then slipped back out of the room.

CHAPTER 2

Rachel's life kinda sucked right now.

Her boyfriend, Sean, had been killed on a mission with us back in March. Grief, pain, and anger kicked at her nonstop from under her own skin. I felt sick around her—her emotions spilled into me, making me want to scream and cry, or throw up, or hit something and curl up in a tiny ball. Spending time with her was a form of penance—I'd survived when Sean hadn't. If I hadn't gone after Isaiah, and if Trevor hadn't followed me, no one would've been shooting. Sean wouldn't have stuck his head over that wall and become a target.

A casualty.

Thoughts like this sometimes flashed through Rachel's mind when she looked at me, but our friendship had survived because I had something she wanted: I could project memories of Sean's thoughts and feelings to her. She wanted to hear them—needed to know all of the tender details. I'd tried to avoid invading their privacy when they were together, but I'd still picked up an awful lot telepathically just from being near them.

I usually visited her in the evenings—Rachel typically skipped dinner and lay in her dusky room, feeling alone and miserable. Hannah checked in every morning, and Cecelia came from time to time as well. Both were frustrated by Rachel's refusal to let them use their abilities to help her, but she wanted to stay in her pain. She knew Sean wasn't out there beyond it.

But earlier tonight, Rachel had gone to the dining hall. Several people splashed yellow surprise at her arrival—she hadn't gone to dinner there in months. She'd joined Cecelia at one of the tables by the windows.

Trevor and I exchanged a glance. *Did she finally let Hannah and Cecelia help her?*

I shook my head. *Doubtful. I can still feel so much pain coming from her.* But she no longer felt nauseous. Instead, she had a sudden, intense craving for the taste of oranges. It was as though the sick feeling had switched off in favor of the craving.

The two words—sickness and craving—bounced through my brain, landing on a single connector between them. My hand flew up to cover my gasp.

Holy crap! Pregnant?

Next to me, Trevor choked on a bite of manicotti. *WHAT?* He stared at Rachel for a stricken moment and then met my eyes.

I put a hand around his neck and pulled a tight mental shield around us. *I'm not sure. If she is, she's not thinking about it.* Trevor's distress was more than concern for our friend; unplanned teen pregnancy was an emotional issue for him—he was the son of a teen mom himself.

How could she not know?

She's been so upset. It's not like any of us have experience with this stuff. Geez, most of what I know about teen pregnancy I learned from seeing "Juno" a couple of years back.

What are you going to do?

I have no idea. Just bringing it up wouldn't be helpful. I tried to give Rachel the illusion that I didn't know about the physical side of the relationship she and Sean had shared.

Can you talk to her?

I winced as I imagined *that* awkward conversation, and then shook my head. *Anything I said would only freak her out. And she needs to know for sure.*

Could one of the healers—?

Probably. I frowned. *But she's so...having one of them examine her...it'd feel like a violation of her privacy. Rachel needs a way to find out that doesn't tip off anyone else.*

Oops.

I'd just shared my suspicions with Trevor, but he'd keep Rachel's secrets. He'd been doing that before I'd even met him.

Would Williamson let us borrow the car? We could pick up one of those over-the-counter tests for her in town.

I shook my head. *I can't ask. He'll see the reason in my thoughts. We can't blab this to all the other minders.*

We could order something online...or with our weekly food pick-up, but that would take days. We can't keep this secret for long.

So Trevor and I had stolen the car and gone to the drugstore.

As we walked back to our church—our little home—we considered the possible fallout. *If only Seth hadn't intercepted us!* Now he knew we'd snuck out and that we'd bought a pregnancy test. Not only did he assume it was for me, he'd tell Williamson and the other new minder.

And the newest minder at Ganzfield happened to be my

mother.

Ugh.

I shuddered. Things were going to get ugly. Our basic decision was either to take the heat—as though we really were the ones who'd needed the pregnancy test—or to violate Rachel's privacy and tell the other minders.

Please. Like that's actually a choice. Trevor quickly dismissed that option. Of course we weren't going to tell.

We were in-synch on this, but I didn't want to put Trevor through that. *Are you sure? It's going to get bad. My mom, Williamson…*

We'll take it. He walked with me as he telekinetically tapped his keycode into the security box by the door to our church. *At least WE know you're not pregnant.* The outside light came on as the door unlocked and Trevor smiled at me in the dim light.

Thank heavens.

I rubbed my hand across my face. Even the thought of dealing with a pregnancy *rumor* for a few days was mortifying—imagining all the I-know-what-you-did-to-get-that-way thoughts made me shudder—a real pregnancy at seventeen would be horrible. Between that and recognizing the cause of Rachel's nausea, I was becoming seriously attached to my technical virginity.

Trevor grinned playfully. *I told you so.*

I snorted. *Okay, you were right. Thank you for protecting my chastity and virginal honor.*

Technically, he added with a laugh, pulling me into the warm, still air of the church.

Technically, I agreed, leaning up to kiss him.

After coming back to Ganzfield a few months ago, we'd considered taking our physical relationship further. But between Trevor's issues with unplanned pregnancy, my mother's telepathic presence in Blair House, and the fact that soulmating was incredible, we hadn't been in any rush. And we always connected as energy before we got too far—like we had a Higher Power chaperone.

We still did *stuff*, though.

My turn tonight. Trevor's words caused a delicious wave of red energy to dance across my skin. We'd learned pretty quickly that if we physically touched one another, we lost control almost instantly and ended up soulmating. So, we'd come up with taking "turns"—using telekinesis.

It was as mind-blowing as it sounded. In fact, that's what we called it.

I kicked off my shoes and dropped my purse in the coatroom as Trevor swept me up and over to the new, king-sized bed in the middle of the church sanctuary. The frame was thick, wrought-iron, and bolted to the floor. I'd bought it for Trevor with the "dirty, dirty money" I now had from my multi-million-dollar stock market accident. Trevor didn't really approve of my telepathic "market research," but how else did he expect a seventeen-year-old, mute, telepathic high school dropout to make a living?

Our hearts raced each other as Trevor's lips found mine. My hands clenched with the desire to slide over the smooth contours of his chest, over his taut stomach muscles, over his—

Trevor groaned. He gently pulled my hands up to grip the twisted iron of the headboard and then covered them with his own.

MY turn, he repeated. He trailed kisses down my neck. I blissfully closed my eyes and opened my mind fully to his, showing him every nuance of my thoughts. My body arched as Trevor's invisible touch made me melt. His lips trailed along the hollow of my neck and left a line of delicious fire in their wake.

Our skins hummed with glowing red energy and my breath came in little pants.

Wonderful, wonderful, wonderful.

I moaned as his mouth moved higher, finding my lips again, and his physical hand gently angled my face up to his. I opened my eyes, met his gaze, and fell into his soul. Our energies pulsed together, glowing with a beautiful, powerful, overwhelming love, bringing us to an intensity that fused our souls together in a magical bliss.

Our still-clothed bodies trembled as we returned to them. Our breathing slowed back toward normal as we gazed into each other's eyes, still amazed with one another, both filled with total adoration.

Distilled essence of intimacy.

I stayed with Trevor, together in peaceful completeness, until he drifted to sleep. I then reluctantly climbed into my own bed up in the loft over the coatroom, since I didn't want him to accidentally throw me across the sanctuary during the night. That sort of thing really killed the romantic mood.

CHAPTER 3

Williamson wants you in his office. Now.

Seth's mental voice pulled me from sleep. How totally unfair was it that he could reach into my unconscious mind? I couldn't even *sense* sleeping people—unless they were dreaming, of course. Light trickled in through the slats in the shutters, but that didn't tell me much—the sun came up before 6 a.m. this time of year.

Narc, I thought sourly at Seth.

Trevor's lanky frame stretched out across the big bed, still in the clothes he'd worn yesterday. My heart seemed to expand at the sight of him. I let him sleep. Since we weren't going to tell Williamson anything, it didn't really matter whether one or two of us stood there saying nothing.

Trevor began to dream. I climbed down from the loft and skirted around the edge of the room toward the bathroom annex, staying out of his invisible reach as his ability acted out the swimming motions that played through his mind. His pillow flew across the room, hit the wall, and landed with a soft plop on the floor.

Get out of range, Seth. I'm going to take a shower first, I thought, in case he was still around. I popped up a mental shield as I closed the bathroom door.

I left a note for Trevor before heading to the main building. Ugh. How much was this going to suck? I adjusted my mental shield along the way, steeling for the confrontation I knew was coming. Two floors above me, Williamson—and my mother—waited with noticeable and growing impatience. A glance at the clock showed me it was just after 7 a.m. I felt Seth check in with them from outside.

Oh, great. Everyone's here for the family meeting.

I fortified myself with coffee in the dining hall before heading to Williamson's office. I didn't bother to knock. They already knew I was there.

You're shielding? Williamson seemed upset.

My mother sat across from him. Her worried green eyes fixed on mine. She reached out with plump arms, as though to give me a hug, but I stayed back by the door and shook my head. She seemed to deflate as she dropped her hands to her lap.

Disappointment glowered darkly from Williamson's mind and, for once, he almost looked disheveled. Were those wrinkles in his shirt? And he didn't spontaneously combust?

Shocking.

He used other's impressions of him like most people used a mirror. Williamson's complexion looked sallow and I noticed the salting of white in his close-cut hair. He still radiated paternal authority and strength, but I knew now that he wasn't as all-powerful as he had first appeared.

His eyes bored into me. *Explain.*

I shook my head, feeling sick at heart. At least Trevor wasn't here, sharing in this sense of disappointment. I felt Seth's mental presence outside but he wasn't gloating. He was actually worried, too. If I still had a voice, I could've tried to tell them all something—given them enough information that they might've backed off for a while.

Maddie. Williamson tried to keep himself calm. *This is unacceptable. First, you and Trevor broke your word to me.*

I felt my jaw tense at the false accusation, but I kept my shield in place.

Second, Williamson continued, *you went off the grounds without taking proper safety precautions, which could've put both you and Trevor at risk.*

A knot of sickly-yellow guilt swept up and lodged in my throat. I guess my conscience agreed with Williamson. But Trevor and I could protect one another, and we'd been careful.

Third, you left us shorthanded while you were gone. What if there'd been an attack?

Again, I pushed down my anger. We hadn't let anyone down. Trevor and I hadn't been scheduled to patrol last night.

Fourth, you need to know that you can't risk a pregnancy on dodecamine. We have no idea how it would affect fetal development. We don't know what it would do to the brain of a G-positive child.

I gasped as a sick wave of cold dismay washed through me. *Oh, my God in Heaven.* Sean had died back in February—three months ago. If Rachel was pregnant, she'd probably gotten at least two shots of dodecamine since then.

My mother saw my distress and started to cry. *Oh! Maddie IS pregnant!*

Well, I could put that fear to rest, at least. I grabbed a notepad and a pen from Williamson's desk and wrote a simple:

I'm not pregnant.

I thwacked the notepad back onto the center of the desk. The pen rolled off the edge and clattered across the floor. Let them assume the test had been negative, if that was where their minds went.

Williamson gave a deep sigh. My mom read the note several times, needing to believe it. The tension in the room eased.

I know I can't keep you from having sex... started Williamson.

Well, I can! My mother had taken to telepathy with remarkable ease. She could hear the thoughts of other minders and read anyone else's when she had physical contact. That's why I hadn't let her hug me when I'd arrived—she might've pick up something even through my shield. *Maddie, how you can justify being so STUPID—so unsafe! And I don't care that you have nightmares. You're going to sleep in Blake House from now on.*

I looked at her hard, forcing my jaw not to quiver. Why didn't they have any faith in me? Why did they still treat me like an irresponsible child? Hadn't I done enough to prove myself?

Their accusations tasted like grey, bitter ash. There was nothing I could say and still keep Rachel's secret, even if I could speak. I couldn't lower my shield and I couldn't send thoughts while shielding. I still didn't know how Williamson did that. I'd been trying to do it for months, but I just couldn't make it happen. So I simply met their eyes in turn, shook my head, and walked out.

Let them try and stop me.

Outside, I had the sudden, intense desire to get Trevor and leave Ganzfield for a while, but that wouldn't happen. I was so tired of it all—of having others listening to my thoughts, of the security precautions, of the threat of attack, of the drama from the new arrivals and the returning survivors who now stayed here at Ganzfield.

The bulk of the mental turmoil faded as I moved across the field behind the main building. Silence—sort of. I could still feel the presence of the people behind me. I also heard some of the sparks waking in the little cinderblock houses by the edge of the lake. But right here, surrounded by the ankle-high grass, the only clear thoughts were those of a few field mice that scurried away from my footfalls.

A light haze burned off as the sky brightened. I walked out to the lake, feeling the coolness roll off it, sensing its depths in the drop in temperature. The water was still too cold for swimming, although a few people did it, anyway. Memorial Day, the official start of summer, had been only a few days ago. I walked along the edge for a while, toward the little, tree-lined alcove where a large chunk of granite jutted into the water. I sat out on the rock and tried to make my thoughts as smooth as the water's surface, but all of the things I could've said kept flashing through my mind.

Pregnant? Geez! I'm still a virgin, Mom. You can have one of the healers confirm it for you. I snorted. Wouldn't that surprise the heck out of Hannah? She had a completely different impression of my relationship with Trevor…and she didn't approve.

I imagined confronting Williamson. *You've been giving Rachel and every other female G-positive here dodecamine without doing a single pregnancy test. Why haven't we been warned about this possible complication?* This wasn't the first time I'd felt the lack of effective communication at Ganzfield. *You're a doctor, for crying out loud! This should've been handled better.*

What about Rachel? How was she going to deal with this? If Rachel was pregnant, would the baby be okay? And, not to be insensitive or anything, but what did it mean for the rest of us?

How would we keep track of Isaiah's movements if Rachel had to go off the meds? She could locate Isaiah better than any of the others could. RVs all connected to their remote viewing targets differently. Some could only find things that were alive. A few couldn't find living things, only inanimate objects—as though the life force within shone like a beacon for some but jammed the signal for others. But they'd all tried to track a single person for the past few months.

Isaiah.

We could get all caught up in the drama of an unintended pregnancy, but Isaiah Lerner was the *real* problem right now. Isaiah had forced Matilda to alter his brain structure, adding both charm and RV abilities to his natural telepathy. I'd burned out Isaiah's speech center in the same fight in which he'd burned out mine. His charming ability was gone—at least, we hoped it was gone. *My* ability to speak certainly wasn't coming back. But Isaiah could still hear thoughts and he still could use his stolen RV skills to locate other G-positives.

The murders had started a few weeks after we'd returned to Ganzfield. Isaiah was tracking and killing G-positives. Eight people had died so far—all in their homes and all from sudden, overpowering strokes. The police hadn't made any connections among them. The victims had lived in different cities and there weren't any public records that could link them to Ganzfield.

But Rachel had seen two of the murders in her visions. I shuddered at the memory. I'd been in-range for one of them. The images flashed up again and stole my breath.

Isaiah'd leaned silently against the pale stone wall. His eyes had stayed on the green painted door, like a cat watching for the mouse to come out of its hole.

Down south, Rachel'd thought. *The Carolinas, or maybe Georgia.*

She'd pulled back with her vision, seeking details like street signs.

Isaiah tensed and Rachel re-focused on him just as the door opened. She glimpsed the sandy-haired guy in a Duke t-shirt with a backpack over one shoulder. Recognition spiked through her. *Tim? Oh, God…*

Tim dropped like a marionette with its strings cut. His legs splayed across the open doorway. Isaiah stepped over him, and then grabbed his limp arms and pulled him back inside. The door closed without a sound.

By the time I got up to Rachel's room, she'd already called Williamson. "Tim Stewart's dead." She rasped the words through a too-tight throat, and tears dripped from her quivering jaw. "Isaiah. I think he…" she drew a harsh breath, "…he was leaving his apartment." *God, he was just going to class. He only left Ganzfield last summer. He wasn't a bad guy—for a charm, at least.*

"What's Isaiah doing now?" Williamson's voice came through her thoughts, stone-hard.

Rachel focused in. Her dismay made her vision swim in and out of focus as she watched Isaiah dump clothing from another drawer onto the floor. Black leather gloves stood out strangely against his pastel polo shirt. "He's trashing Tim's apartment."

None of us had known the second victim, although a discrete charm request for a blood sample from the morgue had confirmed the dead woman had been a G-positive, too. After that, Ganzfield had started filling up as frightened G-positives came to stay here.

Safety in numbers.

Years ago, several people had tried going up against Isaiah. He'd killed them all. *How do you fight someone who can hear your intentions? Someone who can fill your mind with a blast of lethal energy and kill you in a few seconds?* I knew I wasn't a match for him—at least not yet—so I wasn't pushing to lead a mission to take him out. For now, we were playing defense, simply trying to keep our people alive and safe. And I had to hand it to Williamson—he'd made good on his promise to step up security: locks on the building doors, new surveillance equipment protecting the boundary walls, and the patrols, day and night. Hell, if someone launched a missile at us, the sparks probably could divert it into the lake.

I wasn't the only person who felt like Ganzfield was the only safe place right now. Recent "graduates" returned from their colleges or jobs, and some brought G-positive family members. The sparks had added several new cinderblock houses to their little community for the new arrivals, and a cluster of recreational vehicles and trailers housed more people in the field behind Blake House.

Cecelia was back from UNH, much to our mutual annoyance. Heather McFee, the sole healer in a family of sparks, stayed in Blake House, as well. Ann Williamson, Jon's niece, had arrived a few days ago. She took up residence in her old cabin, even though she no longer needed the isolation. She was off the meds and no longer heard thoughts, but this land had been in her mom's family for generations, so she could pretty much stay wherever she wanted.

Many beds in Blake House remained empty, though. The melting snow had washed away the bloodstains from the massacre, but the sense of death remained, clinging to our memories. It sometimes felt like the dead were still here.

Haunting us.

Something moved under the surface of the water. The simple, globular thoughts of fish touched the edges of my mind as a strange rumble stirred them up. On the far end of the lake, two small helicopters lifted into the air. Each was barely large enough to hold a single person, although I knew these two would be remotely controlled by a couple of sparks. The lawnmower drone of their motors came across the water as the helicopters flew low, sending a rippling wake out from the wash of their rotors. When they got closer to the sparks' houses, they splashed-in, one after the other, resurfacing to float on their pontoons. The copters took off again a minute later, repeating the fly-by from another angle.

I nodded absently, feeling reassured. The sparks would never allow another aerial attack on us. Our bigger concern was that some rich skiers would fly too close on their way to a drop on a nearby mountain next winter.

Behind me, I felt a gentle touch from Trevor's mind. I smiled and sent him an image of where to find me.

You left without me this morning. He carried two coffee cups in his physical hands. A plate with two bagels and a bowl of green grapes floated in front of him.

Like you wouldn't have spared me that meeting if the situation had been reversed.

How'd it go? He joined me out on the rock and handed me one of the coffees. He'd even added milk and fake sugar, just the way I liked it.

About as badly as we expected. I gave him a quick mental recap.

So they know you're not pregnant and they don't know about Rachel. Sounds like you did wonderfully.

Thanks, I needed that. I took another gulp of coffee, feeling the lump in my throat as I swallowed. *You're the only one who doesn't think I'm a major screw-up right now.*

Trevor put an arm around my shoulders, pulling me close. *That's because I know you better than they do.*

I smiled, resting my head against his chest, feeling like everything was okay now that he was here.

Any sign of Rachel? I asked.

Didn't see her at the dining hall.

Well, if she's looking for me, we know she'll be able to find me. I knew Rachel would figure out who'd given her that particular little gift. If she wasn't looking for me, she didn't want to talk about it. I wasn't going to push—well, anymore than I already had by putting a pregnancy test in her room last night.

I looked at the bagel in front of me; it didn't appeal. The bowl of grapes was on the other side of Trevor. His hands were full with his own coffee and bagel, so I concentrated, telekinetically picked a single grape, and lifted it back to my mouth. My "turns" with Trevor had improved my skills with his borrowed ability.

Hey, that's my job! He smiled and invisibly picked another grape. I leaned back against the rock, shedding my sweatshirt to use as a pillow. Trevor stretched out along my side, propping himself on one elbow to watch me. He fed me another grape, his unseen fingers lingering against my lips. I concentrated again and did the same for him.

Think we can just stay here for a little while and feed each other grapes? I asked. *I don't want to deal with any of them for a while.*

Absolutely. If anyone tries to bother you, I'll splash them until they go away. A wall of water shot out from the surface of the lake next to us, drenching the tree trunks along the shore.

I was about to try telekinetically splashing a wall of water myself, but we suddenly felt my mother coming toward us. Trevor's smile melted away, and his moral dilemma made me laugh. *Don't worry. You don't have to drench my mom for me.*

Whew, he joked, but his relief was genuine. He really did want her approval.

"Maddie? Honey? Where are you?"

Mom, we're over here. I sent her a little image of the path. We sat up before she came into view. I already knew I no longer had to shield my thoughts—my mom's mind practically shouted her dismay. She'd walked past Rachel in the hall of Blake House this morning and she'd looked upset. Concerned, my mom had "accidentally" brushed against her arm and had gotten a mindful, most of which spilled out of her right now. Rachel hadn't taken the pregnancy test, but she had been full of the *Oh, my God* realization that such a test was necessary.

That's pretty uncool, Mom. I can't help overhearing other people's private thoughts, but you can. Rachel HATES having people in her mind like that. You not only peeping-tommed her head, but now you're leaking it to every minder in range.

She ignored my rebuke. "I just need to know—the test was never for you, right?"

No, Mom, it wasn't for me. But you can't tell Jon or Seth or anyone. You're not able to shield your thoughts, so you need to avoid them for a day or two. You're broadcasting the details of Rachel's intimate life all over right now. It's none of your business. It's none of their business.

"It affects everyone here. Jon and Seth need to know."

Doctor-patient confidentiality, Mom. Think about something else. Go hang out with the sparks or something. Or Ann! Ann won't hear anything from you since she's not taking the meds anymore. If there's anything to tell, let Rachel do it when she's ready.

"That's why you were shielding this morning?"

Yeah. I can't stay out of other people's heads, but I CAN keep their secrets.

My mom gave me a searching look. *Is Maddie becoming so responsible and self-sacrificing that she'd take the fall to protect her friend? Or is she just being a sneaky, lying, difficult teenager?*

I felt her anger and disappointment evaporate as warmth filled her gaze. Something in my chest unclenched.

Okay, she knows you pretty well, too, Trevor thought to me.

My mom's eyes flicked to him, sensing that he'd thought something to me but unable to make out what it was, since he wasn't minder-loud. She'd been furious with him this morning, and now she had to dislodge that particular piece of emotional décor.

"Trevor." She gave him a nod.

"Hi, Nina." Since my mom's arrival, she'd gotten us all to switch to first names. We just interacted too intensely for formality. I still felt strange little tinges of impudence whenever I called Dr. Williamson "Jon." It'd be only a little weirder to call my mom "Nina," like the rest of them did. I'd never tried, though. That wouldn't go over too well.

"You knew about this?"

He nodded. "I was with Maddie when she figured it out."

My mom frowned. She didn't like to think about our "special connection," although she understood that Trevor and I had no secrets from each other. "Well, if I have to avoid the other minders for a while, you'll need to go up and take care of any new arrivals today."

I sighed. I avoided welcome-wagon duty whenever I could— the whole speaking-into-minds thing creeped some people out.

So much for feeding each other grapes in the sun.

Trevor and I got to our feet, picking up the empty plates and mugs as we went. At least my mom was taking Rachel's privacy concerns seriously. She'd taken to telepathy like a natural—which I guess she was. I guess we both were.

I pulled a mental shield around Trevor and me as the main building came into sight. Drew flashed us a big smile and a wave as we passed then returned to the controls of one of the helicopters, weaving and dodging to avoid Grant and Ellen's combined ability. Most sparks now could suppress the engines and cause the copters to stall. A few could grab the combustible parts and rip the machines out of the sky. Something steely-hard inside me gave a grim little nod of satisfaction.

Anyone who comes here to hurt us will get what they deserve.

I started to glow before we got up to the main house and Rachel came around the corner and met my gaze. I met her halfway and, after a moment, self-consciously placed an arm around her. I didn't know how else to respond to the emotional whiplash. First, she felt terrified, then giddy, then embarrassed, then freaked out, then angry, and then a wave of grief hit her. By the time I'd framed something to say, she was onto a different reaction and my half-formed mental words were inappropriate, so I just stood there and hoped that the arm-thing was enough.

Trevor hung back slightly, hesitant and ill at ease. A question formed in his mind—the question that was so central to his own life-long anxieties.

Does she want to keep the baby?

What would Rachel do? I'd always been pro-choice—it just seemed wrong to force a woman to go through a pregnancy against her will. Since meeting Trevor, though, I'd felt my convictions become shakier. A single decision by a scared teenager nineteen years ago could've removed this amazing person from the world and that idea sickened me. I had no right to have an opinion here—it was Rachel's choice—but I knew which decision I wanted her to make. Maybe it was selfish and wrong of me to even have an opinion.

Well, being selfish and wrong never stopped me before.

Williamson's concerns flashed through my mind. What if the baby wasn't developing right? I couldn't say anything to Rachel right now. She had so much to deal with!

Multicolored waves of emotion tumbled through her mind, overflowing her ability to process them. She'd lost the man she loved; her uncle had been murdered; she'd been repeatedly assaulted; and now she faced an unplanned pregnancy. It was too much—she couldn't handle it alone.

But she wasn't alone.

Hey, I'm here. I'm here for you. You're not alone. I didn't know why I, of all people, would be particularly comforting, but I was here and I knew she needed someone. I guess I was better than nothing.

Rachel sniffed, trying to pull herself together. Her quick breaths were gasping, half-crying sounds, like she couldn't get enough air into her lungs. Above us, I felt Williamson's mental touch as he took in the situation. Questions for me began to form in his mind.

Not now, Jon. My shield had gone down when I'd first spoken to Rachel. The secret I'd been protecting was already out— Rachel's turbulent thoughts had broadcast it almost violently to every minder in range. *I'm taking care of this.*

I gave Rachel's shoulders what I hoped was a reassuring squeeze. *Let's go have one of the healers check you out, okay?*

She walked with me to the infirmary with slow, careful steps.

Trevor gave me a questioning look. *Should I be a part of this?*

I'll come find you later.

He was relieved not to be included.

Matilda looked up from her desk in the infirmary. She moved quickly when she saw Rachel's expression. Rachel's whole body shook and she couldn't get the words out.

Rachel, do you want me to tell her?

She paused for a moment then nodded.

Pregnant, probably about three months or so. She just took the test a few minutes ago.

Matilda's large eyes filled with sympathy and she enveloped Rachel in a silent hug. My sense of Ganzfield as a large family intensified. I felt a sudden wave of protectiveness for this place, for our people.

Matilda had Rachel lie back on the exam table and pull up her shirt. She placed her hands on Rachel's still-flat belly. I followed along in Matilda's mind while she concentrated. She found the fetus and yellow flashes of anxiety colored her thoughts. *What will dodecamine do to a developing embryo?*

Rachel lay still, trying to make sense out of her life. It seemed wrong that the person most involved was out of the loop on this.

Rachel, do you want to see it?

She considered that for a few seconds, and then nodded to me.

I relayed the image from Matilda's head. The little thing was only about three inches long. Through Matilda's ability, we could see the tiny fingers.

Rachel gasped, overwhelmed yet again—but this time it wasn't by pain.

The little head looked overly large for the fairy-sized body. Matilda worked her way across the facial features—the tiny, sealed eyes, the low-set ears, the nub of a nose.

Tears streamed down from Rachel's eyes and streaked the hair by her ears. Her feelings seemed to crystallize as she looked at this tiny person—this last piece of Sean.

The baby began to glow with golden light.

Matilda gasped as she felt the strange surge of energy. *What—*

It's okay, I reassured her. *It's just Rachel's ability.*

I guess Rachel didn't need the feed from my head anymore. A sense of wonder filled her, peppering her feelings of loss with little white shards of hope. *Sean isn't completely gone.*

"Can you tell if it's a boy or a girl?" Her voice sounded thin and shaky.

"Let me..." Matilda trailed off, distracted. She felt the baby's developing brain, moving her ability lightly through the miniature structures. I recognized them from my neurology studies, but they were still so tiny, nebulous, and half-formed. I couldn't tell if they were normal or not. Matilda had the same problem. *I'm going to need to read up on fetal neural development.*

Belatedly, she tried to answer Rachel's question. "Not yet."

"Is he okay?" In her mind, her little Sean-baby was male.

"As far as I can tell." Matilda had the same question Trevor had about Rachel's choice.

I already knew what Rachel would do, but her decision wasn't mine to share.

CHAPTER 4

Rachel went back to her room. She wanted time to think and she didn't need an audience for that. I left Blake House, squinting as I stepped back into the bright day.

A shiny, expensive-looking red convertible blocked the driveway, surrounded by a small crowd—all male. Waves of intense, testosterone-laden lust permeated their thoughts—and it wasn't for the car. Someone with platinum hair and a glowing tan leaned seductively against the front fender. She looked to be in her mid- to late twenties. Strategic pieces of her toned physique threatened to liberate themselves at any moment from her too-tight clothing. In the minds of her assembled throng, they were already out.

Another new arrival. Must be a charm. And she likes to make an entrance.

I rolled my eyes. If this unacceptable reaction wasn't the result of charm influence, she'd need to put something else on. Where could we get a nun's habit? I'd never enjoyed the voyeuristic aspect of telepathy—having a front-row seat to other people's sex fantasies made my stomach clench. Most of the time, it was just…*gross*. Not to mention poorly lit, with bad acting and stilted dialogue.

I felt every muscle in my body stiffen—like a cat's fur standing on end—when I saw Trevor. I hadn't recognized his mind because the scarlet-tinged images within it were…*obscene*…and of *someone else?* A wave of orange fire flooded through me as my jaw tightened. I wanted to blast this blonde woman's brain. Not just hurt her—*kill* her. *How dare she!* Furious energy filled me. I could almost feel it spark from my fingertips.

If looks could kill… Oh, wait. Mine actually could. I needed to keep myself under control. I tried to take a steadying breath but tight bands seemed to constrict my chest. Trevor didn't seem to notice my approach; his eyes still followed the newcomer. My blood-red fury at this trampy, bottle-blonde charm increased.

She turned her cool gaze at me and I suddenly felt short, mousy, and plain.

"Is there a problem, sweetie?" Her voice dripped with overly-honeyed condescension. A smile twitched at the corners of her candy-apple pout—she got a kick out of using her power over men. The guys had come to ogle both her and the car when they'd rolled in. She'd simply said, "You all want me, don't you?" Based on her appearance, she might not've had to use charm resonance with a lot of them.

She watched me like a cat playing with an injured bird—the twists of anger and pain in my face amused her. I started to shake with the effort of holding myself back. My vision seemed narrow and red, as though I'd locked on target.

Don't kill her.

I couldn't fry her just for making these guys lust after her, right? I needed to hold it together. Part of me knew my reaction was off-the-charts like this because Trevor was involved. This intense jealousy was just part of the whole soulmate package deal. I needed to calm down before I hurt someone. *Don't kill her.* I repeated my new mantra. *Don't kill her. She isn't making anyone DO anything.*

Stop it, I said into her head. My mental voice sounded weak and pathetic, mostly because I had to hold so much back.

She gave me a bad-girl, cutesy pout and looked at Trevor with new interest. He was still lusting after her and I felt the sudden urge to slap—everybody.

"This one your boyfriend, minder-girl?"

My hand came up and gripped Trevor's arm in a protective, proprietary gesture—MINE. I looked up and met her eyes with an icy stare. *Back. Off. Now.*

"Or you'll do what? Think at me?" She laughed and gave Trevor another long, appraising look. *Ah, hell.* My reaction had drawn her attention to him, setting off some sort of competitive game in her mind. "Tell me, handsome, what's your ability?" Her words resonated with charm.

Lethal energy nearly shot from my forehead. I squeezed my eyes shut, fighting to control it, even though a part of me didn't want to stop it. That part kept growing stronger.

What's up with her voice?

Trevor hadn't answered her question. My eyes flew open. I could breathe again. I had a hand on Trevor now. He'd heard the charm resonance in her words because he now shared my minder-immunity to mind-control.

She's trying to charm you.

The worst of his raunchy thoughts about this woman melted away, replaced with the guarded distrust he usually felt for charms. My fingers tightened around him.

"Don't you want to ditch her and spend some time with me?" Her voice drooled suggestiveness.

Trevor snorted. "No! Why would I want to do that?"

Blondie's vexation grew. I bit my lip to keep from laughing.

"Belinda, you might want to step back. You're about to get your brain fried." Williamson hurried down the steps of the main building. The killing energy in my mind finally simmered back. I took a shuddering breath, feeling my shoulders drop as I exhaled.

"Fried?" She gave Trevor another appraisal. *He doesn't look like a McFee.*

"He's not a McFee, nor is he the one who's about to fry you." *Take the charm command off all of them*, I thought at her. *Now!*

"Make me, little girl." Her lips curled into a shiny, red sneer.

I blasted her Broca's area with a quick, rapier burst of energy, sending the language center of her brain into a seizure. She didn't even notice.

I looked around the circle. Were any of the surrounding people charms? I recognized a head of wavy black hair. *Zack? Can you tell everyone to stop doing what Belinda said?*

"Huh?" Zack seemed to shake himself awake. His unshielded thoughts remained full of explicit images of Belinda and he was rather enjoying them. Normally, Zack shielded his thoughts—making him a one-of-a-kind charm. My voice in his head had surprised him. I'd only "spoken" to him once since we'd all returned to Ganzfield, when he'd sought me out in the dining hall. The memory flashed through me.

What's HE doing here? Trevor's dismay had wrapped around my thoughts and squeezed.

"Maddie. I just—just wanted to say how sorry I am...you know...again." Remorse had flavored each word. "Thanks for not insisting that I be kicked out or anything."

I'd only nodded in acknowledgement. I knew we'd both been at fault. I'd wounded his pride and overreacted when he'd tried to salvage it. His efforts to charm me had been wrong, but I knew he wasn't as bad as some of the other charms.

This Belinda woman was a case in point.

Stop doing what Belinda said, Zack thought to himself. The images in his head disappeared.

Whoa. Did you just un-charm yourself?

He didn't need to find another charm to take off Belinda's command? None of the other charms could do that! Zack's bright blue eyes met mine. His shield snapped back into place, as though he'd suddenly realized his mental fly was open. He didn't answer my question.

"Stop doing what Belinda said," Zack charmed the crowd.

The intensity of dirty thoughts dropped dramatically. Of course, Belinda still looked slutty in her too-tight clothes, so most of the guys still had mental images in a similar vein. Whatever. That was normal. But this pied-piper-of-sex thing needed to stop.

Now.

Apparently, Williamson agreed. "Belinda, things have changed around here."

Belinda intended to say, *Yeah, now that I'm here, they'll get fun again*. Instead, "Mup too dahb…" came from her mouth. *What the hell? What's wrong with my voice?* She turned narrowed viper-eyes at me. *Did she—?*

I risked a quick look at Zack and he met my gaze. A strange play of emotions passed over his face. Even with his shield up, I knew we both remembered the first time I'd done this—because I'd done it to him.

Williamson pressed his lips together, forcing himself not to smile. "I did warn you, Belinda."

What did that little bitch do to my voice? Apparently, this wasn't Belinda's first time framing thoughts to Williamson. She laced her unspoken words with venom.

Oh, great. Another one who hated me. What was it with me and charms? A sad, dark-purple pang passed through me as I remembered Grace. She'd been one of the few charms who'd been a friend. But she'd died—nearly all of the charms at Ganzfield had.

And now we had Belinda here.

Oh, goody.

"You remember the rules, Belinda? No killing, no maiming, no permanent damage, no charming people into sex—"

...and no charming instructors. Yeah, I needlepointed them into a pillow back when I was here. Belinda dripped sarcasm.

Williamson again suppressed a laugh. "Just take it easy while you're here." He seemed fond of Belinda—too fond of her.

Williamson's head snapped up at the direction of my thoughts and his smile vanished. *No! She's young enough to be my daughter!*

Then what is it?

Come back to my office. We can talk about that—and a few other things.

Williamson looked around at the guys still milling around Belinda. "Don't we still have classes here? Get going, everyone!"

Classes. Thank heavens Trevor and I'd stopped attending when we'd started training with the team.

"Belinda, we had several new trailers delivered this morning. Why don't you pick one of them out for yourself and get settled in?" Williamson gestured in their general direction. "I'm sure your voice will return to normal in a few minutes. Right, Maddie?"

I gave her a mean smile. *Yeah. The first time is temporary.*

Belinda blanched, and then scowled at me.

"And perhaps you might consider leaving Trevor alone," Williamson suggested.

Trevor? Isn't he the telekinetic? I heard about him. She looked at Trevor appraisingly. My hackles rose again, sensing her intrigue with the sexual possibilities of an extra set of hands. I itched with an annoying, twitchy desire to slap Belinda repeatedly.

Hard.

I tightened my grip on Trevor's arm. He'd caught her thoughts secondhand and pink embarrassment stained both his cheeks and his mind. I focused in, knowing I might not want to see too closely but unable to stop myself.

A few lustful thoughts about Belinda still flitted across Trevor's thoughts. *Sorry.* He squeezed his eyes shut and tried to think of something else when he realized I was in his head.

I bit my lower lip and looked away. Seeing those thoughts in Trevor made my soul ache. But how could I hold those thoughts against him? She'd charmed them into him—at least the worst ones. And weren't they normal? I heard them all the time from the other guys around here. Weren't all straight guys attracted to women they saw—especially women who intentionally inspired raunchy thoughts? Out in the rest of the world, where guys didn't know to watch the contents of their heads around me, it was even worse. Was I supposed to just ignore them in Trevor? How could I? They hit me in the gut like rocks.

We followed Williamson up the two flights of stairs to his office. He closed the door behind us and Trevor and I took the two chairs in front of his desk. I still held his arm—it gave my hand something to do besides slap people. The contact also kept him in the mental conversation.

Williamson leaned forward in his chair and tented his fingers.

Maddie, do I need to tell you to play nice with the new charm?

I tried to scowl, but it came out more like a pout. *That WAS nice. She's still breathing, isn't she? So what's her deal?*

Belinda? She's our best information source in Washington, D.C.

What? That...that... several rude terms came to mind... *woman is in the government?*

Not exactly. She gets her information...in other ways. Then I saw his meaning.

SHE'S A HOOKER? My jaw dropped as revulsion filled me. She had a G-positive ability, and *that* was what she used it for? What a waste of dodecamine!

Call girl. It's not like she has to have sex with anyone, after all. Really, she's more like a spy. Belinda has a large client list—men in many different positions.

So to speak.

Williamson rolled his eyes. *Don't start that. When she "dates" one of these men, she can charm him into believing that she's...fulfilled his, um...fantasies. She actually spends the time asking him questions and gathering information for us.*

I could see the perverse appeal of having these men pay someone to spy on them. But she could cause so much damage! And what about national security? We were still Americans, after all. What about these men's families? Belinda could "persuade" an otherwise faithful husband or boyfriend to call her. How many good relationships and marriages had she destroyed? Did she care? Her actions might be for our benefit, but they underscored just how dangerous a charm could be. Did she put us all at risk of exposure? And if someone found out what she was doing...

She'd charm them into forgetting. It's happened a few times. Williamson interrupted my building rant. *In fact, if people in D.C. need to "forget" something they've learned about Ganzfield or*

G-positives, I usually call Belinda to pay them a quick visit.

I shook my head. *What she does is wrong on so many levels.*

Aren't you worth over six million dollars these days, Maddie?

That's not the same! I didn't hurt anyone! Besides, it was four-point-something million now. We hadn't cut any corners with the IRS—not after the SEC investigation.

It's probably closer than you like to think.

I huffed, offended. I was *not* like Belinda!

And speaking of what you're thinking, I don't want any more shielding like you did this morning.

My jaw clenched and I considered throwing a brick wall up around my mind again—just to show him that he wasn't the boss of me. No, I needed to be better than that. I needed to be... responsible. Mature. *How about you give me a little credit next time, Jon? It's not like I go sneaking off the grounds a lot, and I always have a really good reason.*

True, but you don't always think things through before you go charging off.

But I usually get a chance to think things through before I get to where I'm going. We're in the middle of nowhere here so it's a long drive.

Trevor snorted.

Williamson smiled. *Okay, how about a compromise? You get a standing pass to use one of the vehicles and go off the grounds when you have a "really good reason," as you put it. In return, I get your word that you'll tell us before you go and that you'll take proper security precautions. Also, if you're shielding to protect someone's privacy again, you let me know. Write me a note, if that's what it takes.*

Deal. I had to admit, I usually liked Williamson's deals.

So we're good? Trevor gave my hand a squeeze as he joined the silent conversation.

We're good, Williamson replied.

We stood up to leave. *Anything else?* I asked.

Williamson frowned as a shadow passed through his thoughts. *One more thing. We think Isaiah has killed again.*

Where?

Just outside Chicago. This time, he took out three people together. A charm and his two children. A boy and a girl—young. Their mother was with them. Her husband and kids just crumpled in front of her.

Oh, my God in Heaven. Killing children? While their mother watched them die? Bile rose in my throat. I again felt the impulse to just *do something* to stop Isaiah. We needed to find a way to take him down, to end this horror.

I'm going out there to talk to Mrs. Davis. I'll take a larger group this time. Your team works well together. I think it's a good model. Zack Greyson is ready to do fieldwork, so he'll come along as the charm. Three sparks should do it. I don't want to leave Ganzfield short-handed—

Williamson broke off as he realized that my attention had turned to Trevor. Alarm had spiked through him at the name *Davis.*

"What was the man's name?" Trevor's thoughts had turned a sickly grey and his face had paled.

I let out a gasp as I understood. *Oh, no.*

"Jared Davis?" he asked.

Williamson's eyes widened as he read the concern in Trevor's mind, as well. He fumbled to pull up the file on his computer, checking the names again.

Jared Davis: age 37.

Rebecca Davis: age 8.

William Davis: age 5.

"I'm so sorry. I didn't know." He meant it. While Williamson kept records of family connections for all of the G-positives who came through Ganzfield, he hadn't remembered Trevor's father's name.

"We—we weren't close."

I wrapped my arms around Trevor, wordlessly trying to send him as much comfort and support as I could. He put his hand on my shoulder and his fingers gripped white.

"Why don't you sit down?"

"No, Jon. I'm okay. I'm just…I'm going to…" Even in his mind he didn't know how that sentence ended.

I'll take him home. Can someone cover our patrol tonight?

Williamson nodded. *I'll get someone to take your places.* A thought occurred to him. *Do the two of you want to go see Jared Davis' widow instead? Maddie, you can get the same information I can. Does Trevor need to go and see his family now?*

"Yeah. We'll go." Trevor sounded far away.

You're sure? I asked.

He nodded.

"You can leave tomorrow. I'll set everything up. Who do you want on your team?"

Trevor looked down into my eyes. "Just Maddie."

You need backup. Some sparks, maybe, and a charm…

"If Isaiah finds us, Jon, we can protect each other long enough to get away. But we can't do that for anyone else. And a larger team would draw attention. No one would think anything about the two of us showing up after—at a time like this. Just Maddie."

Williamson nodded. *I'll set everything up,* he told us again.

Back at the church, I pulled Trevor over to his bed, wrapped my arms around him, and put my forehead against his.

Oh, Trevor. I'm so sorry. I ached to wrap him tightly in so many layers of love that nothing painful like this could ever touch him.

Confusion and contradiction filled him. He mourned a man he'd barely known—he'd only met his birthfather once. *It's stupid for me to care about someone who didn't care about me.* His gut twisted for the half-siblings he'd never met—whom he'd never get a chance to meet now. He felt like crying, but he didn't want to cry.

I brought a hand up to caress Trevor's cheek, trying to soothe him. I wished I was better at this—that I knew how to help him. *What can I do? What do you need?*

Just you. Just this. He wrapped two sets of arms around me, pulling me close—not in a romantic way, but for reassurance and comfort. He got the same sense of wholeness—of peace—from me that I got from him.

I stroked his face gently. *I can do that.*

"I think we need to bring back the rest of my family."

We'd skipped dinner, dipping into our stash of junk food for sustenance. Trevor had been trying the idea on for size for a while and I hadn't interrupted. His mom and grandparents had never made him feel particularly wanted or cherished, so I already didn't like them very much, even though we'd never met. Trevor was too good for them. But it was this good nature that made him want to protect them.

How far are they from Chicago? We leaned against the headboard of his bed and tried to avoid leaving Cool Ranch crumbs on the sheets.

"A little over five hours."

Okay.

"You're not thrilled."

I'm on board, though. I want you to be happy. You want your family safe, so we'll make sure that happens.

"Thanks." I could feel Trevor's own ambivalence, and part of it centered around…me.

Gulp.

You don't want them to meet me?

"Yes…no. It's complicated." His thoughts tumbled out. *I didn't like who I was back when I was with them. I don't want to feel… young and stupid and not good enough. I don't want them looking at you and…seeing someone who's…"different." Different isn't a good thing for my grandmother. I don't want you to see me the way they do—to know what they really think of me…to confirm what I've always suspected they were thinking. And I don't want you angry at them for it. They're my family.*

So, basically, you think we'll all hate each other. I tried not to be hurt.

He gave a sad smile. "Midwesterners don't hate. It's not polite."

So, you think we'll all DISAPPROVE of each other.

"That sounds about right," he admitted.

You love them.

He nodded.

You love me.

"You know how much I do."

Then I will get along with them, even if it kills me. I could play nice. I really could. I'd smile through every disapproval. Maybe I could use my ability to get some insight into how to win a little of their positive regard.

Trevor looked unconvinced.

They used to be college professors, right? I was a complete teacher's pet in school. I can get them to like me.

Trevor gave me another skeptical look. "I seem to remember you ignoring most of your classes."

I gave a little laugh. *Well, yeah. Here. How could I pay attention in class when I could talk to YOU instead?*

He smiled, pinking up slightly with pleasure. I set the chips and soda on the floor by the side of the bed.

You know, you've completely derailed my academic career. I don't know if I've thanked you for that recently.

I pulled myself across him, my legs on either side of his.

"But how will you ever make a living?" He smiled as he wrapped his arms around my waist.

Professional poker player.

He gave me a dubious look.

Game show contestant? I'd rock on Jeopardy!

He considered that one.

How about we just become one another's devoted love slaves and we live off the interest from my millions and millions of dollars?

"That's more like it." He grinned as he kissed me.

CHAPTER 5

"I heard about Trevor's father." Rachel crossed her arms over her abdomen. I'd come up to her room in Blake House because I needed an Isaiah-tracker update. "I'm sorry. I—I didn't see that one."

I was grateful for that, since she'd have given me a head full of memories if she had. She often replayed the killings she'd witnessed through her visions. They filled her with a hot anger that she actually enjoyed, since it temporarily drove out her pain—and her feelings of weakness.

Thanks. I'll tell him. We're going out to talk to—to his stepmother today. The term didn't seem to fit a woman he'd never met.

"I think Isaiah's still in the Midwest. It looked like Iowa from the road signs. Be careful and keep your cell phone with you. I'll call if I see him heading back to Chicago."

We're going to try and bring the rest of his family back here from Michigan.

She nodded, adding that information to her mental map.

"My parents are coming here next week."

Ready to tell them?

"Yeah. I mean, I guess."

Sean's parents are staying in one of the trailers.

"They are?"

You might want to tell them, too.

The trailers were the movie-star kind—not the tornado-bait kind—but I kept away anyway. Many family members of those who'd died in the massacre stayed there—avoiding the places that reminded them of the dead. The combined anguish of the victims' families punched me in the gut when I got too close.

In most cases, telling the parents of a teenage boy that they were about to become grandparents would be a bad thing. It might still be. But perhaps Sean's folks would see it the way Rachel did—like a piece of their son was still alive.

If I didn't have a plane to catch, I'd go with you.

Her laugh didn't cover her anxiety. "Thanks, but I'm not sure I really want to know what they think of me."

It doesn't matter what they think of you. Sean loved you.

Tears came to her eyes. "Thanks, Maddie."

One more thing. If they give you any trouble, tell them I said there was a good chance Gran McFee would've dreamed you two together.

"Gran McFee?"

Their family matchmaker.

She smiled. "I guess you'd know about things like that." *Since you put the ideas into Sean's head that got him to ask me out.*

Sean told you what I did? I felt my face get hot.

She smiled, but her eyes shone with unshed tears. "Thanks. He once told me that he needed the push you gave him."

So, if the parents get mad, be sure to deflect a bunch of that blame onto me, okay?

"Of course. That was the plan all along," she deadpanned.

I snorted with laughter.

Trevor and I took one of the vans down to the airport in Manchester. We'd need the larger vehicle when we returned with his family. I tried to keep my focus on the road. The only other time I'd ever driven one of the big vans, I'd gashed the hell out of one side on the front gate. The combination of controlling the large vehicle and scanning passing minds for intent-to-kill had my heart racing. I gripped the steering wheel with white hands.

The mountains interfered with my cell phone reception for the first part of the trip, but once we got to the interstate, Trevor swatted down his abdominal butterflies and called his grandparents.

"Laurence residence."

"Archer, it's—it's me."

"Who?"

He swallowed hard. "Trevor."

"Trevor's not here. He's at school out east."

"Archer, it's me, Trevor. I'm—I'm coming to Michigan to see you."

"You're coming back?" The voice didn't seem enthusiastic and I felt something sink within Trevor.

"Just for today. Would you mind calling Laurie to see if she and the girls could come to Barton Hills? Maybe for dinner?"

"You want them to drive all the way over here tonight?"

"Yes, sir. I'm bringing someone to meet all of you." I felt his gaze warm me. "We have some important things to discuss."

As soon as he finished the call, Trevor had me pull over and change places with him. Driving gave him something else to think about.

I bought a travel alarm clock and a car cell phone charger from one of the overpriced airport stores. I kept running nervous fingers against the little phone in my pocket. It felt like my personal talisman—a magical object that would keep us from harm. Its silence meant safety; Rachel would call if Isaiah came too near.

The flight packed me into a too-small space with annoyed and anxious strangers for hours. Life had been simpler before telepathy, but at least Trevor's presence helped me deal with the new complexities. And hey, if terrorists tried to hijack the plane or something, I could always blast them.

The mental rumble of Chicago increased as we descended to land, pushing a never-ending babble into my head. *Ugh.* I used to like cities. I really did. *Here we go again. I'm going to try to shield to keep from sharing it with you, okay? One of us needs to be able to focus.*

I want to help you.

I stroked my thumb across his knuckles. *Just get me to the car and drive us out to the suburbs quickly. That'll help.*

Williamson said that a charm named Bill would meet us by the rental car desks.

I nodded and laced my fingers through his. No one was going to charm Trevor on my watch.

Pale yellow anxiety jittered off the man waiting in front of the information kiosk. *"Maddie Dunn." Williamson just said to keep thinking the name "Maddie Dunn."*

I pointed him out to Trevor as I tightened my grip on his

hand. The guy looked to be about thirty and his casual clothes still somehow broadcast how expensive they were.

"Maddie Dunn." But what if they weren't on that plane? "Maddie Dunn." Should I stick around to meet them or can I—

Trevor closed the distance. "Hey, are you Bill?"

Bill's eyes went wide as they darted first to Trevor and then over to me. "You're Maddie?"

I nodded.

Great. We can get this thing over with and I can get the hell out of here. "Bill Davis. Dr. Williamson said you needed some help with a car."

Trevor startled at the last name. "Davis? Any relation to Jared Davis?"

Bill's fear and grief splashed within him. *They know about Jared. That must be why they're here. The girl must be really shy; she hasn't said a word.* "He was my older brother." *And Isaiah killed them—even the kids. Is he still close-by?*

Trevor's eyebrows shot up and he inhaled sharply. *I have an uncle?* "You're...are you going to Ganzfield now?" *He can tell me about my father. Wow. I have an uncle. And he's also a G-positive. He's...he's family. I have family I never even knew existed.*

"As soon as I get you squared away with the car, I'm on a flight east." *Ganzfield's probably the only safe place right now. What're these kids going to do if Isaiah comes after them? They shouldn't be here.*

The rental car agent eyed me suspiciously as I handed her my license and credit card. "We can't rent a car to anyone under twenty-five."

I rolled my eyes. *Blatant age discrimination.* After all, I could put down enough collateral to cover whatever damage they feared I'd do.

Bill leaned in and laid on the charm. "Her age isn't a problem."

The clerk's overly-tweezed eyebrows rose and her lips pursed into a knot.

I don't have time to deal with her attitude. Bill's voice lowered. "You're *delighted* to be able to help her today."

The agent gave me a warm smile as she slid the papers to me. "Just sign here and you'll be all set."

I folded my copy into my purse and grabbed the keys.

Bill frowned. *It doesn't feel right to leave these kids here in danger.* "You two...don't get into any trouble, all right? Get back to Ganzfield quickly. Stay safe."

My lips quirked at the resonance in his voice. It was the first time anyone had tried to charm me for my own good. How sweet. Manipulative, but sweet.

Something caught in Trevor's throat and he nodded.

Bill narrowed his eyes for a moment—*something's off here. Did the charm take?*—but then he turned and moved up the escalator to the Departures section.

Trevor watched until Bill was out of sight and then frowned and shook his head. *Wait. Did he just try to charm us?*

I met his eyes and nodded.

And he's my...my uncle?

Couldn't this conversation wait until I no longer needed to shield my thoughts from him? Right now, all I could do was nod, so I did.

I handed Trevor the cell phone and he called to check in with Rachel.

"You're okay, for the moment." She sounded tired.

We took a shuttle to the lot where the little rental hatchback waited for us, and then followed Williamson's printed directions out Route 290 to the town of Medinah. The mental pressure of the city increased as we approached the city center, and then eased as we left the densest urban areas. My brain felt trampled.

We passed the golf course and pulled up in front of the house. It was nice looking, in a generic suburban sort of way. I took a moment to steel myself—I now had to face the emotional anguish of a grieving mother and widow. The too-warm air of the sunny summer afternoon hit me as I opened the car door.

Trevor hesitated.

I looked at him for a moment, and then pulled the door closed again. *Do you need some time?*

It's okay. I just…

Unwanted. Rejected. Childhood insecurities welled up in his mind, making him feel small and powerless.

I took his face in my hands, bringing his eyes to meet mine. *Trevor, you are an amazing person. A—MAZ—ING. If they never knew that, it is their problem and their mistake. And I know what I'm talking about. I know you better than they do.*

He smiled at his own words coming back at him, and then drew a deep, steadying breath. "Let's do this."

A square-jawed woman answered the door. Her eyes shone too-liquid with unshed tears. "Can I help you?" *What do these kids want? How do I get them to go away and leave Faith alone?*

"I'm…Trevor Laurence." Inside the house, I felt a flash of surprise as someone recognized the name.

So? My sister's been through an unholy hell over the past few days and she doesn't need—

"Let him in, please, Hope."

The voice came from the living room, tired and full of pain. Faith Davis looked like she'd recently been pulled from a river. Buttons misaligned on the shirt that hung off her frame. Her strong features seemed washed out with grief. Faith examined Trevor closely, searching his face for some traits of her husband.

He's about the same height as Jared. His hair has the same texture, although the color is darker. She wasn't sure if she was disappointed that the resemblance wasn't stronger.

Trevor and I took the two empty chairs. Faith sat on the couch, looking hollowed out and fragile with her hands folded in her lap. She never noticed that I didn't speak.

Finally, Trevor asked, "Can you tell me what happened?"

Her face crumpled and she leaned her head in her hands. I saw her memory—the family at the dinner table together as they finished the meal. Faith had gone into the kitchen to scoop some ice cream for dessert. She'd heard the kids giggling at something their father was doing and a warm splash of devotion had welled within her.

Then her daughter's worried voice had called out, "Daddy?" There'd been a soft thud and Faith's world had gone into slow-motion. The ice cream scoop had dropped onto the floor. Her husband and son had lain unmoving and lifeless. Her daughter had convulsed for a few seconds before she, too, had gone limp.

The tears started down my face and I swallowed hard against the rising tide of nausea. Faith still hadn't answered aloud, but she didn't have to. I'd seen the effects of a mental attack before— hell, I'd *caused* them. But this evil, *evil* man had murdered *children.* Something turned hard within my gut. Isaiah could *not* be allowed to get away with this. He had to be stopped.

I bit my lip. I didn't want to cause this woman further pain, but we needed to know more. I floated the thoughts gently into her mind. *Did I see anything unusual? Any strange people around?*

Faith concentrated, trying to answer what she believed were her own questions, but came up blank. She wiped her face and tried to focus what was left of her shattered soul.

My hands shook so I wrapped my arms around myself to stop

them. *We're set,* I thought to Trevor. I just needed to see the mind of the witness. It made my heart ache that we'd upset her and hadn't learned anything new.

Trevor hesitated. "What was he like?"

Faith sniffed and her tear-filled eyes unfocused into her memory. "Charismatic." A sad smile softened her face. "People loved to be around Jared. He was so smart, so funny. He could make the most outrageous plan seem like a good idea."

A wave of overpowering loss filled her and her grief grabbed me by the throat. Her husband, her children—the people who'd given her life meaning—were gone. A tear drew a wet line down my cheek.

Trevor murmured our sympathies again as we stood. At that moment, I felt so *useless*. I wished I had Hannah's ability to soothe with a touch, or even Cecelia's way of comforting with charmed words.

Back in the car, Trevor sat with closed eyes for several minutes, trying to make sense of this new little cul-de-sac on the road of his life. I held his hand, gently stroking my thumb across the back of his fingers. Intense emotions rolled across his mind, leaving it flat. Finally, he took a deep breath and looked up.

You okay? I asked.

Yeah. Trevor paused. *Maddie?*

Yeah?

It was Isaiah, wasn't it?

I gave a solemn nod. *Pretty sure. That was a telepathic attack.*

Yeah. He got lost in his thoughts for a while but I followed behind him, ready to show him the way out.

It's not your fault, Trevor.

If I'd killed him in Peapack, they'd still be alive.

My throat closed. *If I'd just stopped moving when he charmed everyone there to freeze, I could've killed him when he came close enough. Hell, if I'd just had a gun I probably could've shielded long enough to shoot him.*

Maddie?

Yeah?

We've got to stop him.

I know.

Even if...even if it kills us.

I thought of Rachel's growing excitement over the baby. She'd be destroyed if Isaiah ripped that child's life from her. I felt protective of her, of the baby, of my mom, of all of Ganzfield. *Our people.* What would I do to protect them? How far would I go to stop Isaiah? I remembered going over the wall in Peapack—knowing I was outmatched—and I knew I'd do it again for another chance to take down this monster.

Maybe next time I'd bring a gun.

I nodded to Trevor. *Just don't make me live without you, okay? I'm not as strong as Williamson.*

Trevor pulled me into his arms, which didn't work so well in the bucket seats of the rental car. I ended up with the emergency brake handle digging into my hip. The surreal nature of the world we now inhabited struck me again—normal teenagers didn't contemplate destroying murderous telepaths, even if it meant losing their own lives in the process.

Trevor gave a little chuckle at that. *You want to be normal?*

I smiled back, glad to feel the worst of the emotional intensity dissipating. *No. I want to be with you!*

We drove east, passing briefly through the press of cacophonous minds in the city, and then skirted along the southern shore of one of the Great Lakes.

What do you mean you don't know which one it is? Trevor was astonished at my ignorance.

Well, I'm not from around here, am I?

Obviously. Trevor humphed. *So? Which one is it?*

HOMES.

There isn't a Lake Homes.

No. It's a mnemonic. H. O. M. E. S. Huron Ontario Michigan Something Superior.

Erie, he supplied.

It's Lake Erie? I asked.

No, it's Lake Michigan. What did you ever study in school?

No clue. I talked to you through all of my classes.

We passed through a little corner of Indiana before we hit Michigan and turned inland. Near Kalamazoo, we stopped for a snack and a bathroom break.

Kalamazoo's an actual city? I thought it was a cartoon place name.

Trevor rolled his eyes at this further display of the gaps in my education.

The lighter mood dropped away as we closed in on Ann Arbor.

Trevor, I'm going to get them to approve of me even if it kills me. It's not like I could say anything that would offend them, right?

His brows met in a worried line. *It's...weird to bring her into this world. Maddie's...magical, and this is just...normal.*

I raised my eyebrows. *So, you think, after a few hours in the Laurence household of Barton Hills, Michigan, I'll just turn out to be an ordinary girl?*

"No, but I might seem like an ordinary guy to you."

Not a chance.

"You calling me a freak?" he asked, trying to recapture our

earlier mood.

Takes one to know one, Four Arms.

"Enough! I don't have to take this from somebody from *New Jersey*! Are you really a G-positive or do your freakish super-powers come from childhood exposure to toxic waste?"

I cracked up.

We pulled into the driveway of a brown house on a quiet, residential street. Battenburg lace curtains filled the windows that faced the street. It was nearly 7 p.m., but long rays from the setting sun still lit the tidy yard. A quick mental scan didn't turn up anyone who might try to kill us.

...but the evening's still young.

I detached the cell phone from the car charger and pocketed it before I took Trevor's face in my hands and looked deep into his eyes. *Remember, I think you're amazing—and I know you better than they do.*

That going to be our new thing now?

Pretty sure. I like it.

He pulled my face to his for a quick kiss.

An elderly couple waited for us in the arch of the front door. Trevor's grandfather was tall and lanky—much like Trevor—although Archer Laurence looked like he might've lost a couple of inches and had a slight old-man paunch that made his khakis ride up too high. Thin flaps of skin on his neck reminded me of a turtle. His brown eyes had a little more loose flesh around them than Trevor's, but the family resemblance was still evident. He smiled at us in greeting, raising a hand in welcome as we came up the walk. The gesture made something in his side ache and I felt twinges of what might be arthritis from his hand.

Trevor's grandmother wore her steel-streaked hair pulled back severely, like a dancer. She was also tall, nearly the same height as her husband. Liver spots dotted the skin of her neck and arms, right up to the edges of her crisp-collared white blouse. She studied me with unsmiling, raptor-like intensity.

As we got closer, I suddenly realized why.

Trevor, if you could find a way to slip into conversation how pregnant I'm NOT, you'll make your grandmother feel better.

Trevor's eyes closed for a moment of silent realization and mortification before he cracked a smile. *Consider it done.*

I suppressed my laugh, wondering why everyone seemed to have this on the brain, all of a sudden.

We reached the front door. There were no hugs of greeting as Trevor hurried to dredge up the manners he knew his grandmother expected. "Lilith, Archer, this is Maddie Dunn. My…um…girlfriend," he added, slightly self-consciously. I tried not to let my surprise at Trevor's use of their first names show. "Maddie, these are my grandparents, Doctor and Doctor Laurence."

Apparently, I wasn't on a first-name basis with the Doctors Laurence. I pasted on a polite smile as I shook each of their hands.

Doesn't she even speak English? His grandmother was still pretty sure I was pregnant.

Geez, I'm making a heck of a first impression.

"Is Laurie here yet?" Trevor asked as we went into the living room. Decades-old, brown furniture decorated the immaculate room. "I didn't see her car. Maddie and I have some important things we need to discuss with you."

The flashes of thought from his grandparents made me cringe even before Lilith said, "She decided not to come. The girls shouldn't be out late. They both have piano lessons on Saturday mornings and Laurie didn't want them to miss any so close to their recitals."

A surge of pain went through Trevor as he processed that his own mother wasn't willing to drive an hour and a half to see her son for the first time *in two years* because of piano lessons.

I bit my lip. *Do either of your grandparents have heart conditions? Why?*

Because I really want to give them a piece of my mind right now.

You promised to play nice!

Okay, okay, okay.

At least Archer seemed apologetic. "I know she was sorry to miss you, Trevor. And she was sorry not to have a chance to meet you." I could tell she'd made no such comment. Behind him, a magazine slid out of the fan-shaped arrangement on the small table by the couch. It landed on the floor with a loud slap.

Was that you? I asked Trevor. I hadn't felt him do anything with the magazine.

I think it was Archer. Before I went to Ganzfield, I used to accidentally knock things around all the time.

My eyebrows shot up as I gave Archer another look. Another telekinetic? Interesting.

We settled on the two couches set in an L along the walls while Lilith asked us if we'd like something to drink.

"Water's fine," said Trevor. He mentally checked with me, and I nodded. "For both of us."

Okay, now my not-talking thing was weirding them out.

Once Lilith had returned with the tray of water glasses and made proper-sounding comments about dinner being ready in a few minutes, Trevor cleared his throat, leaned forward…

And suddenly realized he had no idea where to begin.

Just prep them for how I talk, and then let me help.

"Lilith. Archer. Maddie and I met at Ganzfield—the school back east. What I'm about to tell you…well…it needs to remain a secret. Ganzfield is a training facility for people with unusual abilities, like us. Maddie's a mi—a telepath."

I felt their skepticism rise and couldn't suppress my smile.

"She was injured a few months ago and can no longer talk, so don't be upset if you hear her directly in your minds, all right?"

Lilith frowned. "Young man, this isn't amusing."

It's not meant to be, I said into all of their heads.

Lilith reacted with the horrified expression of a 1950's monster movie character. Her eyes bugged and her mouth formed a perfect O. *Heavens! What would the neighbors think if they found out that we associated with such a strange person?*

After a quick shock, Archer stared intensely at me. "What number am I thinking of?"

Pi, of course. I smiled. *Which means you're either a math professor or you're ready for dessert.*

Archer cackled. "Trevor, I like her already!"

A little tremor of pleasure rippled through Trevor at this unexpected approval.

Lilith's lips had disappeared in a thin, pale line that clearly conveyed I was definitely *not* making the Christmas card newsletter. She looked at Archer with narrowed-eyed disapproval and regarded her husband's enthusiasm as a form of betrayal. *What kind of strange people has the boy fallen in with? I expected him to make better choices.* She returned to the kitchen and the dishes and pans clattered excessively as she put the finishing touches on dinner. A concern for Archer's health simmered under the rest of her thoughts, causing a constant, nebulous anxiety that made her even less tolerant than she otherwise might've been.

Archer had me guess five more numbers before Trevor told him, "She's not a toy, Archer."

I don't mind, I told him. But I was glad to stop.

"So, Trevor, are you a telepath, too?"

"Telekinetic."

"What? Like spoon bending?"

"More like this." The heavy, glass coffee table rose into the air and hovered halfway to the ceiling. Under us, the couch springs creaked as the weight of the coffee table displaced through Trevor's body.

Archer gave another cackle of delight. "That's amazing!"

Trevor IS amazing, I agreed.

As Trevor lowered the coffee table, Archer gave me a long look. "So, you two are…dating?"

I nodded, feeling a blush warm my cheeks.

"How long have you been together?"

Since October. Nearly eight months.

"Getting serious?"

I nodded again. More blushing.

"Being safe?"

"Geez, Archer!" Trevor turned a mortified red, as well.

After all we'd been through in the past few days, I thought it was funny. *You can tell your wife to stop worrying. I'm not pregnant.*

Archer laughed, slightly embarrassed. *Oh, I guess she picked that up from our thoughts. Wow, mind-reading. That's…neat-o!*

I hadn't expected to, but I found that I liked Trevor's grandfather. I grinned at Trevor. *Hey, he thinks I'm "neat-o!"*

Trevor hid his smile behind his water glass as Archer small-talked me about my family and our flight until Lilith called us into the dining room.

At the table, we obediently folded hands as Archer said grace. The main course was a noodle casserole of some kind, but we didn't eat much. Trevor explained that Isaiah was hunting people like us, and that he'd killed Jared Davis and his two kids. They had no affection for the man who'd gotten their teenage daughter pregnant, but Jared's death still caused flashes of yellow shock in both of them.

"I think you both should come back with us to Ganzfield." Trevor looked from one to the other. "I want Laurie to bring her family, too. Isaiah's getting even worse now—bolder. And he's not too far away. You all need to be somewhere safe."

I'm not going anywhere near the "freak school." Lilith's thoughts stung like acid and I bit my mental tongue. She was important to Trevor. I'd be nice if it killed me.

"What's it like there?" asked Archer, intrigued.

Parts of it are great. I projected a memory of one of last winter's Fireball games. *People at Ganzfield can do some incredible things. It has its good points and bad points, just like everywhere else. But you'd be safe there, and I know Trevor wants you to come.*

Archer looked at his wife's face, taking in her pursed lips and hard eyes, and he deflated inside. "We'll think about it."

I suddenly understood more about the family dynamic that'd made Trevor's childhood so difficult.

"Trevor, clear the table." Lilith rose and carried the glass dish of mostly uneaten noodle casserole into the kitchen.

"Yes, ma'am." Trevor didn't move, but the plates flew one after the other into the kitchen behind her, stacking neatly on the counter next to the sink. Her shout of surprise made all three of us shake with silent laughter.

After dinner, we made our excuses fairly quickly.

"You're not staying the night?" Archer frowned. "We can roll a cot for you into the scrapbooking room, and Maddie can have the couch."

And that's how Trevor found out that his grandmother had turned his bedroom into the "scrapbooking room." I squeezed my eyes shut as I felt him try to push past the stumbling block of emotional pain that caused.

"We can't. Maddie throws nightmares telepathically, and I might bring the ceiling down."

Archer's brows rose. "That happened to me once."

"It did?"

"Woke up covered in chunks of plaster and there was a hole in the ceiling clear into the attic. We chalked it up to termites."

Saying our goodbyes at the door, I spoke into his head. *I hope you'll come visit us—with or without Lilith. I think you'd like it—and you might have an ability like Trevor's.*

Archer's eyes twinkled. "I've been thinking something along those lines myself."

I know. I smiled back at him and he laughed.

After he shut the door, Archer watched us through the window while Lilith's agitation simmered in the kitchen. We picked our way through little clouds of moths around the lights along the front walk.

Trevor shifted the car into gear. "That went well." He was surprised that he actually meant it.

I like your grandfather. I couldn't lie to Trevor so there really was nothing I could say about his grandmother—or his no-show mom. Really, how could they treat Trevor so callously? He deserved so much better.

We made a quick call back to Ganzfield as we drove away. Technically, I don't think Trevor broke any traffic laws—he still had two hands on the wheel while he talked.

Hands-free.

Claire sounded tired when she answered the phone. I could

picture dark circles shadowing her blue eyes almost as if I could RV her. Since the Davis family had been killed, the RVs had been working in shifts to keep track of Isaiah at all times. *"Rick's got him now. He says Isaiah's heading back toward Chicago."*

Brighton State Recreation Area was about twenty minutes from Trevor's grandparents' house; he'd been there a few times as a kid. We parked the car, grabbed our bags, and snuck in past the chain across the drive. Trevor pulled his pen-sized flashlight from the pocket of his bag.

We found a wide clearing that twinkled with the tiny lights of hundreds of fireflies. Trevor took my hand and pulled me down to sit with him. The hard ground pressed through the sleeping bag as I leaned against him. *They love you, you know.*

Tonight's visit still filled his thoughts. *Yeah, I know.*

Really. Your grandmother's primary reason for disliking me is that she thinks I'm a bad influence on you.

Trevor gave a single laugh. *They still wish that I hadn't been born.*

They wish their daughter hadn't gotten pregnant so young. It actually doesn't have anything to do with you.

Something healed a bit within him. *Really?*

You know I can't lie to you.

Yeah, I know. Trevor kissed my temple tenderly. *I'm glad we came.*

And I'm glad your mom got knocked up by a charm at sixteen.

WHAT? He was half-shocked, half-amused.

Well, c'mon. Look at the result! You're amazing!

Freak.

Look who's talking, Four Arms! "Ay-eeeh!" A sudden attack of four-handed tickling could still get a noise out of me.

We rolled over until Trevor pinned me beneath him. Our eyes met in the dim light and we felt our chests press together with each breath. Then his lips were on mine. The starry sky faded and the electric flash pulled us together as energy, pulsing like ocean waves tumbling upon us. We built to a crashing, overpowering, cresting peak, and then floated together back to the world.

The travel alarm had been set for 6 a.m., but we didn't make it that long. My little phone rang at 5:12, a time set strongly into my mind by my first thought of the day: *who the hell would be calling us at 5:12 a.m.?*

I stared at the phone in my hand. The caller ID read "Ganzfield." How was I supposed to handle this? I flipped it open before it went to voicemail. Across the clearing, Trevor was dreaming again. A nearby bush bent sideways, and dozens of tiny leaves flashed alternating sides of forest and mint-green in the pale light as they spiraled to the ground.

"Hmm," I said into the phone.

"Maddie? That you?" Rachel asked.

"Hmm," I said again. I felt stupid, answering the phone this way. Why did I even have a phone anymore?

"I know you're still in southern Michigan, so get moving. I checked as soon as I woke up and Isaiah's bee-lining out 94 east, going at least eighty. He just passed the turn-off for Battle Creek."

Crap.

"Hmm," I said, completely aware of how little that told her. We could at least have worked out a code ahead of time for situations like this—one grunt for yes, two for no, or something. Wait, I could text her. I sent a quick **Leaving now** to her email address. I wondered when she'd check her email—she'd called from one of the Ganzfield land-lines.

I packed our bags in the two minutes it took for Trevor's dream to end. When I could get close again, I gently shook him awake. *Isaiah's coming. He's on Route 94, just past Battle Creek.*

Trevor shocked alert. "That's less than an hour from here!"

We grabbed up Trevor's sleeping bag and ran back toward our little rental car.

Archer and Lilith. Conflicting anxieties tore at him. If we went back to Barton Hills for them, we'd cut into our lead against Isaiah. Trevor wanted to keep me safe, and he wanted to keep them safe—he couldn't do both.

I can't shield Archer and Lilith's minds if he catches us with them.

"He's probably coming for the two of us. If we can draw him away—"

We arrived at the car. *Let me drive.* I dug into my pocket for the cell phone while Trevor pulled out the keys and we tossed them to each other. *You call and warn Archer and Lilith.*

We sped into the sunrise as I practiced throwing a mental shield around us while driving. It wasn't easy, especially without coffee. Fortunately, it was early on a Saturday morning so both automotive and mental traffic were light on the highway into Detroit.

"Isaiah Lerner's in Michigan and is coming this way," Trevor said into the phone. Archer had finally picked up after eight rings. He sounded groggy and confused. "He's probably coming for Maddie and me, but you and Lilith need to get out of the house. Now. Go to Laurie's. Get her and the kids moving, too."

Archer mumbled something about Lilith refusing to have a part in what she called "all that nonsense."

"Then get in the car without her, Archer. If he's coming for

G-positives, you'll draw him away from her." Apparently, Trevor had also concluded that his grandmother was a G-negative. "But Laurie's a carrier and the girls might be, too. You need to stay on the move so he can't find you. Drive on the highways. Change direction every half hour, but don't double back. Call—" he fumbled with the phone, making it display the number back at Ganzfield, which he read off to his grandfather twice. "Ask them where Isaiah is. Tell them you're my family. They'll let you know when it's safe to go home."

"I'm impressed with the way you're handling this, my boy." Something in Trevor's soul blossomed at Archer's approval and, in spite of everything, I smiled.

After Trevor finished the call, he stared at the phone in his hand, trying to figure out what to do next. *Should I call Laurie? Should I call back and try to talk Lilith into going with Archer?*

Let Archer take care of that. Can you call Rachel to let her know we're moving and to see where Isaiah is?

Rachel was relieved to be able to speak with someone who could talk back, and she confirmed Isaiah was coming straight toward us. What would he do if he caught up with us? I could block his ability and Trevor could shield us from bullets but... would Isaiah simply run our car off the road? I doubted it. Isaiah was sociopathic, not suicidal. But what if he attacked us in front of witnesses? Could his actions "out" all G-positives?

If I tried to blast Isaiah, he'd be able to channel along the energy I released, giving him a way past my mental shield. That would be bad. Nothing good could come from a confrontation with him.

We have to run.

My heart pounded as I remembered Isaiah—predatory and cruel—as he'd moved in to kill me. I imagined him gaining on us, drawing closer, trapping us against the cold shoreline of whatever Great Lake Detroit was on.

Next to me, Trevor heard that thought and released a long-suffering sigh.

The stupid rental car map was useless. Little tendrils of panic began to run through me, but then I saw the airport sign and zeroed in. I threw the car into park at the curb on the Arrivals deck, and then tossed the keys to the clerk behind the rental counter as we ran past and up the stairs to the Departures area. There was probably a huge fine for abandoning the car in a tow-away zone—but that was what the dirty, dirty stock money was for.

The screens showed a flight to Chicago leaving in less than an hour. We grabbed two tickets—putting the charge on my credit card—and then ran to the security checkpoint.

Trevor called Rachel again. "He's at the curb. He's getting out of his car." There was a pause. I guessed that Rachel was checking our location against Isaiah's. "He's almost to you guys! MOVE, MOVE, MOVE!"

My eyes met Trevor's for a panicked moment. I tightened my grip on his hand and threw the strongest shield I could around our minds. He pulled me with him as he calmly asked the people ahead of us, "Hi, do you mind if we cut ahead? Our flight's boarding now and about to leave." His voice was all Midwestern and polite, even in the face of danger.

Then we were at the head of the line, walking shoeless through the metal detectors, holding up the boarding cards that allowed us to pass. Isaiah didn't have one. If we could just get past here and out of his range…

I clutched Trevor's hand and pulled him behind the mental shield again as soon as we were both through the checkpoint. We grabbed up our bags from the collection area behind the x-ray machine and booked down the long hall beyond the security barrier toward the boarding area. I felt Isaiah's mental presence at the end of my range behind us as the glow built around me.

Oh, God. He's found us again. I risked a glance back.

There he was on the far side of the security checkpoint, looking right at me. I stopped breathing and went deer-in-the-headlights, frozen by his gaze. His fury at being blocked when so close to his prey lashed orange-hot through his mind.

Even with the distance and the mental roar of all of the other people around us, his thoughts blared into my mind. *How far could I get if I just killed everyone standing in my way?* Isaiah didn't care about avoiding detection anymore. He wanted us dead and he didn't care who he hurt—security people, other passengers, transit cops—so long as he accomplished that goal.

I'd never felt the mind of someone that…*deranged*. He hadn't been this far gone in New Jersey. Was this the result of Matilda's changes to his brain, or had I destroyed the remains of his sanity along with his voice?

No. Killing that many people would slow me down too much and those two would probably get away. I'll need to be closer to kill them through that mental wall of hers. Murdering innocent people wasn't an issue for him—only his calculation of the low odds of success held him back.

Trevor nearly pulled my shoulder from its socket as he tugged me around the corner and down the long hallway. I gasped as the connection with Isaiah snapped.

Our flight was boarding. Trevor held me close as we waited in the slow-moving line at the gate. I couldn't stop shaking. I kept listening for Isaiah's mind. Could he get past security somehow? Thank heavens he could no longer use charm compulsion. If he could still charm...

Trevor called Rachel again. "I see him. He's still standing outside the security barrier. He just seems to be staring down the hall." Was he still watching the place where we'd moved out of his sight—like a parent seeing off a beloved child, killer-telepath style? I tried to swallow the lump in my throat.

I'd frozen.

I'd been face-to-face with Isaiah again and I hadn't been able to move. I felt weak and broken, like when I'd been lying on the floor and he'd been about to kill me.

Powerless.

My heart didn't stop pounding until the plane was in the air. We landed in Chicago about ninety minutes later. Trevor talked to the desk agent and moved up our flight back to New Hampshire. The cell phone battery was getting low, but he made a quick call to Rachel.

"Isaiah's driving back toward Chicago now."

"Good. That means he's not going after my family. Maddie and I'll fly out in less than an hour. We'll be gone before he gets here."

I wrapped my arms around Trevor and pressed my cheek against his chest. Above us, a freakishly-large ceiling fan twirled among the white tubes and girders lining the ceiling. I felt the springs in my gut unwind as I watched it turn.

Trevor then called his grandparents' house and got an earful.

"Young man, I don't know what you think you're doing." Lilith's tone made me cringe, even hearing it secondhand through Trevor's mind. "Your phone call this morning scared the daylights out of your grandfather. He's not in the best of health and shouldn't have all this aggravation."

"Lilith, I—"

"What did you *say* to him? He showed up at Laurie's today and tried to convince her that the kids should skip their piano lessons and go for a drive with him."

"There's a good reason—"

"Something like this makes Archer look like he's getting senile! Really, this whole situation is ridiculous. I know we raised you better. This must be the influence of that strange girl you brought to dinner."

I couldn't help it—I started laughing out loud.

"Am I on speakerphone?" Lilith sounded indignant.

I clamped my hand over my mouth.

"No, Lilith." Trevor's eyes danced with mine as we both held in our laughter. He ended the call as soon as he decently could without being abrupt.

And that's how I entered the Laurence family lore: "That strange girl Trevor brought to dinner."

CHAPTER 6

When we finally got back to Ganzfield, I sought out my mom. I knew she'd need to see firsthand that I was safe. Her hug tightened as she read more of the details of the trip in my memory. I felt a small thread of panic weave through me when it seemed she had no intention of letting go.

Once back in our church, Trevor and I both crashed and slept for nearly twelve hours. In the morning, we finally got up in time for Sunday brunch. Sheets of rain twisted across the lake and the field, winding like enormous kite-tails caught in the gusts. Fat splotches flattened against Trevor's invisible arm "umbrella" over us.

We joined Drew, Harrison, Ellen, and Grant McFee at the table. Grant still got freaked out by my mental-voice-rather-than-talking-like-a-normal-person thing. This morning he had a strange image in his head—me as Trevor's ventriloquist dummy. I sighed and tried to remind myself of how little his opinion mattered. I bit my lip—it didn't matter, right?

Speaking of freaks...the mental temperature in the dining room shot up as pornographic thoughts erupted all around us. Three separate fires flashed around the room as some of the sparks lost control. The flames died back quickly, accompanied by the snickering of others at the tables.

Someone has the hots for the new charm!

I looked up to see Belinda framed in the doorway.

She assessed the room with disdain. *I wonder if the food is as bland as I remember it. I see that the décor is still tasteless, at least.*

Half the room assessed her underdressed assets right back.

She caught sight of me and her diamond-hard anger slashed at my mind. Belinda sauntered with false casualness toward our table.

Geez! Who wore spike heels like that in a rural place like this? She must impale the lawn with every step. I reached for Trevor's hand, not sure which one of us needed the other's protection.

"Why, hello, Little Minder-Girl."

Arrrgh! I hated her fake-sweet tone.

She leaned in as if she were going to tell me something confidential, although her real purpose was to angle her cleavage into Trevor's face. "Didn't anyone ever teach you how to share?"

I felt the killing energy flare up within my mind. I looked down at her stupid shoes and squeezed Trevor's hand harder as I fought to control myself. I knew if I saw the smirk on her face, I wouldn't be able to keep from blasting her.

Back. The Hell. Off.

Little Minder-Girl's too weak to even look me in the eye. She leaned in close to my ear. "Jon won't let you do anything to me. He needs me too much." A twinkly-cute laugh brushed against my cheek. "Why, with a few words, I could have everyone in this room—" A sick, strangling sound cut off her description of the catfight-style, mass hair-pulling she'd been contemplating.

Trevor's invisible hand squeezed her larynx, forcing her silent. I really loved the way he did that.

Belinda's eyes bugged as yellow fear splashed across her mind.

Trevor's quiet voice carried through the suddenly hushed room. "Stop bothering my girlfriend. Go away. Now."

It was wrong how much I enjoyed watching Belinda slink, red-faced and rage-filled, from the building. I kept hold of Trevor's hand, feeling my heart beat rabbit-fast against my ribs. *Thank you.*

He smiled into my eyes. *If someone messes with one of us, they mess with both of us.*

After brunch, I headed upstairs to Williamson's office. He looked up from his computer as I came in. *How'd it go?*

I closed the door and flopped into a chair by his desk. *The trip was a waste of time—at least as far as Ganzfield's concerned.* I gave him the play-by-play of my mental investigation of Trevor's stepmother's memories.

At least Trevor got to see his family and they got to meet you.

I snorted. *Yeah, I made a wonderful impression, especially with his grandmother. I bet by now she's knitting us matching outfits. We can look like twins!*

Williamson rolled his eyes. *I'm sure it wasn't that bad.*

I snorted again and shook my head.

So what was the point of us going? We didn't learn anything that'll help us stop Isaiah Learner from killing again.

Not true. We now have a good idea of how large his remote-viewing range is. He changed direction and went after you from more than two hundred miles away. Of course, he may be able to sense even further;

Charlie Fontaine's range was over a thousand miles. He frowned. *And we learned one more thing, Maddie.*

Huh?

Isaiah saw you two away from the rest of us and tracked you for hours. He went after YOU.

The implication slid into me like a steel knife. *You want to use us as bait again, Jon?*

Not without your permission. He knew that was still a sore point.

Let me talk to Trevor about it. If you can think of a good enough plan, we'd probably be up for it.

Well…

What? You already have a plan?

I'm considering one, yes.

I realized how much of his mind was shielded from me. I only felt the bare essence of consciousness from him. *So? What is it?*

That's the problem. If I tell you—

—you'll have to kill me?

Isaiah might read it from your mind. Or Trevor's.

I pondered that. *Which would basically defeat the purpose of having a "secret" plan.*

Pretty much.

It also means you expect Isaiah's going to be close enough to read us, and that I may not be able to shield properly when he tries. Are we going after him?

Williamson frowned and didn't answer.

Trevor's pretty set on getting Isaiah. After he saw what happened to Jared Davis and his family, he's ready to accept a certain amount of risk for us.

For you? Williamson gave a skeptical look.

For us. Together. Package deal.

Ah. He understood.

How about you? Are you okay with some risk?

I smiled at him. *C'mon, Jon. We both know I'm like a daughter to you! You're not going to set up a plan that puts me in terrible danger, are you?*

He didn't answer and his thoughts had gone completely opaque. A cold-grey wave of energy slid from my throat to my gut. *Uh-oh. Are you shielding because you're thinking about the secret plan right now...or is it because you're not that fond of me and you want to spare my feelings?*

He smiled and humphed. "Knock it off. You know you're one of the daughters I never had."

I warmed at that.

"But I'm trying to assess the risk. I don't want to put you in danger."

Okay. I'll go sound out Trevor—see if he can live with being part of a plan that we're not allowed to know.

"You two are on patrol tonight, all right? We've been short-handed the last few nights. Actually, I think we'll need you to take overnight shifts through most of the week."

Williamson didn't miss my silent groan.

I found Trevor hanging out in the sparks' TV room, which overflowed with people watching the Red Sox game. The four mismatched couches had been garage sale quality even before scorch-marks had been added to the upholstery, and the two in back rested on cinderblock risers—Drew and Harrison's version of stadium seating.

I'd supplied the new television and the satellite receiver, but none of the sparks knew that. My hand-printed sign adorned the wall behind the set:

No matter how the Red Sox do,
it is not the TV's fault.

A few rude remarks had been penciled in around the edges, but the sign hadn't been turned to ash—yet. After all the fried TVs last year, Williamson eventually had stopped replacing them. The first had exploded after the Yankees won by a single run in the bottom of the ninth. The second had melted into a blob of plastic and glass in another Yankee-related fit of anguish. The third had flared up like a fireplace log when a guy had snuck in one night to watch porn. But the fourth TV had crisped in a cloud of nasty-smelling grey smoke during the postseason.

I sat next to Trevor, but couldn't get into the game. Watching pro sports had never been my thing and too many people here looked at me with heads full of anxious thoughts.

Crap. Here comes the thought police.

Before the mission in Peapack, most of the sparks had seen me just as Trevor's girlfriend. Most hadn't thought of me as a minder—because I usually hadn't acted like one. Now, though, I couldn't even say "hi" without reminding people that I was in their heads.

She's like Isaiah Lerner. She could kill me with a thought anytime she wanted to.

Considering that most of the people in this room could set me on fire with nothing more than a strong intention, fearing my ability seemed a little hypocritical to me, but whatever.

If she hadn't gone in to stop Isaiah alone, Sean would still be alive.

That one put a hard knot in my gut every time I heard it.

Geez! It's so creepy how she and Trevor just stare at each other. It's like she's a thought-sucking parasite that's latched on to him.

Ugh. And now Grant had that ventriloquist dummy image in his head again. That didn't even make any sense! I squeezed my eyes shut. I'd had enough. I headed back to the church, alone. Thoughts as grey as the weather filled my head. I didn't want to cause unhappiness for Trevor. I didn't want him to lose friends because we were together. He liked spending time with his friends and I wanted him to have things that gave him joy. *Even if it means hanging out with a bunch of JERKS. DAMMIT! I nearly died trying to save them! I have permanent BRAIN DAMAGE from trying to save them! You'd think they'd be a little grateful or something…even if I didn't finish off Isaiah. At least he can't charm anymore, right? At least he didn't get a chance to send more people to kill us, right?*

I propped myself up against the headboard and spent the afternoon trying to read. I should've been able to relax—the only mental activity in my head was my own—but flashbacks of other people's unpleasant thoughts and the mental touches of the grumpy, wet birds and other little creatures outside made my brain itch.

I pulled out a bright smile when Trevor returned, but I didn't fool him.

"I could've spent the afternoon with you." Guilt muddied his thoughts. He felt like he'd ignored me, even though it'd been my idea to come home early. "I'm sorry I didn't come back with you." He wrapped his arms around my waist and pulled me back to lean against his chest. His cheek rested against my hair and I felt the worst of my bad mood melt away as we listened to the rain patter against the roof.

I wanted you to have some time to hang out with your friends. I don't have to be with you every second.

"I actually *want* you with me every second." His words made a warm red glow pulse within me. "I love you." *And I love the fact that you know what I'm thinking all the time.*

It still amazes me that you feel that way. You're so much better than

I deserve.

Not true. I abandoned you this afternoon.

I don't want you to feel bad! I turned to meet his eyes. *And I don't want to come between you and your friends.*

I'd rather be with you, Maddie. You're more important to me than they are.

Okay, super double bonus points for Trevor.

Best. Boyfriend. Ever.

My vision got all glimmery and I felt the urge to buy him a building or something. *You enjoy spending time with them. I want you to have that. It would make me unhappy if you lost that because of me, okay?*

So, basically, you're asking me to neglect you because it'd make you happy. He gave a laughing snort at my logic, but I knew he understood me.

I loved the way he understood me.

The newly-warm weather made night patrol more tolerable than it'd been for most of the spring. Two people monitored the security feeds in the basement of one of the boys' dorms. Another dozen of us put on Kevlar vests, grabbed two-way radios, and took positions along the perimeter wall. Trevor and I passed our shift in the little patrol house, walking along the wall once an hour, and drinking tepid thermos coffee to stay awake. The near-full moon lit the night with an opal glow, palely outlining the trees.

We'd had a practice drill the last time Trevor and I'd been on patrol. Even the imagined threat was enough to spike everyone's thoughts with bright yellow splashes of fear, and the heavy load of secondhand anxiety had made me feel like I'd drunk about four double espressos. The attack on Ganzfield had been only a few months ago—the danger was still too real. Most of us felt older than we should—our souls had hardened in the past few months. Some people had grown stronger...while others had become brittle.

How useful was I on guard duty, really? My short mental range couldn't detect an attack from very far away. Hell, I couldn't even use the walkie-talkie. Why was it called that, anyway?

Stupid name.

Of course, that wasn't why we were here. If people actually *did* try to attack Ganzfield again, they wouldn't catch us by surprise. And Trevor and I could do a few things to stop them. I'm sure Isaiah, if his remote viewing reached this far, knew he wouldn't get in undetected. That fact might've been the only thing keeping him from coming after us here.

Deterrent—or, at least, mutually assured destruction.

The thought was more comforting than it probably should've been.

The caffeine headache pressed whiningly behind my eye sockets, strong enough to wake me. Maybe we should get a coffeemaker for the church. I could order one online pretty easily. I groaned as I looked at the clock—nearly 4 p.m. The all-night patrol had left us feeling zombie-like and vaguely nauseous.

Trevor and I went to the dining hall in search of enough coffee to make the pain stop. We each gulped our first cups and went for seconds. The day felt off-kilter with the knock to our circadian rhythms. Dinner hadn't started yet, but we sat together at one of the empty tables, holding hands and trying to bring our minds into focus.

A golden glow shimmered into existence around me and I felt Rachel's thoughts come into my range as she walked over from Blake House. My mind snapped into greater wakefulness as she joined us.

So? I asked. *Did you tell them?*

She glanced at Trevor. *Should he be here for this? It's kinda personal. Well, he's a nice guy, I guess. And he pretty much knows everything Maddie knows, anyway.* She shrugged. "I told Sean's parents."

In her mind, I saw their reaction. When she'd first arrived, they'd been polite and distant, unsure of her purpose in visiting them. Her memories showed their growing shock as she'd explained—then the wary scowl as his mother had demanded to know what Rachel wanted from them. *Yikes.* So, not the happy family moment that Rachel would've liked.

How are you doing with it?

"I'm okay. I mean, it's completely embarrassing that everyone's going to know, and I still think my dad's going to kill me when I tell them, but…"

You actually seem better, though.

"It's like Sean's not completely gone, you know?" Her eyes glinted with threatened tears.

I nodded. *I can feel that.*

"Hey, can you sense the baby's thoughts yet?"

Could I? *Ooh! Cool idea.* I focused in. There was something… nebulous, soft and light, fluttering nearly silently against the edges of my consciousness. It was so subtle I hadn't noticed it before. Next to me, Trevor went very still as he piggybacked on the sensations. I smiled as I projected the experience to Rachel. She gasped, and then made the baby start to glow as she envisioned it with her RV ability again.

I had a feeling she'd been doing that a lot. A little shard of cold stabbed into my thoughts and my smile dribbled off my face. Could all this extra mental energy be healthy? Maybe we were irradiating the baby or something. And Rachel still could use her ability, which meant she still had dodecamine in her system.

If old sci-fi movies had taught me anything, this kid might have a problem.

"So, your parents are coming?" Trevor asked.

"Yeah, this weekend." Rachel pulled herself out of her unique form of navel-gazing.

Do you need backup? I asked. *I could be there, if you needed me to be.*

"Maybe. I just don't— Let me think about it, okay?"

I met her eyes. *Just know that you're not alone in this, all right?*

Trevor nodded in agreement.

"Thanks." She gave us a nervous smile and her eyes darted toward the front door as footsteps and conversation drifted down the hall. We changed the subject as Drew, Ellen, and Harrison joined us.

Our second long and uneventful night on patrol drained us. I hated this reversal of sleep and wake. Even though exhaustion soaked through me, the light outside made it hard to sleep. I pulled a pillow over my head and drifted in and out of a half-waking stupor.

Maddie! Meeting in Williamson's office.

Ugh. Go away, Seth! His mental voice gave me a headache—or maybe I already had one.

Four more deaths.

Crap. That was important enough to get up for. My

unintentional noise woke Trevor. *Sorry!*

No problem. He glanced at the clock. *I'm too hungry to get back to sleep. I'll walk over with you and get some lunch.*

He joined Drew at one of the dining hall tables as I trudged up the stairs to the third floor.

My mom greeted me with, "You look tired, honey."

Night patrol. I'm working on almost no sleep here. What's going on?

Williamson looked up from his computer screen. *Isaiah's killed again. The victim was an RV. He also murdered her husband and their two children.*

I closed my eyes as a dizzy-weak ache rolled through me.

"Could we warn people when he's coming? Is there any way we can predict where he's heading next?" My mom clasped her hands in a bundle next to her chest.

Williamson gave me a meaningful look. His thoughts were shielded again.

Oh, there's a way mom, but you wouldn't like it. We could always use your only child as bait.

Her resistance felt like stone. "No! No way!"

I didn't argue—or explain that it wasn't up to her—but she picked it up from my mind and gave me that I'm-considering-locking-you-in-the-attic-until-you're-thirty look. Until I started dodecamine, I'd never known how accurately that look reflected her thoughts.

Is there a pattern to any of this? I asked.

Seth chimed in from outside. *Isaiah kills in different ways. Sometimes the victims just die in their homes, others stroke out in public. But if he gets them at their front door, he goes in and ransacks the place.*

I'd seen that in Rachel's vision. *But why? What does he want from their homes?*

A cold *"a-ha!"* splashed across Williamson's mind, splattering eureka bits to the rest of us.

My eyes widened. *Dodecamine?*

Williamson pulled up some files on his computer, comparing them to one another. *Why didn't I see the connection earlier?* All the home invasions had been committed against *dodecamine-enhanced* G-positives.

The cops didn't find any dodecamine in their homes, did they? asked Seth.

No. Williamson shook his head.

Goosebumps prickled my arms. *He's killing them to supply himself. You and Coleman cut off his old source.*

Isaiah had bribed one of the Allexor Pharmaceutical's employees to divert dodecamine to him. Williamson had located the thief easily—his mind had been filled with his guilt and his greed. After a few charmed words from Coleman, he'd resigned his position at Allexor, given everything he owned to charity, and become an aid worker in sub-Saharan Africa. Apparently, his new calling left him feeling…very fulfilled.

Williamson's twisting emotions rolled dizzy nausea through the rest of us. He hadn't known that his actions would make Isaiah kill to get more of the drug. Suddenly, the emotional spigot shut off. Williamson's shield strengthened and his mental presence vanished.

New part of the plan just fell into place, huh? I asked him.

He gave me a tight, grief-filled smile. "Try not to think about it. You're smart enough to figure it out."

* * *

I left Williamson's office and listened for Trevor's mind. He wasn't in the main building so I went back to the church. His bed was empty. I bit my lip and scowled.

Where is he?

Being away from Trevor made me twitchy. I couldn't sleep as I waited for him to come back. Did he feel smothered by my desire to always be with him? Had he gone somewhere just to have a little time away from me? Was I too clingy? Did he need a break from being around me?

Ugh.

I hated these insecurities. I knew Trevor loved and adored me in the same all-encompassing way I loved and adored him. We both had these stupid little doubts when we were apart—it was one reason we *didn't* like to be apart.

After an hour, I couldn't stay in the church any longer. No one had seen Trevor in the main building and he wasn't in Blake House or one of the other dorms. None of the sparks knew where he was. The butterflies in my stomach had started doing heavy construction so I went to ask Rachel.

She located him instantly. He sat alone on the flat, table-like rock in the little alcove on the lake—the place where we'd fed each other grapes. Trevor had his long arms wrapped around his knees. A look of pain and disbelief filled his face as he stared out at the water. The urge to comfort him pulled me like I was being reeled in on a hook.

Thanks, Rachel! I ducked out of her room and half ran through the field and along the edge of the lake. I sensed Trevor there and a few steps later, started to feel some of his—

Oh, my God in Heaven. The images coming from his mind punched me in the gut. They were vile and…and…*pornographic.* Every muscle in my body tensed. I started to shake and my eyes filled with tears. *What had he done?*

Trevor remembered having sex—crazy, wild, raunchy sex—with Belinda. *What am I supposed to do now? I don't understand. Why did I do this? I can't let Maddie see these memories. I can't hurt her that way. She'll never want to be with me again. And I can't blame her. I don't deserve to be with her. Maybe I should just go—get as far away as I can. I could leave her a note. Hell, I could just swim down to the bottom of the lake and hold onto a rock. After what I've done, I can't be with Maddie anymore. I just can't.*

Belinda. This must be her revenge. Red-hot energy crackled across my skin. My hands balled into fists.

Had she just implanted fake memories or had she charmed Trevor into actually *doing* the things that kept playing through his head? Did it matter? Either way, she'd violated him. Crystalline shards of hate formed in my mind.

I want her DEAD.

Whether Williamson liked it or not, I'd make sure Belinda never had a chance to do that ever again. The blast of lethal energy pressed against the inside of my skull. I squeezed my eyes shut.

Not yet.

Right now, Trevor needed me. With thoughts of drowning himself going through his mind, I couldn't leave him alone. The uneven ground felt like it was trying to trip me with each step but I forced my feet to move toward him. I wanted to scream, and then hurt something until it stopped moving, and then pull myself into a fetal ball and wail.

Trevor's anguished eyes met mine as I came into view. "I'm so sorry." His voice was a hoarse whisper. "I'm so sorry."

You didn't do anything wrong. I bit my tongue and tasted blood. The images in his mind showed him as an enthusiastic participant, but I knew Trevor. He wouldn't have done this willingly. I *knew* him.

Trevor's eyes squeezed closed with pain and he put his head down in his upraised knees. "I did."

Belinda charmed you.

Trevor's face lifted in surprise. "She's a charm?"

Yes. You knew that. She must have told you to forget that when she… when she implanted those false memories. I didn't know whether the memories were false or not, but Trevor had no idea that was even a possibility.

"They're false?"

I nodded. *I think so. I hope so. But can you think of something else now? Please?*

Trevor's brows knit in concentration. *I can't—I can't seem to stop.*

Then we'll need another charm to take her commands off you. It couldn't be soon enough for me. My head felt like it was about to explode! But what if it was a real memory and her command had just been to join in? *Arrrgh!*

Simple plan: I'd help my wonderful, gentle man get free of Belinda's mind-control, and then I'd hunt her down and fry her brain until smoke billowed from her frikkin' eye sockets.

Trevor unfolded himself slowly. Guilt and shame radiated from him in waves of yellow and dusky pink energy. But a little seed of hope—*this nightmare isn't real*—began to take root within him.

I sped up, unsuccessfully trying to get out of range of Trevor's porn-filled thoughts on the eternal walk back. Step one of the plan: find a charm, any charm. A few months ago, that would've been so easy! Now—

ZACK!

He turned to locate the source of the shout in his head. He'd been heading out of the main building, but he changed direction to meet us. His thoughts popped up loudly as he lowered his mental shield.

Behind me, I heard Trevor's unspoken curse and a distinct *not him!*

Deal with it, I snapped. *He owes me.* I couldn't handle Trevor's jealousy right now—not when my own dug into my throat with long, red fingernails.

Zack, we need your help. I bit my lip. *Please. Belinda put some memories into Trevor's head—*

"—and you want me to take the whammy off." *Must be really raunchy to get Maddie this upset. Or to come to me for this.*

My fingers dug into my crossed arms hard enough to leave bruises. *Please*, I repeated. Zack knew I'd blast him if he screwed with Trevor. I felt the killing energy rise just at the thought, but I forced it back down. *Not him. He's not the one I'm going to kill.*

I felt Williamson's *What's going on down there?* float to me from somewhere far away.

"Trevor," Zack said. Charm resonance had never sounded so welcome to me before. "Stop doing whatever Belinda told you to do. Forget anything she made up for you to remember."

The unending tapestry of sexual images in Trevor's mind seemed to unravel. My hands flew up to stifle my sob of relief. Trevor's guilt and anguish deflated as he recalled how Belinda had come up behind him and whispered, "Come with me," as he'd left the main building. He'd followed her around the corner. She'd forced him into stillness, and then filled his head with a never-ending loop of explicit "memories." She'd kissed his lips lightly and flashed a cruel smile. "Forget I'm a charm. Just keep thinking about doing all those things with me."

Oh, God. Trevor hadn't been her target. She'd violated him—

to hurt *me*. Some guys—all right, a lot of guys—would've loved a set of memories like that, but Trevor didn't. It was...an assault. The horrible images were now seared into my mind and no charm command could take them out. She'd hurt Trevor—my wonderful, good, kind Trevor—to hurt me.

And hurting Trevor was—*EVIL.*

I'd only taken a few steps before invisible arms restrained me. I hadn't even realized I was moving.

No. Trevor shook his head. *Not for me. I don't want to you to kill anyone because of me.*

I pushed against his invisible arms. *LET ME GO!*

To Zack, I looked like a furious mime struggling against an invisible wall. Trevor pulled me closer, but I didn't want him to comfort me right now. How could he let Belinda do that to him?

"Zack." Trevor looked over my head. His voice remained calm, but a cringing contrition tightened his invisible grip further. "Could you go and ask Dr. Williamson to come here? Um, now?"

Zack looked at my furious, tear-streaked, murderous face for a moment and then nodded. He disappeared into the main building only to reappear a moment later with Williamson behind him.

Williamson's quick stride slowed as he came toward me and he kept his thoughts behind a shield. "Maddie—"

BELINDA MESSED WITH TREVOR!

I saw him wince. His gaze followed me like I was a rabid dog and he was wondering where he'd left his shotgun. I threw my arms against the invisible wall around me only to have them pulled tightly against my sides.

LET GO of me or I'll BLAST you, Trevor! The raging, overwhelming desire to hurt Belinda was going to make my head explode—and I needed to channel that explosion into hers.

"Maddie." Trevor spoke my name gently. "Maddie, look at

me."

I couldn't. The air rushed from my lungs as I suddenly went limp. *Oh, my God in Heaven. Did I just threaten you?*

Trevor pulled me close, cradling me against his heart as I trembled. I felt a small piece of reason return to my mind so I closed my eyes tightly and tried to wrap my head around that piece.

The term *homicidal rage* floated through my thoughts. Ah, hell. I knew my connection to Trevor made me ridiculously protective, but Belinda had been stupid enough to try to use it against me. I'd just taken "being crazy for someone" to a whole new level. Oh, God. I'd been *horrible*—nakedly, out-of-control furious— and these three people had witnessed it. Dusky-pink shame enveloped me.

Trevor sighed as he felt my rage deflate. He looked at Williamson. "Belinda gave me some fake charm-memories to hurt Maddie. Either she goes, or we do. Now. Today." His voice was iron.

"Technically, she didn't break any of the rules. She didn't actually make you do anything."

Trevor's anger drove spikes of red through him. "Jon, there *should* be rules against it and you know it! Imagine seeing mental images of Elise—"

"Stop. Right. There." Williamson's voice was cold, but canary-colored flashes accompanied his memories—memories of hitting strangers for *thinking* inappropriate things about his wife. At least Elise had been there to charm people into forgetting the assaults. Did that mean all this excessive jealousy was "normal" for minders?

Trevor felt like he had made his point. "Maddie can't get those images out of her head the way I did."

"Sure she can," said Zack. I looked up from where I'd buried my face in Trevor's chest and we all shared the same, "*Oh, that's right.*" Zack was a charm who could shield—and therefore could influence minders.

My stomach turned over at the thought. I didn't want Zack to mess with my head. I needed to know what Belinda had done—but even thinking her name flashed a series of horrible images from Trevor's fake memories across my mind and the urge to fry her threatened to overpower me again. She'd actually kissed him. I wanted to dip him in Purell or something to get her taint off of him.

Maddie, calm down. Williamson's eyes bored into me. *We need Belinda. She's an important resource for Ganzfield.*

Don't defend her! Belinda had known he'd feel that way—she'd taunted me with the fact that Williamson would protect her. Urge to kill—rising.

If you hurt her, I'll have to cut off your meds and kick you out.

You're threatening me? I wouldn't be able to communicate without telepathy and Isaiah wanted me dead. Expelling me would be like catapulting me into the tiger cage at the zoo with a sucking chest wound.

I'm not threatening you; I'm reminding you. Get yourself under control and stay that way. Let Zack help.

I looked at Zack who met my gaze sheepishly. The last time he'd tried to charm me—

Hell, she's still mad about the time I tried to get her to kiss me.

I turned and rested my forehead against Trevor's chest. His arms tightened around me. *It's okay, Maddie. I'll make sure he doesn't mess with you.*

My anger flared anew. Trevor hadn't even been able to protect himself from a regular charm, so how could I trust him to…

Dammit!

None of this was Trevor's fault, but a part of me was still so pissed off at him! How could I be so unfair, so selfish? How could I hold him even partially responsible for being…for being too weak to resist Belinda's mind control? And then, to drag him off to Zack for the fix when he pretty much felt the same, jagged-yellow spurts of crazy jealousy around Zack that I did around Belinda?

No. I had to stop. I had to trust them. I tried to pull in a steadying breath, but steel bands pressed around my chest, so it sounded like a defeated sob.

I shot a thought to Zack without looking at him. *Just take the images and get me calm enough to think straight, okay? I—I need to keep the facts. I need to know what she did.*

He thought for a moment about how to phrase it, and then I felt his shield clamp down more securely over his thoughts, leaving a hollow place in my mental map—an empty shell.

"Maddie, calm down and forget every image you've seen of Belinda in Trevor's mind."

His voice sounded normal, but a fog swept into my consciousness. I felt pieces of thought turn fluid and slippery as they started to seep away. *No!* Panicky tendrils of cold, grey fear wrapped around my heart and squeezed. I couldn't let anyone mess with my head again. I forced the charm command from my mind and whimpered as the pain stabbed behind my eyes.

"Maddie…" Williamson began.

No! I shook my head and wiped hot tears from my cheeks. The effort to block Zack's command seemed to have drained all of the energy from me. *I—I just can't let…no. We'll leave. Cut me off, if you want.* The intense fury had faded. I just wanted to get away. And then possibly curl into a fetal ball and rock back and forth for a while.

"We need you here." Williamson looked at Trevor. "We need both of you."

I can't be around Belinda. One of us has to go. If I see her now, I'll...I might kill her.

"I can't force her to leave. She wouldn't be safe with Isaiah out there," Williamson said.

None of us are. I know you don't want to put Belinda in danger—I didn't care in the slightest if Isaiah fried her just outside the front gates—but she's hurting people here, Jon. She hurt MY SOULMA— Lava-red anger erupted within me again, making the three of them wince as I unintentionally spewed it into all their heads. I took a breath and started again. *She hurt Trevor. I—it's just—she's in danger here, too. So she can take her chances with the killer telepath outside the wall, or the one—*

"Sitcom solution," Zack interrupted.

Huh?

"Divide the property. Park her trailer out on the far side of the lake. She stays on her side of the line and you stay on yours."

We're on patrol tonight. We can't have half the property off-limits. What're we supposed to do if there's a problem on the other side?

"Fine. Just give her a little area, then."

"That's not a bad idea." Williamson looked at me, and I could almost feel his mental fingers rifling through my thoughts. "You'd leave her alone if she stayed in a small area, right? You wouldn't seek her out?"

I'll stay out of her territory as long as she doesn't come near Trevor and me.

"The other side of the lake?" Trevor asked.

"There's a place out behind Ann's cabin that should work," said Williamson.

Will she keep away from us, though? Stay where she's told?

"Sure she will." Zack smiled again. "Just let ME talk to her."

Little clouds of emotionally-charged energy seemed to swirl between Trevor and me as we headed back to the church. Dusky-rose shame. Yellow-grey ghosts of anxiety. Little purple twists of pain.

So…I'm capable of murder.

Yeah. And I'm potentially suicidal.

The downside of a connection like ours was that even our lowest, most horrible impulses were on display to one another. We'd both seen the worst in the other today.

Brittle aches filled me at the nightmare of Trevor harming himself. I squeezed his hand. *I don't ever want you to have to feel that way again. I love you.*

"I love you, too. I would never cheat on you. You know that."

I nodded. *I know that. I knew it today, even when I could see the proof in your mind. I knew it couldn't be real. I KNOW you.* A shadow of anxiety twisted through my thoughts. *It's just—*

What?

Am I a bad person?

Trevor caught my face in his hands, tilting my chin up until I met his eyes. "Madeline Elizabeth Dunn. You are a *good* person. The only people you've ever harmed have been rapists and murderers. They were doing bad things and you stopped them. Your impulses are to protect people. You are a *good* person."

I sniffed and my eyes overflowed. Trevor smiled and kissed my tears away. Tendrils of silver-white energy tentatively expanded between us.

You are a good person.

I sniffed again. *I'm really not sure you have the most unbiased opinion.*

The sound of his laugh flushed some of the twisty, angst-filled garbage from my thoughts.

"I'm not saying that you don't have anger issues. I mean, were you really going to blast me?"

I'm so, SO sorry. I—I can't believe I threatened you. A painful lump stabbed my throat, skewering me with my wrongness. After all I'd thought, done, and tried to do today, I deserved to feel awful.

Trevor's lips pressed tightly together as he recalled my fury. "Yeah. Don't do that again, okay?" He rested his cheek against my hair. *After what I put you through with those memories, I'm the one who should apologize. I wasn't able to stop Belinda from using me that way.*

My jaw dropped as I recognized the blossoms of shame in his thoughts. He actually thought he should take some of the blame. *That wasn't your fault!* Guilt stabbed through me and I wanted to cry. Trevor had taken my internal rantings to heart.

I'm still sorry you had to see those memories in my mind.

And I'd still be seeing them if Zack hadn't been there.

He tensed.

Ah, hell. I hadn't meant to share that thought.

I don't like him. Trevor shook his head. *I've NEVER liked him.*

He's actually a good guy, sometimes, I protested. Wait. Why was I defending Zack? Trevor and I were just beginning to shake off the strained awkwardness between us. I didn't need to flare up Trevor's jealousy right now. Had Zack actually succeeded in charming me, and then made me forget that he had? The thought made a muscle in the corner of my eye start to twitch. Ugh. This was why I couldn't let my guard down around charms…

That's part of what I don't like about Zack. If he acted like a complete jerk, you wouldn't think good things about him. Less competition.

There's NO competition, I'm all yours. I drew his gaze to mine. *Always.* I lightly touched my lips to his, feeling the silver threads of energy weave between us, pulling us back together, mending the jagged little rips in our special connection.

Good. I've always wanted my very own freak.

I laughed, feeling things start to slip back into rightness between us. *Look who's talking, Four Arms.*

The loud, wooden knock startled us both awake. It might've been late Thursday morning—or not. The nights and days since Belinda had charmed Trevor now blurred together in a forgettable confusion of light and dark.

Urgh.

Who'd be coming over here at this hour? Nearly everyone who'd want to talk to us knew that we'd been on patrol last night and would be sleeping now.

Oh.

I recognized the mind outside our front door with surprise. *Trevor, your grandfather's here!*

He rolled out of his bed and padded barefoot out through the doors under my loft to let him in. I lay back in my bed for a moment, yawning up at the ceiling. Maybe Trevor would take his grandfather somewhere else and let me get back to sleep, although neither one of us had gone anywhere without the other since the Attack of the Charm-Whore. I stayed close to protect Trevor from Belinda. He stayed close…to protect Belinda from me.

A sudden awareness of Archer's thoughts made a sick chill

run through me.

Oh, no.

I clamped down with a battleship-strength mental shield.

CHAPTER 7

I quickly pulled jeans and a shirt from the little dresser in the corner of my loft. Trevor kept his clothes out of reach in the little bathroom annex, but he was still decent in his PJ pants and t-shirt.

Archer and Trevor came in together. "—told you in Michigan how I need a large, open place to sleep? This is it." Trevor gestured at the sanctuary, empty except for the rumpled mess of a bed.

I joined them, welcoming Archer with a silent hug, which surprised him. My face felt like it was dripping off my skull.

Why are you shielding from me? A tendril of orange-brown energy wrapped through Trevor's words, like I'd hurt his feelings.

I pointed at Archer and Trevor in turn, and then mimed talking by holding my hand up to my mouth and flapping my fingers against my thumb, like a duck's beak. I felt like an idiot, basically playing charades at a time like this.

Trevor got it, though. *He's got something to tell me, doesn't he?* Little yellow flares of trepidation welled up in him. *Something bad?*

I glanced at Archer, trying to keep the pity out of my gaze.

He gave me a sad smile. "You already picked it out of my head, didn't you?"

I nodded as tears pricked at the backs of my eyes. The aching pain in his left side seemed stronger now. I'd simply assumed he'd pulled something when I'd felt it from him in Michigan.

"What?" asked Trevor, looking between Archer and me. *What's wrong? You're scaring me.*

"I had some medical tests last week. Got the results Monday. Pancreatic cancer." God, it sounded even worse when Archer said it aloud. He tried to keep his voice calm but clouds of dread filled his mind. *The cancer's already spread. The pain's going to get worse—much worse.* The doctor's clinically-cold words seemed tattooed into his thoughts. *"I'm sorry to tell you the prognosis is very poor. Expected survival rate for a case as advanced as yours is about two months, possibly less."*

Trevor sat down heavily on the edge of his bed, gripping the headboard for support. After looking around and assessing the limited seating options in the big, empty room, Archer tentatively settled on the foot of the mattress.

I let my shield drop. Trevor gripped my hand like a man-overboard clutching a lifeline. Emotions churned dizzy circles through his mind.

Oh, no. No, no, no.

"So," Archer tried to sound nonchalant, "If I'm going to kick the bucket in the next few weeks, I wanted to see this amazing place first. Lilith didn't want to come, so yesterday I just got in the car and started driving. I stopped after about nine hours, stayed at a motel overnight, and hit the road early this morning. Once I got to Vermont, I called the number you gave me, Trevor, and a nice girl gave me the directions to get here."

He turned to me. "When I got in, I think it was your mother who sent me over to this church, Maddie. She had green eyes like yours...and they had that same 'I'm-trying-not-to-show-pity' look that yours had a few minutes ago."

I gave him a watery smile. *Did she get a hand on you?*

He nodded. "Even gave me a hug. Nice lady." I saw my mom in his mind.

That's her.

"Is she a mind-reader, too?"

I nodded. *If she touches you, she knows what you're thinking.*

"Matilda," said Trevor. Our eyes met and I felt my eyebrows climb my forehead.

Archer's brows furrowed in confusion. *Didn't she say her name was Nina?*

She and Morris have never done anything with cancer, I told Trevor.

"Now they have their chance." His eyes held a fierce determination.

I turned to Archer. *How do you feel about trying a miracle cure?*

A huge grin spread across his face, wrinkling the skin near his eyes. The bright little spark of hope illuminated him from within. "What've I got to lose?"

"Please, open your shirt." Matilda's expressive eyes reflected her somber thoughts as Archer related what his doctor had told him. She laid her hand against the pale skin of his abdomen and closed her eyes as she concentrated.

Oh, my. It's quite advanced. Fatal within a few months...but I don't think we should give up.

Trevor's outward calm covered a roiling nausea and horror. *He can't be dying. Archer can't be dying.*

I tightened my grip on his hand. *She's going to try to help him.*

"Please, lie down." Matilda indicated the exam table in the center of the infirmary. While Archer settled himself, she picked up the phone. "Morris, we have a new case and I need your help."

Do you want Hannah and Heather? I asked her. *They're upstairs.* I could hear them above us in Hannah's room, having an animated discussion about lipids.

Matilda nodded.

Hannah, Heather—

"*Holy crap!*" Apparently Heather wasn't used to thought projection.

The expression bothered Hannah, but she concluded that taking the name of poop in vain really wasn't blasphemous.

New case down here in the infirmary, I told them. *Matilda wants you to come.*

Their feet thudded on the wooden stairs.

"Hey, Maddie. You scared the *hell* out of me a second ago." Heather grinned, although traces of her fear still fluttered within her. She'd thought Isaiah had been about to fry her.

Hannah winced at Heather's word choice.

"What can you sense?" Matilda watched them closely.

Heather rolled her eyes. *Oh, great—pop quiz!*

Two new sets of eyes swung toward Archer, who pinked up uncomfortably. *All these young ladies looking at me and I'm lying here half-dressed. But they're doctors, right? I must be getting old. They all look like children to me now.*

Next to me, Trevor started to shake. *He's going to die. Archer's going to die. Dammit! No! It's not fair! I just lost my father. I can't stand losing my grandfather, too!*

I squeezed his hand and leaned against his shoulder. What could I say?

Hannah and Heather flanked Archer and each placed a hand on his arm.

What's this? Archer wondered. *Are they doing some sort of supernatural religious ritual?*

I shook my head. *They're healers. Right now, they're using their ability to look through your body to see where and how badly the cancer has spread.*

Hannah located two tumors as I watched her thoughts. Three. Four. She hadn't even reached the pancreas yet. I felt Trevor's growing panic as he followed them through my ability. Each new discovery made him feel like he'd swallowed a nail.

I gave Archer what I hoped was a reassuring smile. *Do you want to see what they're doing?* I immediately regretted making the offer. How could it help to show him how bad it was?

He smiled back. "You read my mind, Maddie." *I'd like to see a few more amazing things before I die.*

I focused in on projecting the images in Hannah's mind— vivid, three-dimensional, and overlaid with patterns of energy that pulsed in various rhythms. Archer's circulation throbbed a double drumbeat throughout the various systems. Fizzy little micro-zaps of electricity hummed from every neuron. Hormones flavored the various organs. And the tumors...well, they felt... *wrong.* Seen through the mind of a healer, the pockets of tissue obviously didn't belong.

The door burst open, breaking everyone's concentration.

"What'd I miss?" asked Morris.

Hannah shook her head, refocused, and sunk her mind back into Archer's systems for another eternal-feeling minute.

Oh, this poor man, thought Hannah. *I don't think we can do enough to help him.*

This guy is so screwed, thought Heather.

I chose not to convey these assessments to Archer.

Matilda moved into teaching mode. "Options?"

Both Hannah and Heather hesitated.

"Palliative care," said Hannah. "Pain medication could keep him comfortable."

Trevor's jaw quivered.

"We could remove the tumors surgically." Heather looked between Matilda and Morris. "What do you think? Can we try it?"

Hannah shook her head. "I found twenty-one tumors."

Across the room, Morris sucked in his breath in a little hissing grimace.

That's a lot. There's only so much we can do to rev up the body's natural healing. We don't know how much a person can handle. And this patient's older and sicker than the people we usually treat.

"I suppose we could try." Matilda clasped her hands in front of her. "Once the malignant cells are removed from the pancreas, we might be able to re-create adequate insulin production."

Archer sat up slowly, the pain in his side biting into him with the motion. He started re-buttoning his shirt.

"I don't want to get your hopes up." Matilda's accent gave a subtle melody to her words. "We've never tried to treat cancer before, and yours is rather advanced."

Archer smiled at her. "If we do nothing, I'm dead in two months. Trevor and Maddie here seem to think that you might be able to do something to change that."

"It wouldn't be easy on you, and there's no guarantee of success."

"Doing nothing is a guaranteed failure. I'd like to see what you can do."

Matilda nodded. "All right. Come back here at eight

tomorrow morning. Don't eat or drink after midnight. You'll be unconscious for the procedure and we wouldn't want you to aspirate anything."

Archer frowned. "Oh, I'm allergic to some of the anesthetics."

Matilda patted his hand. "Don't worry. We don't use them."

"Up for some lunch?" Trevor's giddy relief danced around him like sunshine on the ripples of the lake as we left the infirmary. *Archer's going to be okay!*

I'd only taken two steps from Blake House before I suddenly found myself lifted twenty feet in the air. I let out a shriek of surprise, drawing startled attention as I "flew" down the path to the main building.

Archer thought it was hilarious. "Don't drop her!"

I chose to ignore the stares. Trevor's delicious joy washed through me and I started to laugh. He pulled me into his arms on the porch of the main building and gave me a smacking kiss in front of his grandfather and everyone. Once we were inside, however, the crowd of minds around me assaulted my senses.

What are they so happy about? Isaiah Lerner's coming to kill us all.

I'm gonna lose my job if I stay here much longer. Why can't Williamson and the other minders get it in gear already?

If I hear the sound of helicopters again, I don't think I'll be able to stop screaming.

I could feel their thoughts squeezing against me, like riding a too-crowded bus. I closed my eyes and tried to breathe as my mood crumbled with the pressure.

Trevor sensed the crowd's effect on me. *Picnic?*

I nodded gratefully. *Please.*

The two heaping trays of food floated above head-height, out of jostling range in the busy dining hall.

Amazing. Archer's eyes reflected his sense of wonder. *And that's my grandson.*

My mother's minder-loud thoughts cut through the crowd, flaring with awareness of another mind whenever someone bumped or brushed against her. *There you are, honey!* She started toward us.

Trevor reached back through the line for another sandwich.

"I see you found Trevor." My mom put her hand on Archer's arm in a "gesture of support." *Oh, dear. How's he doing?*

I rolled my eyes. *Subtle, Mom. Why don't you just ASK him how he's doing? He'll tell you, you know!*

"You spoke with Matilda this morning?" she asked.

Archer smiled. "Looks like there might be a way to make my terminal cancer...well...non-terminal." He held back a laugh as he caught my eye—he knew exactly what my mother was doing with her little "gesture of support."

She blushed and released his arm. "I'm so sorry! I shouldn't pry."

"No apology necessary. I'm just thrilled at the possibility for another chance." Archer looked at Trevor and a warm, teal-blue flash of pride flowed through him. *I want to get to know the incredible young man my grandson's become. It shouldn't take a cancer scare to get me to appreciate what's important in this world. I'm not going to waste this second chance.*

We settled out at the edge of the lake, pulling some of the sparks' metal chairs and benches across the clumpy, brown-sugar sand of the tiny beach. Fast-moving clouds reflected on the water's surface and sent dark shadows rolling over the surrounding hills. A cool breeze threatened to steal our paper napkins.

Archer looked out at the water. "This place is wonderful." The view wasn't the object of his admiration. *I should tell the people I care about what I think. You never know how long you have.* "Trevor, Ganzfield's been good for you. I am so proud of you, son. Look at the man you've become."

Trevor lit up as his grandfather's praise warmed him like a burst of springtime. I couldn't contain my smile.

Archer took another bite of his sandwich, washing it down with a gulp of the pale, flavored water we euphemistically called "lemonade," despite the fact that no actual fruit was harmed in the making of the beverage.

"I have to say, though, I'm not thrilled with the fact that you two are living together…and in a church, no less."

The smile slid off my face. Apparently, our choice of building added an extra layer of sacrilege to our "shacking up."

Trevor's face didn't seem to change, but something wilted inside him.

My mother joined in, emboldened in the presence of an ally. "I completely agree!" *Finally, someone who sees things sensibly!* "You're both much too young to be in such a serious relationship."

Ugh.

Pressure pushed at the back of my eyes. Why couldn't Archer have left it with the positive comments? His approval potently affected Trevor, but his disapproval wounded him even more strongly. And now my mother's thoughts filled with all of the things she'd held back—concerns, disapprovals, things she didn't say because she feared voicing them would drive me further down the "wrong road." *Maddie needs to focus on going to college, not playing house in the woods with a boy with no solid prospects for the future. Her hormones are doing her thinking for her.*

I rubbed my hands across my forehead and then down over my eyes. Did people actually use the term "prospects" anymore, or had my mom been reading too much Jane Austen? Oh, man. I was way too tired and wrung out to deal with this stuff today.

Can we have this discussion another time? Like…never? Never works for me. *Trevor and I had patrol last night and we're working on about three hours of sleep here.* I dove for the subject change. *How's the thing with Dorothy going? Has she let you cook anything in her kitchen yet?* My mother loved to cook, but Dorothy guarded access to the Ganzfield kitchen like she'd sworn a sacred oath to protect it.

"And what about college?" My mom ignored my attempt to divert her. "How are you going to manage that? Will the two of you go to the same school?" *Will that get Maddie back on track? Really, though, boyfriends shouldn't factor into college decisions.*

Mom, no one's going to college with Isaiah still out there.

"Nina, Archer, please understand. Maddie and I…this relationship isn't temporary."

"I know you two feel that way now," said Archer, "but people change over time."

My hands curled into fists as I forced myself to count to ten—slowly. *They're double-teaming us!*

My mom picked up the thought. "Now you understand how I usually feel. I know you two believe that you have a 'special connection'—whatever that means—but what you want when you're seventeen may not be what you want when you're twenty-five or thirty."

Arrrgh! Splinters of orange energy poked behind my eyes and I smothered the impulse to pull out a couple of chunks of hair—my own or someone else's. Did they think we were stupid?

That we couldn't tell the difference between puppy love and the I-can't-live-without-you kind? I really wanted to give them a piece of my mind—and with projective telepathy, that took on a whole new meaning. *Mom—*

Trevor stood up quickly, yanking me with him. "Please excuse us." He met my eyes. *Don't say anything you'll regret. After all, they mean well.*

I folded my arms across my chest but kept my thoughts to myself.

"Maddie has a headache and we both need to get some sleep since," *despite our immaturity,* "we have a twelve-hour patrol tonight then Archer's surgery in the morning. Nina, can I please ask you to make sure Archer has a place to stay for the night?"

My mom nodded. Her eyes widened as his words registered. *He's taking care of Maddie—watching out for her. And they do have a lot to deal with right now. Maybe I pushed too hard. But I'm her mother. I just want what's best for her.*

I felt their eyes and thoughts on us as Trevor and I walked away. As the church door closed behind us, much of the pressure of the outside world seemed to stay outside.

Sanctuary.

I groaned and rubbed my hands across my forehead in an effort to dispel the headache that pulsed at my temples. *I hate that they assume we're going to break up.*

Trevor pulled me close. *Let's cut them some slack. It's not like they know everything about what we have together. Next time either of them starts in, let's just smile and nod.*

And then keep doing what WE choose?

Exactly. He brushed his lips across mine then dropped kisses along my neck.

I felt my tension unclench as dancing swirls of red energy

licked my skin. *Trevor, you're making me melt.*

He chuckled against the hollow of my throat, sending little eddies of electricity shooting down to my fingertips. *Then I must be doing this right. How's your headache?*

What headache?

He pulled me down on the bed next to him and looked into my eyes. "Maddie," his voice became serious, "I'm going to spend the rest of my life with you. And as much as I want both of our families to give us their blessings, in the end, the only person's opinion that truly matters to me is yours."

Overwhelming, dizzying, amazing—a tear slipped down my cheek as my emotions overflowed. *I love you so much. Forever, then?*

"I'll be your date to forever."

My date to forever.

The world dimmed around us, our souls connected, and forever started that afternoon in the church.

The giddy, residual energy of soulmating still buzzed through us as we started our patrol. Since we'd missed dinner, we brought sandwiches and coffee out to the little guardhouse. The metal folding chair creaked as I set the thermos down on the cinderblock "table."

So, Williamson wants to use us as bait again.

"He really thinks Isaiah will come after us?"

I rubbed my hands up and down my arms. The air cooled as the light ran out of the sky, but that wasn't why I felt a chill. *He really, really wants us dead.*

"Your mental shield's strong enough to keep Isaiah out. We should know the plan."

If I were Jon, I'd probably want to set up a trap for Isaiah. Make him come to one place, and then have a shielder there to attack him. I gasped. *Zack!*

Trevor frowned. "What about him?"

Zack's been spending a lot of time in the main building. Maybe Williamson's training him for this. Only a few of us can shield, and we've already been cast as "bait."

"So, we sit somewhere, wait for Isaiah to arrive, and then Zack…what? Just pulls out a gun and shoots him?"

It may be just that simple. If we look vulnerable, I think Isaiah will come for us. He really wants to kill us.

"What else does he want?"

Ah, the Christmas list of a homicidal maniac!

Trevor snorted.

The idea hit me with a nearly audible ping. *Wait, you're completely right.*

"I suspected as much."

Dodecamine. He needs to keep his supply up or he'll lose his abilities.

"So, we just need to cut him off?"

Cut EVERYONE off. Anyone who needs a booster has to come to Ganzfield to get it.

"How do people get it now?"

I think the healers FedEx it out a few doses at a time.

"So, if we cut off the shipments, he'll be forced to come to where we are. No more killing people to re-supply."

We'd also need to protect the supplier. Hannah said it's made in New Jersey.

"Okay, so two places where he could get dodecamine. He'll have to come to one of them."

And we'll be there, seemingly alone and defenseless.

Grey tendrils of anxiety snaked through Trevor's thoughts. "I hate putting you in danger."

I squeezed his hand. *You know I feel the same about you.*

Trevor humphed a half-laugh. "We're really doing a bad job of staying out of it then, huh?"

Terrible.

His thoughts shifted. *Archer—I didn't get a chance to talk to him again this afternoon. Will the procedure work? Will he be okay?*

You know, it's because of you that Archer even has this chance.

"What if it doesn't work?" Something in his voice sounded like a young child, lost and alone.

I took his hands in mine. *Matilda's a genius. She can heal anything.*

He rolled his eyes. "Except comas, apparently."

I laughed. *Yeah! What's up with that?*

"Actually, I had a lot of time to think about that, once." I knew the exact nine-day stretch to which he referred. "I think G-positives may have a unique reaction to an overload of our abilities. It kind of resets the brain and it takes a while to boot up again."

I considered that. *We do a lot with energy. I wonder if Matilda senses all the different forms we use? Maybe something happens in a range she can't detect—that none of the healers can detect. Like it's causing a seizure or something, keeping us off-line.*

"I just never, *ever* want to see you like that again."

I'll do my best to avoid it.

We grabbed breakfast with extra coffee before searching out Archer in one of the spare rooms in Trevor's old dorm. Orange bursts of trepidation sparked like tiny fireworks from his mind.

"I've been worrying about it all night," he confessed. "How, exactly, are they going to do this without drugs?"

The pain in his side stabbed, hot and sharp. I cringed with every step as we walked to the infirmary. I hadn't realized how heavily medicated Archer must've been yesterday—or how much more he'd hurt after stopping the pain meds in preparation for the procedure.

Guilt flavored Trevor's anxious mind. *I should've stayed with him. I could've explained more about how the healers work.* "The healers can knock you out with a touch—overload the brain. They'll repair the incisions before you wake up, too, so you shouldn't have any pain with recovery."

"Amazing!" Archer's eyes brightened. "I'm so glad I had a chance to see this place. I never imagined such things were possible."

"Once you're okay again, we'll take you to see a Fireball game. I think you'll like it."

I swallowed hard, trying to focus through the secondhand pain. *You also might want to try dodecamine. See if you can move things with your mind.*

Archer's face lit up at the prospect and for a moment, he looked much younger. *Wouldn't that be something?* We clomped up the stairs at Blake House. "I called Lilith last night and told her about this."

And she thinks we're all insane, I finished for him.

He laughed. "How did you know?"

I tapped the side of my head. *I have my ways.*

The other healers barely glanced up from the notes and charts spread across the desk—their battle plan. Matilda settled Archer on the exam table then shooed us out. "I'll call you when we're done. I think this will take several hours, possibly most of the day."

Back to the church? I asked Trevor.

"Can we just walk a while, first?" His thumb chafed circles against the back of my hand while jangled emotions scampered like squirrels just under his skin.

I nodded. *Sure, lead the way.*

We crossed the field and went out to the lake, taking our time before settling on the dining table rock in the little alcove. I'd come to think of this as one of "our" places. Trevor ran impatient fingers through his hair as he gazed over the water. *He has to be okay. If this doesn't work…* The thought made his stomach heave.

I leaned my cheek against his back, wrapping my arms around his waist. Nothing I could say right now would help. We just had to wait. My eyelids drooped and I forced my eyes extra wide, fighting to stay awake.

I didn't win the fight.

I dreamed the existence of G-positives had become public knowledge. Most of us were herded into camps. Sinister men in dark uniforms threatened to kill Trevor unless I helped them hunt down the charms hiding in the State Department. I woke up with a startled gasp.

"That was a weird dream."

You saw that? I looked up to meet Trevor's eyes. He'd rearranged us out on the rock and now my head was pillowed on his leg. Trevor ran nervous fingers lightly over my hair, as though stroking a cat.

He nodded. "Don't worry. There are still enough Ganzfield charms out there to keep that from happening."

Actually, the scarcity of reliable charms did worry me. What if the wrong people found out about us? Could the few remaining charms act quickly enough to keep our existence secret? No wonder that stress came out in my dreams.

I shook off that line of thought—we had enough to deal with today. *I meant to stay awake with you. How long did I sleep?*

"About three hours."

I winced. *I'm sorry. I left you alone.*

"I enjoy watching you sleep. It's peaceful." He smiled. *Except for your bizarre dreams, of course. But I'm used to them.*

Should we go back and get an update?

Trevor nodded, not even thinking the words.

As we got closer to the infirmary, I focused in on Matilda's thoughts. She visualized with her ability as she directed the scalpel around the tumor. The meticulous work focused her concentration sharply, as though her mind cut into the tissue along with the blade.

I flipped channels, finding Heather next. *This area's not doing well. I gotta get the blood supply back to this tissue A-sap.* I felt her energy pull on the tiny capillaries and they seemed to flush and warm.

Hannah stood at Archer's head. Her hands touched his temples, ensuring that he remained deeply unconscious. The prayer in her thoughts was as automatic as breathing.

Morris's thoughts felt gritty and dirt-brown. *We've been at this for hours. How much more can this old man handle? How much more of this can we do to him?*

The pressure of Trevor's grip on my hand pulled my focus back outside. The blood had drained from his face.

You caught all that? I asked, already knowing that he'd followed along with me. This sharing abilities thing—well, if I'd heard all that solo, I would've softened it up a bit before relaying it to Trevor. He didn't need the raw version right now.

We picked at flavorless food in the dining hall for a while, and then a silent cheer made me glance toward Blake House, like a dog hearing one of those whistles.

Heather's gleeful thoughts became clearer with every bounding step she took toward the main building. *We cured cancer! TERMINAL cancer! We ROCK! I LOVE being a healer!*

I pulled Trevor up, abandoning our trays on the table. Once I had a hand on his arm, Heather's thoughts became clear to him, as well. Joyful relief spiked through him. Heather met us on the steps with a huge grin and we all ran back over to Blake House without a word.

Green elation and amber giddiness swirled through everyone in the infirmary. Matilda surveyed the people gathered around Archer's annex bed with a teal-blue glow of pride. *We did it. This was the right call.*

Hannah smiled with closed eyes as she said a silent prayer of gratitude.

Archer looked up at Trevor with a tired grin. "Well, my boy. Looks like I'll be sticking around for a while."

Trevor swallowed hard and tried to make words come out, but then gave up and just put a hand on his grandfather's shoulder. *He's okay! Oh, thank God!* Joy, love, and relief kaleidoscoped out of him. I held back my overwhelming reaction with a hand over my mouth.

In contrast to the exuberance around him, Archer seemed drained and weak, but the sudden release from constant pain made him feel like he was floating. A slap-red patch of newly-healed skin on his neck faded to pale within a few minutes.

Not a mark on him.

Archer's eyelids drooped and he stopped following the conversation. We left him alone to sleep in the annex. He had a slight smile on his face, like he was in on a private joke.

In the next room, Morris gave a wistful sigh. *If only we could write this up in one of the medical journals. Fame, fortune, and glory.*

Heather's thoughts still danced with glee.

Williamson touched in mentally. *What's all the fuss about?*

I grinned. *Miracle cure.*

Excellent. I felt his satisfaction. *Carry on.*

Our relief gave way to exhaustion. Trevor and I stumbled back to the church. He collapsed face-down across his bed and was asleep by the time I came out of the bathroom. Sleep pulled at me as well, so I dragged myself up the ladder to the loft and threw a pillow over my head to smother the daylight.

The phone in the church rang just after 5 p.m., startling us both awake. I kept forgetting that we had a phone here. It'd been installed during the security upgrade—after I'd lost the power of speech. Drizzly little currents of anxiety ran through Trevor as he picked it up. I reached the bottom of the ladder just as his world tilted.

Oh, no.

I wrapped my arms tightly around him as the ache that started in his heart overflowed his entire frame with pain.

Matilda's voice carried to me. "—your grandfather's heart stopped. His body's ability to heal would no longer respond to our ability. We think the repairs from removing the tumors took too much from him. We worked to restart his heart for nearly an hour but he didn't respond."

Archer was dead.

Trevor sank to the floor and I slid down with him.

No, no, no.

He started to tremble.

I'm so sorry. I'm so sorry, I repeated, uselessly. I held on tightly and wished I could do something to make everything better.

The afternoon light faded around us.

CHAPTER 8

She'll probably call the police.

I stared at the little yellow pool of light under the desk lamp while Williamson considered my words. The world seemed strangely flat and colorless—Trevor's grief had left me drained and weak. I'd come to Williamson's office in the middle of the night, once Trevor had faded into an aching sleep. It seemed somehow disloyal to be discussing his family problems with someone else, but those problems might just show up at our gate tomorrow—with a police escort.

Every charm we had in the Midwest is now here. Williamson didn't look up from his computer screen. *I don't have anyone to send to talk to her.*

Too bad mind control doesn't work over the phone. I never thought I'd be disappointed by the limits of charms. *Lilith Laurence needs to know that her husband died. If I could, I'd call her myself. She doesn't like me anyway.*

I worried about how Lilith would treat Trevor if he called.

Would she hold him responsible for Archer's death? We needed an option that both left Trevor emotionally unscarred and protected the secrecy of Ganzfield. Could we risk sending someone out to Michigan? Should we? I normally felt so sure of the right thing to do, but tonight my mind felt muffled in a fuzzy, dull-grey blanket that frayed around the edges. I just slumped in my chair and wanted someone else to solve this problem.

Two other exhausted people filled in for Trevor and me on patrol. Everyone was getting overworked and ragged, and fear nibbled at the edges of all of our thoughts. We had to do something to change the situation with Isaiah. We couldn't go on like this indefinitely.

Go home, Maddie. Get some sleep. We'll deal with the rest of this in the morning.

Déjà vu hit me as the church came into view, glowing faintly in the moonlight—a strong flash of the first night I'd come here, escaping the dorm where I'd been throwing nightmares. I'd accidentally trespassed into Trevor's life that night. I watched his sleep-slackened face with dark-adjusted eyes. A coil of energy wound within me. I wanted to soothe his pain—find a way to fix it—and keep him from being hurt again. Trevor deserved to be happy.

But I had no idea how to make that happen.

Dr. Williamson and I floated high above Ganzfield as we debated the true nature of soulmating.

"I contend it is a literal connection of souls." I smoothed my white satin choir robe and adjusted my halo. "We're essentially beings of energy who can leave the shells of our bodies."

Williamson's black velvet robe and mortarboard absorbed

the light around him. "I postulate that our minds interpret the sharing of energy that way because we lack the proper mental framework or sensory receptors to understand its true nature."

I woke up with a snort. Since when was I on the side of the angels? And when did Jon "postulate?"

Trevor held a book in his hands but he wasn't reading. "I'm with you," he called up, meeting my gaze with a tired smile. "I think we're actually souls."

You caught that?

He nodded.

I gave my dreamcatcher a drive-by hugging on the way to the bathroom, and then came back and joined him in the big bed, wrapping my arms around his waist and snuggling my head against his shoulder.

"I'm trying to work up the courage to call Lilith, but—" His voice broke. *I just don't know how to tell her.*

I talked with Jon about it last night, after you went to sleep. I felt like I was confessing something. But he didn't have anything useful to add.

Maddie?

Um-hmm?

Did I—? Is it my—? He couldn't finish, even in his mind.

I hugged him tighter. *NO. It's NOT your fault. NO. When Archer got here, he knew he had terminal cancer. You gave him an option he never knew existed. You did everything you could to help him, and it worked! You made the right choice. His body just wasn't strong enough to take it.*

But he would've had two more months if I hadn't said anything. Trevor's anguish bled from him.

Two more months in pain. I felt it yesterday, Trevor. It was bad. And he knew it was only going to get worse.

He rubbed his hand though his hair. Dark strands fell over his ears and threatened his eyes. I reached up and pushed them back from his forehead. A deep wave of silvery tenderness filled my heart and swelled up into my throat.

Let's go see Williamson before you call so he can set charms at the gates for when Lilith calls the cops on us.

He gave a mirthless laugh. *She probably will, won't she? We'll deal with it.*

Trevor pulled me closer. *I don't know what I'd do without you. You'd talk out loud a lot more.*

Lilith called the police.

Trevor had phoned her from Williamson's office less than an hour ago, and now two of North Conway's Finest were buzzing in from the front gate. I sighed. So much of my life these days seemed to involve acting normal in front of law enforcement officers.

Dew still clung to the grass, wetting our shoes as Cecelia and I escorted the cops into Blake House. I listened for the officers to notice anything strange. I'd give Cecelia a mental heads-up if she needed to charm them.

Tag team.

"We received a phone call from a distraught woman in Michigan. She claimed the people here at Ganzfield had killed her husband." The older man seemed apologetic. "It sounded crazy, but we have to check it out."

"Of course you do," said Cecelia. *And with a few words from me, you'd confess to murdering him.*

I raised my eyebrows at her but she just smirked.

Archer's body still lay in the infirmary. Matilda had called the coroner last night, but they'd had no reason to send someone after-hours…until Lilith's phone call. The ambulance pulled slowly up the driveway and the medical examiner joined us as we entered Blake House.

The report said the deceased had end-stage cancer. Is this a case of assisted suicide? I'll need to run a tox screen.

No problem. Archer's bloodwork would come back clean.

Trevor ached as he finished filling out the paperwork, making arrangements for the return of Archer's body to Michigan. *Oh, God. I can't even attend the funeral. I can't risk bringing Isaiah down on the rest of my family.* Dirty-yellow guilt flared through him. *I can't even show my respects properly. Lilith, Laurie — they'll expect me to be there.* He glanced at me. *Maybe if I went alone —*

Cold horror trickled down my neck and I shook my head at him. *No! If Isaiah caught up with you —* I suddenly found it hard to breathe. Trevor, unshielded and vulnerable, as Isaiah closed in on him… Even the idea kicked me in the gut.

An invisible arm wrapped around me protectively. *Sorry. I won't go alone.*

I took a shaky breath. *His body is still here for a few more minutes. Do you want to say goodbye? Maybe we could have a small ceremony or memorial here.*

He gave me a sad smile as he remembered my dream. *We're souls, Maddie. He's not in there anymore.*

Once the police and coroner had gone, Trevor went back to the church alone. I ached to comfort him—to take his pain away—but Trevor actually wanted his grief for a while, to roll it around on his tongue and get the ashy taste of it. It was a way for him to honor Archer: to miss him, to feel bad because he was gone, to mourn him.

Come find me when you don't want to be alone anymore.

He squeezed my hand, and then released it. *Always.*

The dining hall still had breakfast stuff out and I tried to remember the last time I'd come solo to a meal. The thoughts of the people at the other tables pressed much more strongly into my mind without Trevor's comforting presence. I tried to find someone's thoughts that were worth listening to.

—but she's so smokin' hot. I totally want to—

—and I'm going to fail thermodynamics and probably burn the place down after—

—seeing someone else. He's totally ignoring me now. Maybe I should—

—dead guy in the infirmary. I'm surprised the cops aren't here more—

—after she got naked and started touching my—

—such a bitch. I should charm her to shut the hell up! I don't care if she is my sister, if she—

—Katie should play goalie again today. She's better than Mel, and Mel can work on her—

—so sexy, I lost my mind. I can't believe I got to do it with an older woman. She must be…what? Twenty-five? And when she—

Ugh. It was like flipping TV channels and finding a bunch of porn. Half the guys in here seemed to have Belinda on the brain. *The male minders have it so much easier.* The obscene thoughts we picked up all the time didn't bother them the same way they upset me. I didn't want anyone else's erotic images thrust into my head…except Trevor's.

I rolled my eyes. Geez. Did I actually just think the word "thrust?"

How…Freudian.

Another wave of dirty thoughts from a stranger hit me and I gagged on the coffee I'd sipped. No wonder Ann had quit. Without Trevor, I'm sure I'd have overloaded months ago.

I squeezed my eyes shut but the Belinda porn continued. She must be getting visitors out at her little trailer in the woods. But why would she bother giving these guys these memories? What could they offer her? They knew what she was and how she worked, didn't they? Would they actually pay her for fake memories? Did she thrive on their lust or something? Was she running a fake sex charity? Whatever the reason, the images had killed my appetite and made me itch to blast someone. I took my coffee and started to go.

I ran into Rachel at the front door. Orange flashes of nervous energy electrified her and her face seemed vampire pale. She looked like she was about to be sick.

Oh.

The Belinda stuff suddenly faded into inconsequence.

What time are your parents arriving?

"In about nine minutes." She bit her lip. She saw them in her mind. They were near the turnoff in North Conway.

Need some company?

She nodded. We sat in two of the mismatched rocking chairs that littered the wide front porch of the main building. Rachel's thoughts jumped around her head like hyperactive children in a moon bounce. Nausea pressed up within her.

Good thing I didn't eat anything.

"Maddie? Can you, just..." *talk* "...um, tell me some things? Anything? Just distract me?"

The first two things that came to mind—Trevor's loss and the weirdness with Belinda—didn't seem to be the soothing topics Rachel needed.

What do you want to hear about?

"Well, how about your family?"

You've met my family. My mom's the only family I have.

"I've been thinking a lot about family recently."

That makes sense. Okay, my dad died in a car accident when I was four. My mom's parents…well, before she was born, doctors told them that they'd never be able to have children. They were both over forty when they had their little "miracle baby," as they always called her. Both of them died when I was six, within three months of one another. I suppose we have some distant relatives on that side, somewhere. We've never been close to any of them, though.

"And your dad's side? After…after he died, did you have any contact with his family?"

I paused for a moment, feeling the tendrils of concern running through Rachel—and finally understood why she asked. *His mother, my Gramma Dunn, was my favorite grandparent. I probably shouldn't have had a favorite, but I really did. She treated me like I was older than I was—talked to me like a person and not a kid, you know? She died three years ago. I still miss her.*

Rachel stared at the disappearing end of the driveway, but the view didn't register. What did she need me to say?

You know, Sean's parents aren't the only McFees. Most of them are really big on this whole extended-family-takes-care-of-our-own thing. Your kid's gonna be part of the pack of red-haired fire-giants.

She smiled at that.

Hey, once you tell your parents, go find Drew. Let him know he's going to be an uncle.

"Sean was his cousin, not his brother."

Most of the McFee "uncles" are cousins of some once-removed variety. Let Drew and his mom bring you into the McFee family if Sean's parents won't do it.

Rachel's ambivalence pulled at her as her desire for privacy conflicted with the fact that she wanted a connection to Sean's family for her child. She hoped her baby would be a part of something larger—a family, a community.

I gave a little laugh at that. *It takes a village to raise a G-positive child?*

She drew in a tense breath. "Especially this one." Cold tendrils of apprehension shot through her. "Matilda's worried about what dodecamine exposure might've done to him." Her voice dropped to a whisper. "I've had three boosters since Sean died. The last one was less than two weeks ago."

I didn't mention that I already knew the risk. *What does Matilda think will happen?*

"It might affect how his basal ganglia develops. He might develop a new and different ability, or he might have more than one. Or he might have brain damage that causes seizures or mental retardation." She bit her lip.

Or he could be a perfectly healthy kid who'll someday set things on fire with his mind.

She laughed. "I guess wanting something 'normal' for this baby is asking too much."

Or too little. C'mon, your kid is going to be fine. Even if he's not "typical," he—or she—is going to be loved....cared for...spoiled rotten.

"But if he has brain damage—"

We'll find a way to cope. It's not so bad.

She suddenly flushed with embarrassment, worried that she'd insulted me. "Maddie, I didn't mean—"

I shook off her concern. *Not a problem. The fact that you forgot is simply proof that we can adjust to this sort of thing.*

"I just don't notice that the way you speak is all that different, anymore."

Thanks.

I felt the touch of two new minds coming up the driveway. I didn't need to say anything—Rachel had them glowing at the end of her little golden thread. She stood up, still biting her lip.

You want some privacy to talk to them?

"Stay. I mean, if you don't mind…"

Do you want to know what they're thinking, or should I shut up?

"I don't know," she admitted. Her stomach heaved like a ship caught in a storm.

If you need me to do anything, just think it to me, okay?

She nodded in a quick, bird-like motion. He eyes stayed fixed on her approaching parents. She paradoxically felt relieved that they'd arrived safely—finally out of Isaiah's reach—but she also viewed their approach like that of her own firing squad.

I knew the Fontaines had first met when they'd worked on Project Star Gate. They still lived near Washington, D.C.— Rachel had watched Isaiah intensely whenever he'd headed in that direction. Noah was an RV like his brother Charlie had been, and the resemblance between these two large, heavy-set, and balding men was strong. Paula was a healer. She had her blond hair cut matronly short and was plump without being unattractively heavy. Neither used dodecamine to enhance their abilities anymore, although both had been early recipients of the treatment. Since they'd both been adults when they'd first started dodecamine, their abilities had never been great—more party-trick level than superhero ability—but they'd been part of Ganzfield since its founding.

They parked around the side of the boys' dorm. *Look at all of the cars here,* thought Rachel's mom. *I've never seen Ganzfield so full.* True enough. The place normally housed about eighty people. We now had more than two hundred.

Paula enveloped Rachel in a huge embrace. *Rachel seems to be coming out of her grief. Good. I've been so worried. And something about her feels...different.*

Was that from her latent healing ability or maternal instinct?

Rachel's dad grabbed his daughter up in a bear hug.

"Mom, Dad. This is Maddie."

Hi.

Both of them startled at my voice in their heads. *Oh! She can project thoughts like Jon!*

Rachel mentioned her before, but why is she here now?

We pulled up chairs. Rachel opened and closed her mouth a few times, willing something to come out. Nothing did.

"Are you okay, honey?" Her mom put a hand on her arm. "What is it?"

Rachel flushed bright red as she realized and experienced the full horror of the moment. "Mom, Dad, I—" Her voice broke as her parents leaned in closer. Concern lined their faces.

Help! she thought at me.

Just say it. It'll be easier once you get those first words out.

"I'm—I'm pregnant."

Cold shock splashed through both Paula and Noah.

Oh, no. No, no, no. Paula's feelings twisted with an aching purple.

WHAT? Noah's face flushed as his rage pummeled his feelings of shame and concern into submission. *I'll kill him!*

I looked at him sharply. *Don't say that to her. You know Sean's already dead.*

His eyes filled with a challenge. "How is this your business?" Heated emotion churned in him like boiling water. I had a brief flash of a cartoon guy with steam coming out of his ears. I'd never seen the real-life equivalent before.

I kept his gaze. *Rachel's my friend and she's been through a lot. This is tough for her. Don't make it harder. Don't say something hurtful right now.*

Paula started crying. *Oh, my poor baby!* She pulled Rachel into another hug.

Her dad felt like he was about to explode—crimson energy enveloped him. When he looked at Rachel, his soul seemed darkly bruised. There was a male pride—a protectiveness toward his only daughter—that had been violated.

Sean loved her. He would've done the right thing. As soon as I told him that, I wondered if it was true. Despite being the same chronological age as Sean, I felt so much older. He'd been infatuated with Rachel, but he'd been so immature. I didn't know if he could've been responsible enough to be a good father.

Still, at this point, it didn't hurt anyone to give him the benefit of the doubt.

Rachel and her mom cried and held onto each other. The emotions flowing off the two of them would've oversaturated a *Lifetime* movie.

Noah looked at the two of them, and then pulled his hands down his face, as though he could scrub off the excess emotion. His eyes fell back on me.

"Is she—? I mean, we're Catholic, so—" he didn't know how to put it.

She's keeping the baby.

"How is she going to…I mean, college…and the cost of raising a child. She's only seventeen."

It's covered.

"It's covered?" He raised an incredulous eyebrow. *That's hundreds of thousands of dollars. I seriously doubt this girl understands the financial reality of the situation.*

I know what kind of numbers I'm talking about. Either Ganzfield will take care of it, or I will. Mental note: get Nick Coleman to set up a trust for the baby. Being at the top of Isaiah's hit list and all—well, I probably shouldn't put that sort of thing off.

"What's it to you?"

I smiled. *Think of me as your grandchild's fairy god-minder.*

Noah gave a dismissive scoff. The word "grandchild" floated around his mind, searching for a place to land.

Seriously. I introduced Sean to Rachel. He died on a mission with us. I owe it to the two of them to make sure their kid is okay.

"And you're a Vanderbilt or something? You're talking about a huge amount of money. Do you even know what you're committing to?"

I gave him a tight-lipped smile. *Jon Williamson taught me a few things about the stock market.*

"Ah…" He looked at me as though I'd been hiding secrets from him. The quick-fire edge of his anger seemed to be dissipating. I suspected that it would've stayed sharp if Sean were still alive and potentially punchable.

Look, there's no one to force to the altar with a shotgun, and no financial problem. Rachel's afraid that you're going to disown her for this, so now would be a good time to let your daughter know you still love her. Noah did love his daughter. I could feel the caring protectiveness that fueled the intensity of his anger. I hoped that he wouldn't direct that anger to Rachel, but there was only so much I could do.

He gave me a long look as my words sank in. I stopped breathing, but I didn't shrink from his stare. Finally, he nodded. "Yeah." He stood up and, after a few seconds of hesitation, put his hand awkwardly onto Rachel's shoulder.

* * *

I approached the church like a thief. Trevor wanted time to grieve alone. I needed to honor that even though I felt a pull to go to him, to soothe his pain away.

Inside the sanctuary, Trevor's face looked pale and troubled, even in sleep. I paused for a few seconds just to watch him breathe and clenched my hands into fists as I resisted the urge to brush the hair from his forehead.

I grabbed my laptop and headed back to the main building. Four other people already occupied the library—people who'd disrupted their lives to come here and be safe from Isaiah. Now they tried to telecommute or keep up with their college courses online. Too bad they couldn't let their professors know why they had to leave. I bet fleeing a serial killer with superpowers would be a valid excuse for missing final exams.

I tucked myself into an empty chair and wrote an email to Nick Coleman, the charm lawyer who'd set up my investment account a few months ago. Coleman wouldn't evacuate unless Isaiah headed to New York, but he had his own helicopter standing by if he needed to leave quickly.

Nick, I need you to put together trust paperwork for Rachel Fontaine's baby. Enough to cover everything, including college. While you're at it, you may as well make up that will you keep telling me I need. Set aside a chunk for my mom, but list Trevor Laurence as the primary beneficiary.

I humphed. Trevor would probably give all of the dirty, dirty money away to charity or something.

Geez. This was so surreal—sending an email to my charm lawyer to make arrangements for the money I'd accidentally made while mind-reading in the stock market. And why did I feel like this was more of a phone call situation? When did *anyone* deal with stuff like this?

I halfheartedly surfed a few sites while I was online. I really didn't know what to do with myself. Everything seemed less worth doing if Trevor wasn't doing it with me. It'd only been a few hours, but I was in Trevor-withdrawal.

This was probably unhealthy—co-dependent or something. My mom would have a few choice psych terms for it. But the sense of missing a chunk of my soul kept growing stronger—a twitchy discomfort, like steel wool scrubbing under my skin.

Maybe I should go upstairs and confront Williamson with what we'd guessed about his secret plan.

Maybe I should go see how Rachel and her family were doing.

Maybe I should stop being all clingy and needy and just deal with the fact that Trevor didn't want me around all the time.

Ouch.

I scowled. What if Trevor got sick of me? Part of me knew he felt the same incredible connection I did, but the other parts said I wasn't good enough for him—and they were shouting that first part down. *I'm a bad person. I don't deserve to be as happy as I am with Trevor. God or the universe or karma will put things right before too long, and then I'll be alone and miserable. What does Trevor even see in me?*

I wanted to go to him right now and feel the peace of his arms around me. I ached to lose myself in the warm brown of his eyes. Trevor made me want to be a better person, to try to be worthy of him. Everything was better when he was part of it.

I ran my fingers through my hair. I felt like an animal in a cage, pacing behind the bars. My eyes fell on the book that'd been left on the table in front of me—Hemingway's *A Farewell to Arms.*

Yeah, I missed being wrapped in four arms right about now.

My ninth-grade English teacher had been obsessed with Hemingway. We'd read *Farewell to Arms, Sun Also Rises, For Whom the Bell Tolls,* and *Old Man and the Sea* that year. I picked up the book and flipped through the pages, trying to re-establish the story in my mind.

We could feel alone when we were together, alone against the others. We were never lonely and never afraid when we were together.

I groaned. Yeah, that about covered it. I resisted the impulse to just go and find Trevor right now…and just *force* him to allow me to comfort him. *Arrrgh!* I needed to calm down. Forcing comfort on someone isn't the way to comfort him. *God, I'm such a loser. Clingy and needy and co-dependent and stupid.*

I slumped back in the chair and listened to the minds around me. The whole building hummed with their mental babble. More telecommuters worked downstairs in the living room. Directly above me—in his office—I sensed Williamson shielding his mind, probably because I was down here.

Across the hall, an RV named Rick concentrated on Isaiah. He was old by Ganzfield standards, about thirty, and he had a nerd-cool sense about him—like a keyboard player or something. In his mind, Isaiah registered as a nebulous spark of green-white energy. That spark flickered against a three-dimensional map of the surface of the earth. Water felt black and cool in Rick's mind, while living things seemed to pulse and shine a deep red-orange. *I'm ninety-four percent sure he's near St. Louis.* It was so different from Rachel's remote viewing—another variation in how RVs experienced their ability.

Two other RVs worked on computers. One updated tracking

information on their map representing Isaiah's movements and where he'd killed. The other checked his trajectory against the map that showed the known G-positives still away from Ganzfield—seeing who might be Isaiah's next target.

I got up impulsively, not sure where I intended to go but just feeling restless. I popped open the door and startled backwards. *Holy—!*

Zack treaded slowly on the stairs from the third floor, as though trying to avoid making any noise. His blue eyes flashed surprise at seeing me burst from the library. For a moment, we just stared at each other in shock. No one had snuck up on me since—well, since I'd become a minder.

I flushed. I'd been avoiding him ever since he'd seen me lose it so badly. Williamson understood the intensity of my connection to Trevor—he'd had that with Elise—but Zack had just seen the crazy.

Good shield, I finally told him, as the silence stretched between us. *I can't hear you at all.* It was true—he was an empty shell in front of me. My ability didn't even register a person here.

"Thanks."

I suddenly remembered how many times I'd seen Zack around the main building over the past few months. Was Williamson training him in shielding as part of his plan for taking down Isaiah? Did Zack know the whole plan, including what Williamson wanted Trevor and me to do? Was that why he still kept his mind so completely hidden from me right now?

My eyes narrowed as I concentrated on him. *I don't think it'll work if Isaiah RVs you, though.*

Zack paled. Did he feel like he'd given something away?

Maddie, come up to my office. Williamson's order filled my head.

I passed Zack on the stairs. He escaped quickly, making no

effort to keep his steps quiet anymore.

I flopped down in one of the empty chairs in front of Williamson's desk. *Good job with Zack. I completely missed him just now. If I hadn't come out when I did, I'd never have known he was there.*

I asked you not to think too much about this.

Trevor and I can shield well enough to keep things secret. Besides, if Zack was in on it, why shouldn't I know the plan? I could shield more strongly than he could.

How's Trevor doing?

A painful ache filled me. *I didn't come here to talk about Trevor.*

He read the situation in my mind, which answered his question. *Stupid minder connection.* I felt exposed and vulnerable with all my angst hanging out.

I want to know the plan. I stood up—the idea of sitting here and getting a lecture right now made me want to blast something. *Trevor and I will come back when he's ready. You can explain it to us then.*

Williamson didn't reply. I stared hard at him for a few seconds. I still couldn't figure out what he was shielding.

And at that moment, I decided I just didn't care.

I headed back to the church. Trevor didn't want me around right now, but I just needed…I didn't know what I needed. I felt…*broken* without him with me. I half-ran to the front door and fumbled to enter my keycode. His pain called to me from within.

Trevor opened the door before I finished typing in the code and pulled me close. I shut my eyes and took a shuddering breath as the tightness in my chest unwound. The woodsy guy-scent of his skin soothed me.

This may be really selfish of me to ask, but PLEASE let me comfort you now, okay?

He kissed me tenderly on the top of my head. "That's kind of the opposite of selfishness, you know?"

Not the way I feel it.

"Maddie, it's just—" His voice broke. *When I'm with you, I'm so happy...and it just seems...well...disrespectful not to hurt for Archer right now.* He pulled back to search my eyes. *Does that make any sense?*

I nodded. *You and I basically got over the trauma from the massacre in a day—a lot of people here are still shell-shocked. I was messed up from being attacked before I came to Ganzfield, but being with you made it better. So, I understand what you mean. We just seem to—*

—make each other whole.

Yeah. And you want to feel broken for a while—to feel his loss.

You understand. He gave me a relieved smile.

I smiled back. *What kind of soulmate would I be if I didn't?* The itchy, Brillo-under-the-skin anxiety that'd been building within me all day melted away now that I was here in his arms.

He laughed softly and pulled me close again.

"I spoke to Laurie today." He gestured toward the phone. The yellow-grey anxiety stuck to his thoughts like old gum on the bottom of a shoe. "She's really upset. Lilith told her that you and I—"

I felt the rest in his mind. *"It's all your fault. Mom said that you and your strange girlfriend lured Dad to that cult for some wacko cure. My father is DEAD because of you! I hadn't even known he was sick!"* Her voice had risen with each accusation, and then she'd hung up on him.

I tightened my arms around him. *Trevor, I'm so sorry.*

His anguish rippled through me in dark waves. He'd yearned for their approval for so long. Trevor had never felt like he'd earned a proper place in his family—and now that family held him responsible for his grandfather's death.

Probably just as well that those two women were in another time zone, because I really wanted to slap them both right about now. I leaned up and met Trevor's eyes. *They're wrong. It's not your fault. I swear, it's not your fault.* My hand touched his cheek.

Trevor shuddered.

A grey sliver of anxiety stabbed into my thoughts. *That stuff she said…you don't believe it's MY fault, do you? That's not why you wanted to be away from me?*

He shook his head. "No. Really. I just needed…I mean… Archer raised me…like a father. I—I needed to feel that loss. I feel like I should."

Can I just stay here with you? I promise I won't try to make you feel better.

Trevor's poignant smile made my heart pang. "Just having you here makes me feel better. I want you to stay, but I need to be sad for a while, okay?"

We ended up on his bed, where he rested his head in my lap. I stroked his beautiful, dark brown hair as he showed me memories of his grandfather from his childhood.

In one, fourth grade Trevor had stayed up late, keeping vigil at the dark front window. A thrill of joy had hit him when he'd seen the lights of his grandfather's car. Holding up a report card, he'd watched his grandfather's face for a smile of validation. "Well done, son." Archer had tussled Trevor's hair.

In another, Lilith's sister had scowled coldly at the little boy over fancy china. "I don't know why you kept him at all. If my daughter ever had a baby out of wedlock, I'd have made her give the little bastard up for adoption."

Archer's face had flushed red with shame. "He's still family."

Even if he is a bastard, Trevor added.

I tensed. *Please don't ever use that word.*

"That's what I am. Illegitimate. A bastard."

No! I know what the word means, but I feel how ugly it is. That sort of ugliness isn't part of you.

"Archer thought so."

Archer NEVER thought that word around you that I know of. Trust me on this—I would've noticed.

"Maddie, you're doing it."

Doing what?

"Trying to make me feel better."

Sorry.

"You're not sorry." A twinge of a smile tickled his face.

I can't lie to you. I'm not sorry. I want you to feel better, but I'll stop trying for the moment. Please, continue.

"Thank you."

But watch your language. You're talking about the man I love.

"Fine. Where was I?"

You were showing me your Midwestern, conservative upbringing.

Trevor mentally eulogized his grandfather for a few hours. We missed a meal or two, but neither of us was hungry. Eventually, we just sat together quietly. It was as though looking through the memories gave Archer's life a sense of completion. Trevor drifted to sleep and I climbed up to my loft and let the exhaustion take me, as well.

CHAPTER 9

Tell us the plan or count us out.

Trevor held my hand as we leaned against the wall in Williamson's office. We'd been at breakfast downstairs when I'd received his mental summons. Trevor had been adjusting in the four days since Archer's death, but he still had moments when his grief hit him in the head with a brick.

The whole minder "family" had shown up for the meeting. Seth listened in from outside, and the office windows were thrown wide, letting in a warm, sleepy breeze that smelled of fresh hay. My mom sat in one of the chairs in front of Williamson's desk, bristling with maternal protectiveness. Ann sat in the other.

Ann?

She sat overly-straight, seeming almost prim. Her thick, black hair draped between her slender shoulders in a girlish ponytail. She seemed paler than I remembered, and the large, hazel eyes above her high cheekbones were wide with anxiety. *Please don't let me overload. Please don't let me overload.*

Williamson had convinced his niece to re-start dodecamine. She was a minder again.

Was this part of the plan to take down Isaiah? I could tell that Ann had even less of an idea what that was than Trevor and I did. She picked that thought up from me and met my eyes. *It's just temporary. I'm stuck here until Isaiah's gone so I might as well help out.*

I nodded. *You don't seem to be overloading.*

Matilda's got me on a lower dose now. I just have to have more frequent boosters.

Like me.

Exactly. She'd gotten the background of the new treatment regimen from reading Matilda.

Williamson frowned at Trevor, and then at me. "What do you think you know?"

I minder-talked him through our conclusions.

His mind remained impenetrable, but his frown deepened into a scowl. Finally, he gave a long exhale. "I might as well fill you in. You seem to have figured out most of it."

He dropped his mental shield and his ideas gusted out like a strong wind. *It all comes down to dodecamine. Isaiah only enters the homes of those on the drug. I've done the math and figured out how much the victims probably had on-hand. He's getting an average of more than one cc a week—about five times the normal dosage.*

Whoa. Isaiah needed even more than I did and I was a *major* rapid burner.

He might be hoarding the meds, but probably not. Williamson tented his fingers. *It's consistent with the amounts he smuggled out of Allexor. Based on these numbers, Isaiah might have enough of the drug to keep his abilities for another four or five weeks.*

So he'll be neutralized in about a month, one way or another, I thought.

Williamson looked at me. *You know he's not going to just sit back and let his abilities fade.*

I nodded. *Yeah, I know.*

Williamson frowned. *We're also working on a deadline on our end. Rachel will only be able to track Isaiah for about two more weeks. She can't risk additional drug exposure in her condition.*

And she's the best tracker we've got now.

By far, he agreed. We'd lost nearly a dozen RVs in the attack, and Rachel's Uncle Charlie had been killed at Eden Imaging. We didn't have many left who were up to the task. *While many of the others can tell us WHERE he is fairly accurately, Rachel's gift also allows us to see his actions over any distance.*

The door opened and we all jumped. None of us had felt Zack's approach.

"You're late," said Williamson.

"Sorry." He looked for a place to sit.

Huh? What was Zack doing at a minder meeting? Was he here because of his shielding? Or because he could shake off other charms' commands?

Zack leaned against the far wall. He nodded to the rest of us, but his gaze seemed to linger on Ann. This might've been because she stared back, openly in shock.

"Have you met?" asked Williamson. "Zack Greyson, my niece, Ann."

"How are you doing that?" She looked at the rest of us, seeking confirmation that she wasn't the only one experiencing Zack's invisible-mind effect.

Yeah, I confirmed, projecting to everyone. *Zack's a charm who can shield. Weird, huh?*

"*You're* calling *me* weird?" Zack raised an eyebrow at me.

I flushed pink, remembering how Zack had witnessed my

losing it. Ah, hell. Surrounded by telepaths—think of something else. *I'm just saying. Not many people can sneak up on a minder. You just surprised a whole room full of them.*

Zack gave me a smug smile.

Jagged yellow bursts of energy flashed through Trevor's mind.

Oh! I popped up a nearly-invisible spiderweb shield around the two of us. *Trevor, I love you. I adore you. You have nothing to be jealous about. And pretty much everyone in this room can hear your thoughts.*

Sorry. He flashed me a chagrinned smile. *Give me a second.*

No problem.

Only Williamson seemed to notice that we'd cut off from the "hive-mind." He glanced at us sideways and shook his head slightly at me.

How strange! My mom had put a hand on Zack's arm. She and Ann were doing the equivalent of poking him with a mental stick.

That's wild! Ann seemed to have recovered some of her color.

He was good. None of Zack's thoughts came through his mental invisibility cloak.

"That's kind of...amazing. I didn't know that was possible for a non-telepath." Ann's thoughts jangled neon bright.

I turned back to Williamson. *Okay, Jon. So the dodecamine is all here at Ganzfield or down at the pharmaceutical plant in New Jersey. He'll come after it here or there.*

Or when it's in transit.

Trevor and I shared a flash of surprise. We hadn't considered that. Cold washed through me. Could Isaiah fry the driver of a moving vehicle? After the crash, he'd kill any occupants who survived then take the drugs they were transporting.

I met Williamson's eyes. *So Trevor and I are going to New Jersey?*

"Why do *you* need to go?" Pearl-grey blossoms of concern flowered from my mom and flavored everyone's thoughts.

Isaiah wants Trevor and me dead, Mom. If we're splitting our forces, the two of us need to be at the location that looks more vulnerable.

Williamson nodded in agreement. "Maddie and Trevor will go to Allexor."

"No." I saw her jaw clench.

Uh-oh.

Mom, it's okay—

"*IT'S NOT OKAY!*" Her words reverberated through both our ears and our thoughts. "That man almost killed you!"

"Nina, I'm not going to send them alone." Williamson frowned.

"Jon, they're just kids!" she said, trying to appeal to some common-sense element of his personality that I knew didn't exist.

"They won't be in danger. They may be the bait, but Zack's the hook."

Zack's coming with us? Trevor's dismay splashed rust-red energy across my mind—and everyone else's.

"We'll also send some sparks and a healer." Williamson intentionally ignored Trevor's reaction. "Who do you want?"

"Drew." Trevor recovered quickly. He looked at me. "How about Harrison, Ellen, Grant, and Melanie?"

Not Grant, I thought back. He still felt weird around me. *Hannah should come, if she's up for it.*

"Dave?" Trevor asked.

He won't want to come without Claire. Can the other RVs spare her?

Probably. Her talent's local, interjected Williamson. *She'd actually be more useful with you, since she sees images when her targets are in range. If Isaiah's going there, she'll be able to show you what he's doing before he actually reaches you.*

"Maddie, you are *not* going." My mom's emotions fluttered like a brightly-colored kaleidoscope. If she weren't so upset, I'd appreciate how trippy it looked.

Mom, I'm going. They need me.

Her fists clenched helplessly. *My God! Maddie's going into danger. She won't listen to me. How do I get her to listen to me? What do I say? How do I stop her? How do I keep her safe?* She drew in a ragged breath. *I can't—I can't stop her! My baby's going to be in danger and none of these people seem to care!*

Mom... The pain and wordless accusation in her eyes stopped me and I sighed. *I guess every parent has a moment when she realizes that her little girl is all grown up and wants to hunt killer telepaths.*

Outside, Seth cracked up.

"Not funny." My mom scowled at me.

A little funny? I tried to get a smile out of her—and failed.

"So," said Williamson, pushing ahead, "when Isaiah comes for Maddie and Trevor, Zack charms him so Maddie can move in close enough to blast him."

"You can charm minders?" asked Ann, still staring at Zack. Pale pink tendrils flowed through her mind. Fascination. Wonder.

Wait—is Ann interested in Zack?

My thought pinged around the room and I winced.

Oops.

Ann flushed, and her feelings shaded deeper with embarrassment.

Williamson's eyes narrowed as he looked at Zack like he was a cockroach—a *diseased* cockroach.

From outside, Seth's exasperation came through. *Geez, Maddie! You aren't one to talk! For eight months we've all had heads full of*

"Ooh, Trevor's so amazing!" "Trevor's so handsome!" "Trevor's my perfect soulmate!" His mental voice whined with falsetto parody.

Shut up, Seth! My cheeks grew hot as a wave of pink embarrassment flowed through me—and then continued on through Trevor.

If a minder who overloads thinks a guy who shields without having to think about it is interesting, just let her think it, okay? Not all of us have pathetic little mental ranges like yours.

I felt something else behind his words, but now I was too pissed off with Seth to ignore it. *At least I can project thoughts, unlike SOME people. Since you can't, want me to ask Zack if he has a sister?*

"Can we get back to the subject at hand?" Williamson frowned in annoyance.

I wish I could shield. Ann was still embarrassed.

I wish Seth could, I thought sourly.

"I'd still be able to talk, Maddie!" came the thin sound of a shout from outside.

"ENOUGH!" Williamson didn't raise his voice often and it got our attention. "Isaiah probably hasn't figured out that we've cut off the supply yet. He'll probably move quickly once he does, though. He won't want to risk waiting until he begins to weaken."

So, Trevor and I are the bait. Zack's the hook. Claire gives us the heads up when he's coming, and the sparks fry him from a distance if we mess up. Oh, and it'll all happen in the next few weeks since Isaiah won't wait until he's out of dodecamine.

"That's pretty much it," said Williamson.

I met Trevor's eyes. *Does this work for you?*

He nodded. *We can stop him this way. He's desperate enough to come after us, and he knows he needs dodecamine.*

I sighed. Maybe the world would be a safer place if none of

us had the drug—if production just ground to a halt and we all reverted to nearly-normal people.

But that wasn't going to happen. And, most of the time, I really didn't want it to.

My mother brushed past me as she left the office, still simmering angry-red because the rest of us intended to put her only child into a dangerous, even lethal situation. What could I say? What she wanted—keeping me here behind the walls—wasn't going to happen.

Ann? I stopped her at the top of the stairs. *What you said before—have you ever been able to shield?*

She shook her head. *I've tried.* Feelings of inadequacy bubbled up and fizzed across her mind.

Can you show me what you did?

She thought about shielding. Nothing happened.

Her thoughts reminded me of the first time I'd attempted to borrow Trevor's telekinesis. I'd tried to think a soda can into motion rather than just using my mind's natural programming to make the energy move the way I wanted it to. The shared memory made Trevor smile—a rare sight these days. I squeezed his hand and smiled back, and then borrowed his ability to brush the hair out of his eyes with invisible fingers, reminding him I had the hang of it now.

Could I help Ann? I focused on exactly what I did when I shielded—the way the energy seemed to well up, how I visualized it, and how it...just how it *felt*. Then I sent her the most detailed memory I could.

She concentrated intently, pulling the details out and running her mind across them, as though we were two old women comparing the patterns of our knitting. *Can you show me once more?*

I centered on the memory again, focusing on the tiny impulses involved.

A single comment from Williamson's office floated out through the now-quiet hall. *"Zack, do I need to remind you not to try to charm ANY of the minders?"* Williamson only had one person in mind. Ann flushed again and dropped her eyes.

I bit my lip as I tried not to laugh. *You should've seen what he put Trevor through.*

Trevor wrapped a possessive arm around my waist. *Completely worth it.* The surge of silvery energy that passed between us gave me a delicious shiver.

I sent the shielding memories to Ann a second time, feeling her pull them in and attach them in her own head. Then I felt her mind go grey and foggy—*unreadable.*

You're doing it!

A bright spark of excitement burned though the shield. It suddenly collapsed, revealing her thoughts again.

Ann, did you just shield? We both heard the surprise in Williamson's mental voice. He stuck his head out the door.

Ann nodded. The little zings of pale-green energy she emitted matched her excited smile.

Neither of us could tell if Williamson was proud of her, or of me, or of both of us—but we both saw the teal-colored emotion well up within him.

My jaw dropped. *Wait, you see colors?*

"You can see them, too?" Shock flared like sunlight within her. *I thought I was the only one! I don't think Uncle Jon or Seth see them.*

I looked at Ann again, viewing her through new eyes. She'd been leaving Ganzfield the first time I'd met her so I'd never really thought of her as another minder. I'd had no idea that we had so much in common. *Keep practicing your shielding while I'm gone. Call—ah, hell.* We wouldn't be able to talk by phone. Stupid brain damage! *Email me. We can discuss ways to improve it.*

Ann shook her head. "I just shielded for the first time in four years as a minder. No one's been able to teach it to me before. We'd assumed I just couldn't do it. No way. I'm going with you."

Jon? I asked. We all turned to look at him, still standing in the doorway of his office.

It'll be dangerous with Isaiah targeting the group there, but maybe learning to shield will give her a reason to stay this time. But I don't think her interest in Zack is—

Ann gasped and pinked up.

Uh, Jon? You know we can hear you, right?

His shield popped up, leaving us wondering where that last thought had been headed.

"Ann can go," he said, finally.

Trevor and I sought out the team members immediately. If we were going to leave in the morning, we had less than a day to prepare. We found Drew and Harrison on opposite ends of the firing range, suited up in Kevlar as they pointed handguns at each other like old-fashioned, pistols-at-dawn duelers. Both radiated power, even at that distance, as they focused on suppressing the other's weapon. Trevor pulled invisible arms around us as we held back, waiting for them to lower the guns before trying to get their attention.

"Drew. We're going after Isaiah," Trevor said. "You in?"

Drew let out an enthusiastic whoop.

Harrison? How about you? I asked.

"Hell, yeah!" He echoed his brother's whoop.

What's the yelling about? Hannah poked her head up from behind the barricade. *No one seems to be injured.* She turned back to her book but I caught her attention.

New mission. We think we have a way to stop Isaiah. We should have a healer with us.

I'd have to ask Ann if she saw a color for lack of enthusiasm. I got nothing. *Rachel's pregnancy—*

C'mon, Hannah. You've trained with the team, and the others can take care of Rachel. We'll be back long before the baby's born. This will only take a few weeks, at most. Isaiah would come after us before he ran out of dodecamine.

"Let me think about it. I'll talk to the other healers." Hannah headed back toward the infirmary.

The rest of us descended on the Fireball field. More than a dozen sparks moved across the grass. The largest group practiced fundamentals—bouncing a flaming ball from one to another across a large circle. At the far end of the field, four more people juggled flaming batons.

I smiled. Sparks *loved* playing with fire. Their bright joy gave me a contact high.

"Ellen! Mel!" Drew's cousins turned. "C'mere a sec!"

The two stepped away from the Fireball practice and joined us. As Drew relayed the invite, Ellen and Melanie also whooped. Was that a new spark thing, or just a McFee thing?

"You're gonna want us to coordinate our abilities, right?" asked Mel.

Trevor and I shared a glance. "We can't give details right now."

Ellen humphed. "That's a yes."

"You're asking Jonah Parker, right?" Mel wasn't going to let it go. "He's the best at directional control when we work together."

She turned to Ellen. "He increased our range—what? Forty percent that time?"

"At least," she agreed, nodding. "Hey, Jonah. JONAH!"

One of the jugglers froze his flaming pins in mid-air as he searched out the source of the shout. When his eyes landed on our group, Ellen waved him over. Jonah's focus shifted to the unmoving torches for a moment. The flames died as though they'd been snuffed by giant, invisible fingers, and the still-smoking pins dropped to the ground as he turned and started toward us.

I didn't know Jonah well; I don't think we'd ever spoken to each other. He had a dark mahogany complexion, slender build, and was only a few inches taller than me. His hair had been shaved very short, which gave him a clean-cut appearance, although his prominent cheekbones and watchful, almost-black eyes made him look somewhat exotic close up.

Jonah wasn't a whooper. He simply nodded seriously and said, "Okay."

We finally tracked down Dave and Claire down by the lake. Drew's shout gave them enough time to get presentable before we came into view.

Dave whooped—definitely a McFee thing.

"You really want me instead of Rachel?" Claire asked. "I'm not that strong an RV. I can't see things more than about fifty or sixty miles away. Rachel's the varsity team—I'm more like the JV."

JV RV? I grinned. *Pretty sure we'll just need local stuff on this trip.* Claire had no idea why Rachel wasn't going on missions anymore—and I wasn't going to be the one to tell her.

Trevor changed the subject. "We'll leave from the main building at 8 a.m."

"Hey! Dibs on one of the new tents!" Drew grabbed a couple of shiny bundles off the shelf and tossed them to Trevor, who caught them in mid-air and added them to the growing pile of gear in the main building's basement storeroom. The tents had been custom-made of a flexible aluminum fabric called pyreflect and could withstand heat of up to three thousand degrees for up to a minute. We took six of the ten, along with four of the standard, blue nylon tents for the non-incendiary among us.

Trevor picked up a ground cloth. *I hope it doesn't rain too often.*

I frowned. Trevor would have to sleep shelterless for the next few weeks.

Wait, why would he have to? Didn't I have millions of dollars?

Jon! I called up to the third floor. Sometimes I just loved telepathy. *Does your pharmaceutical plant have open space for a new building?*

It's got acres of open space. Why?

I want to put up a new hanger or garage or something.

For Trevor?

Exactly.

Actually, we were going to put in another building a few years ago. Poured the slab but the contractor had an accident on another site and delayed the project. The state changed the tax rules in the intervening time and the project was no longer cost effective, so it was scrapped. Perhaps we could put up a Morton building or something similar on the slab.

What's a Morton building?

Pre-fab equipment garage. The crew can set them up in a day. He flashed me an image of a large, metal structure.

That'd do it.

I'll order one. I'll have Coleman get the permits, so we'll probably have them by the end of the day.

I sent a dose of happy up to him. *Thanks! Have him bill me or something.*

This one's on me. Williamson still felt responsible for Trevor freezing in the unheated church during his first winter at Ganzfield. *I'll also get a couple of trailers delivered and hooked up, so you'll all have showers and kitchens, too.*

Bonus! I grinned. *You have no idea how much better that'll be than camping!*

Maddie, I sleep in my car when I'm not here. I know EXACTLY how much better it will be.

Thanks, Jon.

This is it. We're going to stop Isaiah this time. I can feel it.

I wished I shared his confidence. Now that we had an actual plan, the thought of facing Isaiah again dropped a rock in my gut. *I hope so.*

Allexor's security staff has been told to expect you tomorrow afternoon. Zack knows who to talk to when you arrive. You'll all need to keep a low profile. Most of the people who work there make pain relievers and drugs that treat anxiety disorders. They don't know anything about us or about our abilities, and we want to keep it that way.

I'll bring a few good books. My lips twitched. "Drew" and "low profile" worked so poorly in the same sentence. *Good news, guys.* I relayed the trailer and building information to Trevor and Drew.

"Sweet," said Drew.

The situation didn't seem too dangerous if we'd have hot showers and dry places to sleep. Almost like a vacation.

Almost.

* * *

Maddie? Trevor thought to me. We were alone again, back in the church, packing our personal gear.

I looked down over the edge of my loft to where Trevor stood. *What's wrong?* I asked, feeling his uneasiness even before I met his eyes. I stumbled down the ladder and landed in his arms.

"I feel like we're missing something. Isaiah's not stupid. He calculates the odds of success, like he did in Detroit. And he'll be able to RV us. Why would he come into a trap?"

Desperation? Cold dread trickled rusty tentacles through me and I frowned. *But you're right—he won't just walk in if he thinks we have a good chance of stopping him.*

"Maybe he'll come armed."

But he knows we survived after he shot at us, so he might guess you can stop bullets. And Isaiah could tell that the sparks kept his gun from firing—he heard it in their heads. I felt a humorless laugh bubble up. *Maybe he'll drive up in a tank.*

"That's actually not impossible."

No problem. The sparks could stop a tank.

"Probably," he agreed.

Drew would LOVE to stop a tank. It would make his day.

Trevor smiled at the thought. "Yeah."

That's not the only thing bothering you, though.

Trevor bit his lip as he looked away at nothing in particular. "They had the funeral yesterday." He'd found the obituary on the website of a Michigan newspaper. Neither his mother nor his grandmother had contacted him to inform him of it, and he wasn't listed in the obituary as one of Archer's survivors— although both of his half-sisters were. Grief and hurt churned within him.

The intensity spilled across our mental connection, catching my breath. Trevor was so tired of the emotional pain, and I ached to take the pain away. My hands slid up to frame his face. I met his eyes and we sank to the floor together as the light of the church dimmed around us. The connection was gentler this time. We pulled together with a glowing fullness that lifted our souls with a rhythm like a beating heart.

We returned to the trembling bodies that lay entwined on the smooth wood of the floor. The afternoon light painted everything a warm gold. We looked into each other's eyes, still feeling the perfect connection with the other's soul. His finger traced the edge of my lower lip—no, my finger traced his.

Something shifted within Trevor, like he'd been underwater until his lungs burned, and then had finally broken the surface and drawn a deep breath. *If they don't want me, I don't need them. I don't need their approval anymore.*

Lilith and Laurie? I asked, even though I could tell whom he meant.

I—I can't let them cast this…shadow over any more of my life. I don't need to beg for scraps of affection. He stroked the side of my face. *Not anymore. Not when I know what it feels like to be cherished.*

It doesn't have to be either-or. I'll adore you, no matter what.

I'm not completely cutting off ties with them. If they don't, that is. I just know that their opinions don't define me anymore.

I kissed him tenderly. *If you're going to base your self-image on MY opinion of you, you're going to get a huge ego.*

The sparkle returned to his eyes. *Oh, well. You know me better than they do.*

Stop stealing my line!

He smiled. *It was MY line first.*

I snuggled against him, feeling the warmth of his arms around me and the fullness of his soul. There was peace and contentment within him now, and I felt my own soul react to it. The restlessness I'd felt within myself calmed.

Trevor was whole again.

And we were whole together.

CHAPTER 10

"Maddie, you don't have to do this."

Mom, we're going.

My mom crossed her arms as she watched us load our gear into the big black van. She scowled as she briefly considered grabbing my bag and making a run for it—anything that would keep us from leaving this morning. Guilt pinged within me; I actually felt bad for my mom. Since last fall, I'd gotten comfortable with the concept that regular rules didn't apply to me. But she hadn't had as much time to get used to it, so she kept trying to enforce some of them. Back in our previous life, I hadn't given her too much trouble. She didn't know how to set parental limits for a seventeen-year-old, lethal telepath.

"Nina, it's going to be okay. I'm not going to let anything bad happen to her."

Aww. I really didn't deserve this wonderful guy, but there was no way I'd ever let him put himself in danger and go up against Isaiah to save me.

Well—not *again.*

My mom's too-bright eyes fixed on his face. "Keep her safe or I'll never forgive you."

Trevor nodded. "If anything happened to Maddie, there'd be nothing left of me to not forgive." His brows knit in frustration. "Wait, did that make sense? You know what I mean. I'd die to protect her."

My mother pulled Trevor into a hug, which made a happy-green flash of energy flow through him. I tried not to let him read in my thoughts that she wanted to get a hand on him to see if he really meant it.

Claire gave Rachel a nervous smile as she slid into the front passenger seat. Rachel didn't notice. She frowned as we packed up without her—she'd been part of the team since before there was a team.

You going to be okay staying here?

Rachel scoffed. "Safer than the rest of you. I'm not the one he keeps tracking down."

Ellen looked up sharply. *Wait—Isaiah's coming after us? I thought we were going after him!*

Don't stress, I told her. *Isaiah's in—where is he, Rachel?*

"Phoenix." I saw her vision of him at a desk. Early-morning light draped across the wall behind him as he focused on a computer screen.

I wonder how he communicates these days? As far as we knew, he couldn't project thoughts like I did.

Rachel frowned, thinking. "I haven't seen him talk or use sign language. He pretty much avoids other people. But he's been on the computer a lot recently. Maybe he does everything online."

Everything except kill. Isaiah still did that in-person.

It was disconcerting—he had to deal with the same disability

I had. It was like he was a parallel-universe version of me—the evil one with a beard. I humphed. If this were a movie, I'd soon discover that he was my real father or something—Darth Lerner to my Maddie Skywalker. Ugh. I shuddered.

Not funny.

Dave hopped into the driver's seat. "Let's go, everyone."

My mom stood next to Rachel as we drove away. Both wondered if we'd all be coming back alive. I tried to swallow the lump in my throat and brace myself for the long drive. The thoughts of everyone in the van filled my mind—the babble of nearly a dozen mental voices, loud and close.

Inescapable.

"Okay, Claire-voyant," Dave grinned at Claire as he pulled the van out through the gate, "lemme know when we get near the speed traps."

She flashed a smile back at him. "I always do."

"You got the music covered?"

"What music?" she asked. "The radio?"

The van swerved a bit as Dave ransacked the dashboard. "This thing doesn't have an iPod dock?" *Four hundred miles without music? What are we, barbarians?*

Claire tried to get a radio station to stick, but the mountains cut off each signal after only a few minutes.

I leaned against Trevor's shoulder. Mustard-yellow anxiety trickled through him. *What will Isaiah do when he sees where we are? Will he come after Maddie again? Can we really protect each other?*

Behind us, Ann's minder-loud thoughts pinged like sonar against mine. *I hope I don't overload. Could one of these sparks accidentally blow up the van's gas tank? Is Zack seeing anyone? Would he ever be interested in a minder like me?*

I popped up a mental shield before she got an unintended

answer to that last one from my memories. Actually, Ann and Zack might make a good couple. He wasn't intimidated by minder-girls—I knew that first-hand. She was a little older than he was—nineteen to his seventeen. That wasn't too much of an age gap, was it? Zack had come back to Ganzfield more serious— more mature—than when I'd first met him. I flicked out a mental feeler, but still didn't sense anything from him, even though he sat only a few feet behind me. Actually, he had chosen the seat right next to Ann. Was he interested in her?

You're not matchmaking, are you? Trevor asked.

Nah. I rubbed my chin, and then caught his eye and grinned. *Ooh, maybe I should. Think of the huge untapped market for a telepathic matchmaking service!*

Maddie? Ann's tentative thought made me gasp. Had she overheard my exchange with Trevor just now? *You just shielded, right?*

I cleared my thoughts before answering, imagining a blank wall. *Yeah.*

Mind if we practice a bit now?

Sure!

Working with Ann, I found that her thoughts had a soft-yet-strong texture, although her self-esteem seemed deflated. *I couldn't handle all this last time. Am I really capable of being a minder?* Nearly an hour of shield practice helped her gain a fragile confidence. Her thoughts glowed a satisfied green.

After stopping for lunch at a Friendly's in Connecticut, we swapped out drivers again and Ellen had a turn behind the wheel. Ann's eyes grew wider as we drew into the outskirts of the Bronx. Route 287 would've taken us around the City.

I scowled. *Why are we driving directly through the Bronx in heavy traffic?* The population shot up around us, pressing the thoughts of thousands of minds against us. Humming, buzzing, bubbling up through Ann's larger range—I felt it hit her like a riptide, knocking her feet out from under her and making it hard to breathe.

Then the same wave hit me. I squeezed my eyes shut and pressed my fists against my clammy temples. I may've whimpered, although the sound didn't register with me. Gah! My skull felt like it was trapped in a vise and someone was turning the crank. This was *so* much worse than the last time I'd been in New York!

I felt Trevor shift next to me, vaguely sensing his hands on my shoulders. He was saying something, but I couldn't make out the words. Unseen hands pulled mine down from my face, trying to get me to look at him. Concern and pain flashed in his eyes.

Finally, his words registered. "Maddie? Can you shield?"

I scowled. Trevor knew—he *knew* that shielding wouldn't keep out other people's thoughts! Why was he asking stupid questions right now? *Dammit—my head's about to explode here!* Shielding just kept me from being read by other minders and there was only one other—

Oh.

I concentrated on blocking my thoughts. My shielding felt weak and crude—like wet clay slapped up around the inside of my skull—but the intensity dropped like someone had turned down the knob in my brain. An entire stadium of cheering fans still stomped and did the wave between my ears, but they no longer blew thousands of those evil air-horns directly into my soul. Good thing I hadn't been driving—although I would've taken the *right* road. I guess no one had told Ellen about not driving minders through big cities. Looking back at Ann, I saw a bleary double image of a tear-streaked face that probably matched my own. After all, we'd had thousands of minds' worth of thoughts bouncing back-and-forth between us.

Feedback loop—minder-style.

Urgh. Dizzy and drained, I buried my face against Trevor's chest and hoped I wouldn't yak all over his t-shirt. He was shaking and breathing fast. I simply focused on keeping up my shield as the thoughts of thousands of strangers gushed like a fire-hose through my head. The population density dropped off as we crossed the G.W. Bridge into New Jersey. The individual thoughts of the people around me lifted out of the torrent and became understandable once again. After a few more minutes, the van shut off.

I looked up and had a mediocre déjà vu moment—we'd pulled over at the Vince Lombardi rest stop on the New Jersey Turnpike. Except for the resters and stoppers, the meadowlands—the sprawling, tall-grassed swamp of North Jersey—had almost no other minds.

A smooth hand pressed against the side of my face as Hannah did a quick assessment. Trevor ran nervous fingers through my hair. I reached out and caught them.

"You've never had such a bad reaction to a city before." He tipped my head up and searched my eyes. "Did you and Ann do something to each other?"

I nodded, still shielding. Dropping it seemed premature— potentially dangerous. Right now, I felt small and vulnerable and I wanted to keep my blankie wrapped tight around my head.

A groan came from behind me and I twisted to look back at Ann. Zack had a hand on her back and he hovered protectively close. His eyes never left her face.

"Maybe my coming wasn't such a good idea," she whispered.

I didn't say a word.

* * *

The side door squealed open and some coffee appeared in my hand. After a few more minutes, the last of the overload dissipated. I lowered my shield tentatively, feeling like the stupid person in the horror movie who opens the door of the creepy house and calls out, "Hello?"

Trevor's relieved smile warmed me. *There you are.*

I sighed. *Next time, let's go AROUND the city.*

You okay?

No permanent damage, thanks. It hit you, too, didn't it?

Just secondhand. Not as badly as it hit you.

I looked back. *Ann? Are you okay?*

"Oh!" She startled and blushed as she peeled her eyes away from Zack. Little fireworks of *I think he likes me!* shot through her head.

I snorted. Yeah, she'd made a full recovery. Giddy tendrils of her euphoria seemed to reach out for me. I felt my batteries recharge slightly, but that may've been from the coffee.

So that's "overload."

Ann nodded, and then frowned. "You've never overloaded before?"

Not like that! I've been overwhelmed with too many thoughts, but—gah! That was like getting a concussion from the inside. Who knew there was a critical mass for multiple minders?

"It's happened to me with Seth—twice." Ann's brows knit together. "He has this problem with almost every minder, though. I'm glad you were able to shield when you did."

Me, too. I leaned back against Trevor's shoulder and absorbed the relative quiet while it lasted.

The rest of the group filtered back to the van a few minutes later, flashing thoughts of concern that turned to relief. We got back on the road and Claire RVed us toward Allexor's facility in New Brunswick.

Ooh, neat.

When Claire used her ability, rippling silver tubes shot out from her mind horizontally, gently curving with the surface of the earth. Once she located her target, her focus seemed to slip through the connecting tube as though through a wormhole. This gave her a fish-eye vision of the other side, like the distorted view through a security peephole.

Cool. Ann watched it, too.

I flashed her a conspiratorial smile, which she returned.

We pulled up to the front gate of Allexor Pharmaceuticals just after 5 p.m. Metal fences topped with wicked-looking razor wire ran the perimeter, and a line of cars streamed out of the employee parking area. The acres of nearly-flat, manicured lawns still showed light and dark stripes from the gardening crew's mower. Several low buildings clustered well away from the perimeter fence. Something about the place felt ominous and forlorn—like a nursing home filled with unmoving people, gazing into the distance. *Abandon all hope, ye who enter here.*

Trevor snorted. *Wasn't that the motto on the "Welcome to New Jersey" sign we passed?*

Ann and I both cracked up, drawing confused looks from the other people in the van.

Geez. Minders.

Are they laughing at something in MY head?

We got ourselves back under control as Drew rolled down his window at the security booth.

Zack leaned closer to the window. "We're here to see Martin Martinson."

We are? I was out of the loop on some things, apparently. I stared at the sign that warned of "Severe Tire Damage" if we tried to back up. Signs like that always made me feel a nervous itch to defy them. Good thing I wasn't driving.

The guard at the gate looked at the van full of tired teenagers and his mind filled with skepticism. "Can I see your ID?" he asked Drew.

"You don't need to see his identification," Zack deadpanned.

Stop quoting Star Wars! I tried not to laugh.

Ann couldn't contain her giggle.

The guard waved us through.

Personally, I thought Trevor had a better claim on Jedi-powers than Zack did. I mean, could Zack suspend a droid and a box of tools in mid-air while standing on his head? Doubtful.

True, thought Ann, *but that's not actually the "Jedi mind trick," now is it?*

I'm just saying, if Zack and Trevor were ever trapped by the snow monster on the ice planet Hoth, only one of them would be able to get hold of that out-of-reach lightsaber.

Ann grinned. *Wow, Maddie. You seem to know an awful lot about Star Wars.*

Doesn't everyone? Isn't it a basic component of cultural literacy? Like Shakespeare, or, um…the Bible? After all, it wasn't as though I'd called that snow monster a *wampa.*

Oh, my God! Ann laughed. *You actually know the SPECIES NAME of the snow monster?*

I pinked up. Okay, I wasn't used to having another telepath around all the time. I'd need to watch my thoughts a bit more.

You think I'm like a Jedi? Trevor grinned, amused that I'd betrayed my nerdly credentials.

I popped a shield around our minds and met his eyes. *I TOLD you you'd get a huge ego from my views of you.*

Trevor flashed a wave of adoration at me in return.

And you're definitely more of a Jedi than Zack.

He beamed at that—not that he felt particularly competitive with Zack or anything.

We continued up the curving road to the manor house that served as the administrative center of the corporate campus. Martin Martinson walked out to meet us as we rolled to a stop at the front door. He seemed a little too short and slender for a man—almost elf-like. His close-cut, mud-brown hair probably would be curly if it got longer, and he wore an expensive-looking grey suit with a yellow print tie. His thoughts were strangely... *smooth.* Unruffled. It didn't strike him as odd that a dozen high school kids were about to camp out on the property? We looked like a group who should be on their way down the shore, not guarding a pharmaceutical company.

"Dr. Williamson told me to expect you. Welcome to Allexor Pharmaceuticals. We have the site prepared according to Dr. Williamson's specifications. If you'll follow me, I'll drive you to it now."

I wondered at this strange unflappability. Had someone charmed Martinson into believing that anything Williamson asked was reasonable? Was this his natural state? Was he simply well-paid enough not to care if strange things happened here?

Think he's charmed? I asked Ann.

She shrugged. *Or something. His mind feels...weird.*

Maybe he really IS an elf.

Ann swallowed her laugh.

Martinson gestured, and a younger man zipped a white golf cart to his side. Drew drove the van behind the little vehicle as it followed a road around the building. He didn't even need to touch the gas pedal to keep up and his impatience built in sunset colors around him.

We passed several institutional, one-story buildings. The orange and brown panels under the metal window frames looked faded and out of style. We made another turn and saw a large area—nearly a football field—surrounded by an eight-foot-high, chain link fence. Blue construction tarps spread across each panel, blocking the interior from view, and large yellow signs proclaimed, "Danger: Construction Zone." For some reason, it reminded me of building blanket forts in the living room as a kid.

Martinson stood to open the padlock on the gate. "The crew drilled and placed the sills on the slab this morning. They set up the fencing this afternoon. With the tarps up, you should have privacy here." He gestured to the closest building. It looked like all of the others. "That's Building Sixteen. Dr. Williamson said that was the one where you needed access."

Zack nodded. "Thanks."

What's so special about Building Sixteen? *Wait. Is that where they make dodecamine?*

Zack gave me a subtle nod, not turning his head toward me. He was still shielding so well I would've walked past him in the dark.

Drew pulled inside the gate and parked the van next to a huge, open slab of concrete that dominated one corner. Metal beams traced a long rectangle across its surface, with gaps that might be doorways at either end. A pile of scrapped wood pallets stood off to the side. At the far end of the fenced field, two trailers nearly touched the edge of the enclosure. Electric and water hookups trailed off both of them and into Building Sixteen, along with a snaking green cable that I hoped was an internet connection.

"The pre-fabricated building goes up tomorrow morning."

Martinson gestured to the slab. "The installation crew will be here by eight."

Zack nodded. "Good."

Zack was doing all the talking and suddenly I felt—*sidelined.* I knew I could no longer manage some of the basic tasks on a mission—like talking to this strangely unflappable man— however, seeing Zack confidently handling the situation made me feel obsolete. *Useless.* And I couldn't even read his stupid, shielded mind.

You need to do everything? Trevor asked.

I shook my head. *Sorry. I don't know where that came from.*

Long day? He could feel how tired I was.

Yeah. Any idea how we're going to handle dinner?

Umm...

Zack just took care of it while I was having my existential mini-crisis, didn't he?

Martinson got into his little golf cart and putted away. Seriously, it would've been faster to walk.

Uh-huh. Trevor smiled. *They're delivering pizza.*

Ah. It was my turn to smile. *Jersey pizza.* Like bagels, the quality of pizza seemed inversely proportional to the distance a place was from New York. Jersey pizza—with the drippy orange grease that would run onto our hands as we fed ourselves the narrow, folded-in-half-lengthwise slices—was simply the best pizza on the planet. We'd be able to *feel* our arteries clogging, slowly killing us with each incredible bite—but what a way to go.

Trevor laughed. *Hungry?*

Oh, yeah. I'm sorry, but they do NOT do pizza right in New Hampshire. I mean, what are they using for sauce? Ketchup?

Speaking of New Hampshire...

I handed him the cell phone. *Remind me why I'm the one still carrying this thing.*

Conversation died out at the sound of Trevor's, "Hey, Rachel."

I couldn't hear her response over the sudden flashes of concern.

Where's Isaiah now?

Is he coming for us, or are we going after him?

Why are we in New Jersey again? Nothing good ever happens to us in New Jersey.

Why isn't Rachel with us? Is it because Sean died around here and she can't handle coming back?

Trevor put his hand over the receiver. "Isaiah's still in Phoenix."

The others relaxed and started talking again. I considered the other concerns for the group. The most difficult issue would be the sleeping arrangements. We needed to place ourselves so that both Ann and I were far enough away from the others—and from each other—to avoid sending or picking up dreams. I scanned the enclosed space and frowned. Suddenly, the football-field-sized space didn't look big enough.

Ann? What's your range?

I used to hear at one-ninety, detect at three-thirty.

I shook my head. No, definitely not big enough, particularly with the stronger connection between minders.

But I'm not at full strength on the new dosage, and I don't share dreams.

You don't?

I hear them from other people, so I need the distance to sleep well, but I'm not projective like you and Uncle Jon.

But you can shield now. I'm pretty sure that shielding and projecting are related.

Oh. She considered that. She didn't know whether this was a good or bad development. The idea of being a projective telepath intrigued her on one level, but sharing thoughts and dreams unwillingly scared her.

I humphed. *Tell me about it.*

We clustered the tents in the corners, leaving the center of the rectangular area open. Ann and I were diagonally across from each other. Trevor set out his tarp and air mattress on the concrete slab about twenty feet in from my little blue tent. The corner opposite the trailers filled with the metallic tents of the sparks. I hadn't heard the discussion that put Hannah in one trailer and Zack in the other, but it worked. While Claire's tent was pitched by the trailers, I got the impression from her and Dave's minds that it was mostly for show.

The pizza arrived as we finished setting up. Drew and Harrison scavenged some scrap wood from the construction debris and flashed up a little campfire in the middle of the manicured lawn, in the exact center of the fenced area. I could almost feel the horror of whoever's job it was to keep this place looking like a golf course. We pulled a few of the air mattresses into a loose circle around the flames and ate pizza as the sun dipped from the sky and the light evening breeze cooled the air.

I looked around the group. Claire and Dave sat hip to hip. Their bright blue eyes seemed to match, although she was slender and dark-haired, while he was burly and barrel-chested with the standard-issue, McFee red hair and blotchy freckles. They talked and laughed with Ellen and Melanie.

On their other side, Drew and Harrison debated the best way to get a good color change out of the flames, and parts of the fire flared red, yellow, white, and blue in turns as they showed each other various techniques.

Jonah Parker was quiet, both in and out of his head, and he

cast a light presence here, especially with so many large, vibrant McFees around. I focused on him for a moment, trying to figure him out. I knew that Jonah was a descendent of the first known pyrokinetic, William Underwood. I floated a quiet thought into his head.

What happened to bring me to Ganzfield?

The memory played through his mind. Three years ago, a distant cousin had visited him. Two weeks after a cheek swab to look for the "genetic abnormality" the cousin claimed to have, he'd been thrust into a new world of sparks, charms, and minders. He'd never told his mother or grandfather about his ability, despite the fact that he'd inherited it through them. They were both strongly, charismatically religious. He feared they'd regard his power over fire as demonic and evil—and the joy he felt from it as wicked and prideful.

I gathered from their conversation that Hannah and Jonah were part of the same group that met in one of the Blake House classrooms on Sunday mornings for an informal church service. How strange—Ganzfield had an actual church on the premises, but the faithful met in a classroom.

Yeah, I asked about that when I first started sleeping there. Trevor's shoulder pressed against mine. *The people who started the group a few years back wanted to meet in a place with heat.*

Lucky for us. I smiled sideways at him.

Ann and Zack sat together across the circle from Trevor and me, shielding as they talked to each other. Half-eaten slices of pizza hung forgotten in their hands.

I pulled a mental shield around Trevor and me. *I can't read either of them. Are they interested in each other?*

He half-choked on a bite of pizza. *Seriously? You can't tell? They're both shielding right now.*

They're into each other. Totally enamored. He was so much better at reading body language than I was.

Think that's okay?

I think it's fantastic that he's interested in someone who isn't you. But Ann's...well, I worry about her.

He's a good guy.

She's had a rough time of it. I felt a little flare of jealousy at the remembered flash of the time he'd spent with her, before I'd gotten to Ganzfield. Trevor had been one of the last people she could stand having around last time she'd been on dodecamine. On one hand, I could completely understand that—Trevor's genuine goodness really did feel wonderful to minders. On the other hand, the thought of her "connecting" with his mind made me pink up with delayed jealousy.

Trevor snorted. *So, I was jealous of Zack and you were jealous of Ann?*

I could see the humor in it—now. *And now they seem to be interested in each other.*

So this could be a good thing?

I smiled. *Or at least in our benign self-interest.*

I lowered the shield. *Ann, should Trevor and I take the first watch, or do you and Zack want it?*

Ann flushed. When she dropped her shield to answer, her mind blossomed with Zack-related giddiness. *We'll stay up and talk a little more.*

I looked at the time displayed on my cell phone. It was a little before eight. *Wake me at ten.* We quickly set the order of the night's watch—Drew and Harrison at midnight; Dave and Claire at two; Jonah and Hannah at four; Ellen and Mel at six. With so many of us, we didn't have long watches. They weren't too much of a priority at this point. Isaiah was still far away and Allexor had enough existing security to keep out most other threats. I sent a quick text to my mom letting her know that we'd arrived—although Rachel probably had told her.

Another side benefit of being an RV—Rachel would always know where her child was…and what he or she was doing.

I kinda pitied the kid a little bit.

Trevor gathered up some additional construction debris as we left the fire. He sat on his air mattress and put a ring of wood scraps at the ends of his range, marking a circle so the others wouldn't accidentally approach too closely while he slept.

The others noticed when Trevor joined me in my tent, but after eight months as a couple, we really weren't the objects of gossip anymore—more like part of the social landscape. Only Jonah's morally-tinged disapproval registered at the outermost reaches of my range.

I popped up a shield around our minds, since we were still in Ann's range. I couldn't hear her thoughts—she must also be shielding. *Quiet.* I felt the strains of the day leaving me and the sense of completeness filled us. The minds and voices within the enclosure gently touched the edges of my consciousness and I drifted to sleep in Trevor's embrace.

Two hours later—which felt like ten minutes—Ann's hushed voice called my name from outside the tent.

I'm awake. Trevor's arms were still around me. My forehead was damp from where it'd pressed against Trevor's neck.

I'm awake, too, he sent to us both.

What? Ann's surprise flared bright yellow. She hadn't heard his thoughts from inside the tent until he dropped the shield at the sound of her voice. He'd been borrowing my ability to shield us both while I slept.

You stayed awake and shielded me?

You hate sharing dreams with other people, and Ann was still in range when you fell asleep.

Tears tickled the edges of my eyes and a lump filled my throat. *Thank you.* I was so unworthy of this consideration. In the dark, I felt the tender brush of his lips against my forehead.

Trevor scavenged a few more pieces of scrap wood, built the fire back up, and then slid down to sit next to me. We talked silently through the uneventful shift, shielding together so as not to disturb Ann. I felt her mind in the isolated little tent in the far corner. Her foggy shield slipped as she drifted into sleep.

Only a few stars were visible in the hazy sky when we woke Drew and Harrison at midnight for their watch. The two sparks shared my unspoken view that the two-hour shifts definitely beat the all-nighters we'd been doing at Ganzfield. The air felt damp as I watched Trevor settle down to sleep on the air mattress in the center of his no-man's-land bull's eye. I curled up in my now-lonely tent, feeling his mind disappear into unconsciousness. The solitude felt empty; I was glad I was soon pulled down into sleep, as well.

Maybe it was because we were back in New Jersey.

I had the van attack nightmare again for the first time in months. I cried out as Mike punched me in the jaw and Del ripped my shirt down the front. Suddenly, Trevor pulled them away from me, scooping me up in his arms as the world shimmered and changed into our beautiful beach in Aruba.

"I thought we were done with that one."

"So did I." Ah, the magic of dreams—*I could talk again!* I

wasn't broken and defective in Trevor's imagination. I rubbed my jaw, trying to use the lucid dreaming technique to make the pain dissipate. It didn't work. Trevor slid down onto one of the beach chairs under the grass umbrella, pulling me into his lap as he did.

"You sure do have to rescue me a lot." My voice still held a quiver.

"You're worth saving. And besides, you rescue me, too."

He leaned in to brush a feathery kiss across my lips. I put my hand around the back of his head, pulling him closer. The kiss deepened and his arms tightened around my back.

"Oh!"

We pulled apart at the sound of a familiar voice. Ann stood on the beach, wide-eyed.

Ann's in our dream?

The shock woke all three of us up.

I let out a long breath. *Ah, hell. We're going to need a bigger boat.*

Trevor came quietly into my tent, his little pen-sized flashlight in-hand. *Are you okay?*

I nodded, feeling moderately creeped out. Ann and I had known the enclosure area might put us into range to receive each other's dreams, but it hadn't occurred to me that she might be able to *enter* my dreams the way Trevor did. That had an icky, "three-way" connotation to it that twisted my stomach.

Ann's confusion whirled in her head, distant but still readable. Her emotions pulled between a deep curiosity about what'd happened and a purple-hot *let-us-never-speak-of-this-again*. After a long half-minute, her curiosity won. *So, uh…was that your dream or Trevor's? I couldn't tell.*

Um, both.

Both?

We share dreams, sometimes. It started as mine, though.

You can DO that?

Actually, I usually just share nightmares. Trevor's the one who can change them like that—make them all wonderful.

Trevor gave my hand a squeeze. The physical contact allowed him to follow the mental conversation.

The first part—?

Crap. You saw that? I sighed. She *would* have to have seen my worst memory, too.

Those three guys…attacked me last year. They died. I—I killed them.

Are you all right?

Before tonight, I would've said yes. But with that nightmare still fresh in my head… *Hey, we get access to a lot of personal stuff—um, can you just keep this thing private, too?*

She understood. *Of course.*

So, Trevor can—

Yeah? he asked.

You can hear us? She hadn't noticed that he was following along.

Maddie and I have a special connection.

And that turns you into a MINDER? Her incredulity seemed to fill the empty field between us.

A little bit. When I'm with Maddie.

Oh, she responded, although she was completely confused. *I wondered why you were at that minder meeting, and then Zack came in…* She trailed off, embarrassed at where *those* thoughts might lead.

We'll talk more in the morning, okay? Right now it's— I had no idea what time it was.

Trevor checked his watch with the pen-light. *1:48 a.m.*

What he said.

Ann paused. *I think I missed an interesting eight months.*

Trevor and I both smiled at that. *Welcome back.*

CHAPTER 11

Coffee.

There was a serious, dangerous lack of coffee here. When Claire woke up, I planned to ask her to RV the closest coffeemaker in the surrounding buildings so I could break in and get some.

Instead, Drew and Harrison made a Dunkin' Donuts run. They returned with ample supplies, which we inhaled with pleasure and relief around the little fire circle. Once the caffeine had reattached my soul, I grabbed my little notebook and started making a shopping list. I wrote down the coffee-making essentials, and then I passed the list around. Trevor got it first and added some luxury items like milk, cereal, bread, and sandwich meat. Drew added marshmallows.

Claire was worried. "Do we have money for these things?"

I never thought about how to pay for things like this anymore. *It's covered,* I told her. Of everyone here, only Trevor knew about my dabbling with stock options.

Across the little fire circle, Ann nearly shot coffee out of her nose. *WHAT?*

Okay, I guess two people knew now. There's no privacy with another minder around. *Long story. Short version: Trevor and I are set for life.*

She cracked up, surprising Zack, who was sitting next to her. "What's so funny?"

"Maddie." Ann didn't explain further, which caused Zack to look at me searchingly. As usual, his thoughts were blank to me. It still creeped me out sometimes—it felt as though he was an empty shell.

Like a zombie or something.

I leaned against Trevor, making contact without even thinking about it. Trevor reacted instantly, locking eyes with Zack across the circle, suddenly wary and protective. I tossed up a shield around us both, but Ann had already felt a whiff of it.

What's going on? Ann looked from Trevor to Zack.

I really wished I could shield while still sending intentional thoughts. That'd be really useful right about now, as Ann's mind filled with several unpleasant possibilities. *Please tell Ann it's nothing.*

"Maddie says it's nothing." Trevor's eyes still focused on Zack. Most of the others watched the silent exchange. Only Drew and Harrison remained oblivious as they inhaled donuts and discussed Fireball.

Zack let out a long exhale and looked at me. "I'm going to have to tell her, huh?"

I nodded, feeling my stomach sink. He was no longer the immature jerk who'd tried to charm me a few months ago after I'd broken through his shield and taken his voice.

Ugh.

Neither of us came off looking very good in that story.

Zack's eyes widened as he became aware of the circle of onlookers. He bit the inside of his cheek as he looked at Ann. Tangled emotions choked her mind and closed her throat. Ann and I both flinched as his thoughts suddenly popped into our heads with air-horn blast intensity, and Zack inwardly cringed as he showed her memories of how he'd tried to force me to kiss him. I could feel the hurt building in Ann, purple-red and aching.

I dropped my shield. *Don't be too angry with him.*

The pain within her suddenly flared yellow and red as her eyes narrowed.

I drew a quick breath. *Jealous? Of...ME?* Geez! We had one twisted little love-square going on here, didn't we?

Zack's leaving out the part where I blasted his brain. I flashed her the memory of how I'd broken through his shield and temporarily taken his ability to speak. It served the dual function of showing her that I had no interest in her would-be boyfriend and changing the subject.

Ann looked at me from under furrowed brows. *That's what happened to you? Why you can't talk anymore?*

I nodded. *Except mine's permanent. Isaiah did this to me—after I did it to him.*

But Zack?

Zack's not the same person who did that. I hope you won't hold it against him. I don't anymore.

And Trevor? she asked.

He still eyed Zack coldly. *I'm working on it.*

Drew finally noticed that the circle had gone silent. "Whoa. What's up? Minder-chick fight?" The image in his mind involved spandex costumes and professional wrestling moves. The ridiculous image broke the tension—sort of.

* * *

We made ourselves scarce when the huge truck arrived with the components of the new building, but the driver's thoughts hit me anyway. *This is the weirdest thing. I thought this building was going out to that farm in Clinton. It's been on the schedule for months. Why are we putting it up here? And what's the rush? Usually I drop this stuff off at least a day before the crane arrives, but it's coming in right behind me.*

I grinned. *Coleman strikes again.*

Most of the group hung out in Zack's trailer all morning, watching movies on someone's laptop. Dave and Claire went to the supermarket on a food run. Trevor and I curled up in my tent, as far as possible from everyone. We read a book together, unsuccessfully trying to drown out the drama in the enclosure with the drama on the page.

I felt Zack's thoughts pop into my consciousness a few times as he and Ann talked in her tent. He lowered his shield periodically, letting her see his mind clearly, and our stronger minder-to-minder connection sent me a big bundle of yearning, hurt, confusion, jealousy, lust...

Ugh—too much information.

I wanted to tell Ann to just forgive him, already!

Trevor pulled our shield up around our minds. Hey, he was getting pretty good at that. *Maddie, stay out of it.*

But I just—

Stay out of it, he repeated. *None of our business.*

But I feel partly responsible! And they both like each other! And they'd be such a good couple!

He looked at me bemusedly. *You really like matchmaking, don't you?*

Only since we met. I'm so happy with you. I just—I just want other people to be happy, too.

And it's not because you think you know what's best for everyone?

I laughed. *Okay, that's part of it. But my meddling is kindly intended.*

I know it is. He closed the book with a smile. *But now you leave me no choice but to find something to distract you.*

Little flecks of red energy began to ping off of his skin. He rolled above me, bringing his mouth to mine for a searing kiss. *Oh, yeah—sign me up for the deluxe distraction package!* My heart thudded wildly against my ribs as my legs slid around his, the fabric of our jeans suddenly rough and thick against our skin. Unseen hands turned my thoughts to jelly. *What had I been trying to—? Oh, never mind.* Trevor could do things with a single, invisible touch—

I was alive with a scarlet glow as the beautiful intensity washed through me in waves. The world began to dim and Trevor traced the edges of soulmating in delicious teasing. When we finally came together as energy, we were drawn into a passionate singularity that finally burst forth as an explosion of white light. Every cell in our bodies seemed to hum as we lay trembling, wrapped together, our minds still linked and filled with adoration for one another.

The crew completed the building by 3 p.m. We even got additional panels installed in the fence, enlarging the area by another forty-eight feet on each side. Would that be enough? I really hoped so. Ann and I had already had *way* too much "sharing time" today.

Once the construction crew was gone, we all checked out the

new structure. The building's metal sides accordioned in large, corrugated waves. The roof was over twenty feet above us, rising to thirty in the center. It was definitely large enough that Trevor wouldn't bring it down in his sleep—if he slept in the middle, anyway.

"So, this is all for you, Trev?" asked Drew.

"Just at night."

Ann turned to me. *Got a few minutes?* She'd arrived alone and I picked up that Zack had gone to check on something outside our little tarp fortress. *I need to...um, can we discuss a few things?* I sighed. I guess sharing time wasn't over for the day, after all. Wait, maybe I could help them work through this. They really would make a great couple...

I gave Trevor's hand a quick squeeze. *I'll be back in a little while.*

The two of us walked along the newly-expanded fence line. Ann's tent looked lonely in the corner.

Think this is far enough? She frowned with concern.

I don't know. I hope so. I don't like throwing nightmares.

Can I—?

I understood and nodded. We sat down cross-legged on the grass and looked at each other. The thoughts simply flew between us. This was the way that Williamson had instructed each of us— an intense transfer of thoughts, words, and images. However, our interaction included more emotion than we usually had with Williamson.

Minder "girl-talk."

Her feelings for Zack bubbled up from her like a fountain. *I've never been...drawn to someone like this before. But...is he really a good guy? Am I making a mistake? Are we moving too fast? Do I really like Zack as a person, or am I just attracted to him because I can't hear his thoughts? Are you really okay with what happened before? Do you really think he's changed?*

The euphoric excitement within her swept through me, making me grin. *You REALLY want to know what I think?*

Absolutely.

Yay! It's not "meddling" if it's requested. Our thoughts wove together in a tapestry of communication. *I think you two would make a good couple. He seems much better now than when I first met him. I don't like not being able to read him—you actually LIKE that in a guy? And you know that he might be able to charm minders, right?*

She gave a quick nod. *Yeah, but he's told me he won't try charming me. Do you think he likes me? I like not having his every thought in my head, but…sometimes I'd really like to know what he's thinking, you know? Is he really interested in me?*

Ann, he's really into you. Even when you and I can't read him, Trevor can tell stuff like that. I found myself smiling, surprised that I felt energized by the exchange. It was…well, it was *fun* talking to Ann like this. Williamson and Seth were male—it was a different dynamic. My mom was *my mom*—there were things that I just couldn't discuss with her. Ann and I shared a special perspective. Now that the stupid jealousy thing seemed to have simmered down all around, we could be friends.

I just love that I can be so close to him without being overwhelmed by his thoughts. It's exhilarating and peaceful, all at the same time.

I'm really happy for you two.

When you met Trevor, how—I mean, how did you know?

I blushed. Among the many thoughts and images that flashed through my mind, soulmating featured rather prominently.

Is THAT what you were doing this morning?

I felt the heat tint both my thoughts and my face. *Sorry, I thought we were shielding.*

You were, but then there was this flash of energy…

Gah! I scrunched my eyes shut and shielded. This was a private, Trevor-and-me thing. I didn't want to talk about it with someone else. I could see the pamphlet now:

There comes a time in a telepathic relationship when you'll feel the urge to connect as pure energy. This feeling is normal.

Maddie?

I dropped the shield. *Yeah. It's just that...well, it's so...intense. We're pretty private about it.* I gave a quick laugh and rolled my eyes. *At least we try to be. Sorry about this morning.*

Not a problem. You know how it is—we see all kinds of personal stuff. It's just part of the whole telepathy thing.

You're doing really well this time.

Ann shrugged. *It feels easier now. Maybe it's the lower dose. And the nastiest charms at Ganzfield are gone. Since the—since this spring, I guess—the place has a lot less of that terrible, cruel feeling now.*

Although everyone's still scared.

Not so much in this group, though. She waved a hand in the direction of the new building. Excited voices echoed out to us.

And yet, we're the ones Isaiah is probably coming after. Ironic, huh?

But you can shield Trevor's mind from Isaiah, right?

I nodded. *And he's stopped bullets to protect me.*

So, your special connection—?

I blushed again. *Probably related to the thing you felt from us this morning.*

I wonder— She began to flush, too, and didn't finish framing the thought. She didn't have to.

Maybe. If Zack—if Zack's the right one for you, you might be able to. My face warmed even more. *It's...well, you have to be totally open to the other. No shielding, no holding back. I don't actually know how it works.*

Ann's eyes drifted away, as though she could see the past in the middle distance. *I didn't want to be a minder again. I thought—I thought I wanted a normal life.*

I get that now. I don't think I could've stayed without Trevor. I focus on him and other people's thoughts fade into the background.

Now all we need to do is find some girl who can shield and who can stand Seth.

I cracked up. *I think it'd be easier to find one who can shield than to find one who can stand him.*

He wants to do the right thing—

—but he's just so obnoxious about it!

She nodded enthusiastically.

I stopped smiling. *He's still hurting, you know.*

I know. Pearl-grey concern bubbled up within her. Seth annoyed us, but it was like he was family—our minder-brother or something. *He felt all those people die, didn't he?*

Yeah. It was horrible. Did Zack ever talk to him? Do some of that "charm-therapy" stuff?

She shook her head. *I don't think Seth let him try.*

I sighed. *I can understand that. Zack tried to help me with the Belinda thing—*

What Belinda thing?

I bit my lip. *Belinda planted some...nasty memories in Trevor's mind. Made it so he couldn't stop thinking about them. Seeing them—I kinda went ballistic. Zack cleared them out of Trevor's thoughts, but...I don't know, I just couldn't let him mess with my head after the time he—* I cringed away from that line of thought. *But then Zack charmed Belinda into a small part of the property.*

Ann winced. *Yeah, I heard her talking when they brought her past my cabin, but I stayed inside. She was...well, REALLY mad at you. Actually, she seemed pretty angry at everyone at that point.* Her memories included several harsh words she didn't frame to me.

I haven't seen her since, although half the male population of Ganzfield seems to have Belinda sex memories.

THAT'S who that was? I just thought they'd all been watching the same porn.

We laughed. *Nope. She's really twisted, but Jon thinks she's too useful.*

He's not—?

No. I sort of asked. I don't think he's felt that way about anyone since Elise.

Ann grew sad. *You know, she was like a mom to me before she died.*

I didn't know. I'm so sorry.

Isaiah   he killed my parents. Jon and Elise took me in when I was six. Then Isaiah killed Elise. I was thirteen. She'd gone down to D.C. to charm someone in the State Department who'd found out about Ganzfield. Isaiah followed her onto a Metro train and gave her a stroke. She died in seconds. Jon saw him in the minds of two of the witnesses he tracked down. I've seen his memories.

I'm so sorry, I repeated, knowing there was nothing else to say.

If you get the chance, Maddie, please—

Cold slivered through me, but I nodded as I met her eyes. *I'll end him. I promise.* I wanted to kill Isaiah for what he'd done to so many families. To Trevor. To Ann. He'd ruined *so many* lives. I felt a surge of righteous wrath, which quickly morphed into a shudder as I remembered the feel of his oily-black killing energy spreading through my mind. What would he do when he came for us? Would we be ready? Did I really stand a chance against him?

Ann seemed to shake herself. *So much for girl-talk, huh?*

I laughed breathlessly, feeling a little queasy. *Well, if two telepaths can't silently discuss killing their shared mortal enemy using only their minds, I just don't know what we'd have left to talk about!*

Do you want to practice shielding now? Maybe I should, as well...

Actually, I want to seek out my charming, mysterious, could-be boyfriend right now.

I felt a wave of Trevor-longing, myself. *Let's go find out what all the shouting is about.*

"ARENA FIREBALL, baby!" Drew yelled in greeting.

A series of skylight panels near the roof peak let in a portion of the afternoon sun. At either end of the building, two rectangles looked like they'd been drawn on the siding with charcoal, and several scorch marks already marred the walls.

There goes our security deposit.

Ann edged along the wall to Zack. He leaned against the side, watching with interest and keeping out of the way. Ann's heart seemed to leap as she laced her fingers with his. Even with my pathetic face-reading ability, I didn't miss the way Zack lit up. Against the far wall, Hannah sat in the corner and read a book, ready to heal the inevitable burns. She gave a vague wave in our direction, but her eyes never left the page.

Trevor played goalie at the far end of the building. Fireball rules were basically the same as soccer, played by using the sparks' abilities to move a burning sphere with their minds. I'd seen enough games over the past few months that I even knew many of the players' favorite moves.

Trevor and Drew faced the combined team of Harrison, Dave, Ellen, Mel, and Jonah. Jonah had the "ball"—a bunch of burning rags tied to a lopsided wire frame—hovering over him. He kept it above him as he ran, passing quickly to Mel, who made the shot. Trevor caught the ball in his invisible grasp, and then lobbed it the length of the building where it hit the wall just inside the rectangle of the far goal.

Drew let out a whoop in Harrison's face. "That's twelve to three, baby bro! We are DESTROYING you!"

Harrison grinned as he flipped a rude gesture back at him.

I edged over to be near Trevor. I knew he sometimes played Fireball, but his ability gave him such an advantage that he usually didn't. The telekinetic portion of their ability was the most difficult for the sparks. To Trevor, it was easy, so it took a lot of the fun out of playing.

Totally unfair, I teased. *You should play with one invisible arm tied behind your back.*

I am, he admitted with a rueful grin. *But don't tell them.*

I laughed. *Maybe I should send you distracting images.*

With Ann here? He caught the ball as it flashed at the goal over his head. "Drew!" he yelled as he lobbed the ball to his position. Ellen and Dave promptly double-teamed him.

I glanced over to where Ann and Zack stared into each other's eyes, oblivious to the ball of fire whooshing around in front of them. *Not a problem.* I wondered if they'd notice a bomb going off.

You're okay with that? He indicated the two of them.

It's different from how Rachel and Sean were. Ann and Zack are both shielding. I'm not forced into voyeurism against my will.

The ball flashed directly at Trevor's head. He blocked the shot and the ball bounced loose and rolled across the cement floor, leaving a sooty, uneven trail.

Where'd you get the ball?

We found a bunch of wire coat hangers in Hannah's trailer closet. And Drew sacrificed a t-shirt.

The game continued until the score was fifteen-four. Trevor begged off a rematch, and the sparks divided in more equal numbers for the second game. We slid down to sit against the wall in the corner opposite Hannah and watched the sparks play.

The sound of a helicopter approaching jolted the action to a halt. Icy shards of fear filled the sparks as the chop of the rotors fanned terrible memories to life. I strained to hear the thoughts of the approaching people.

Ann had the range advantage, so she relaxed first. "It's just Martin Martinson. He had a meeting in the City."

The City. That reminded me—I hadn't heard back from Coleman. I checked my phone and found that he'd sent me a message this morning.

Call me.

I rolled my eyes. Coleman *knew* I couldn't talk.

Would you? I asked Trevor.

Sure. He took the phone from my hand as soon as I'd speed-dialed Coleman's direct line. I still thought it was funny that I had my *lawyer* on speed-dial—just like all seventeen-year-old girls.

"Nick Coleman." The speakerphone gave his voice a tinny resonance.

"Hi, Nick. This is Trevor Laurence, translating for Maddie Dunn. You asked her to call you?"

"Oh, right! I didn't consider her speech issue when I sent that message. Sorry about that; I should've said 'contact me.' I wanted to go over the documents that she requested before I sent them to her to sign."

Shouts erupted as someone scored a goal.

"Where are you?" Coleman asked.

"Homemade sports arena in New Brunswick, New Jersey."

"Wait, are you with the group at Allexor?"

"Yeah. We both are." Again, Coleman was well informed.

"Actually, that's extremely convenient. I'll be flying out this weekend for my next…treatment. I know that at least two other, um, Ganzfield alumni are planning to come out from New York with me, as well. I can bring the papers for signatures then. Let me just make sure I have things the way she wants them."

"Go ahead." Trevor looked at me quizzically. *What've you been up to now?*

"It's pretty straightforward. Primary beneficiary: Trevor Laurence. Also bequeathing $750,000 to her mother, Nina Dunn, and a trust in the same amount for the child of Rachel Fontaine and Sean McFee, with Ms. Fontaine as the trustee."

I nodded. *That sounds right.*

Trevor stared at me, shocked into silence.

"Hello? Are you still there?"

Trevor shook himself. "Uh, yeah. Sorry."

"I'll bring out the paperwork when I come. I also took the liberty of drawing up the papers to give Maddie emancipated minor status so the will and trust will be valid, even though she won't be eighteen until next year. If that's all right, I'll have the judge sign them tomorrow."

Trevor didn't respond.

"Still there?"

"Yeah, that'll be fine." Trevor distractedly passed along my affirmative nod. He hung up without saying goodbye and pulled me bodily from the building.

He turned to me as soon as we were outside. *What was that about?*

My will.

And you put me in—

For just under three million dollars.

Why?

If anything happens to me I want you to have it.

Trevor's mind felt like it was about to erupt. *Maddie? "If anything happens to you?" Do you realize that I wouldn't want—that I don't think I could stand to—* "I'm *not* living without you." Anguish snaked through his gut at the thought of it.

I hugged him close, trying to quell the twists of fear that slithered through me. *If you commit suicide, I'll kill you.*

Not funny.

Not meant to be. Okay, maybe a little. But seriously, don't you DARE. What if I have to fake my death at some point?

What? He looked at me with raised eyebrows. *You think you might have to…to fake your death?*

I shrugged. *We did it once already, remember? It happens. Promise me you'll go on, even if I'm not there; even if you're sure I'm dead. If I'm not, I'll come find you as soon as I can. If I am, then…well, try to be okay again.*

Wait. In what reality is this a normal conversation? He shook his head and relaxed as the absurdity hit him.

I smiled. *If you wanted normal, you shouldn't have fallen for me.* I could've pushed for his promise at that moment, but he was no longer upset so I decided to let it slide.

Freak. He kissed me.

Four Arms.

Another group shout came from inside the building and we returned to watch the rest of the game.

We called in to Ganzfield for another Isaiah update, and then Drew and Harrison went to pick up dinner at the front gate, which we had delivered from a local Chinese restaurant. We ate around another little fire; the building components had been packed with wooden pallets and spacers so we had a huge pile of scrap. After dinner, Drew tore open a bag of marshmallows and the sparks toasted their own by focusing the heat from their minds. Aferwards, only two of them needed Hannah to heal their burned hands.

Trevor used his ability to hold two marshmallows over a glowing red part of the fire until they turned golden brown and melted inside. He gave me one, ate the other, and then repeated the process. Hannah, Zack, and Ann stretched out wire coat-hangers as impromptu skewers.

The moment's tranquility made me smile, but it fell off my face as I suddenly remembered what Coleman had told Trevor and me. *We're getting some visitors this weekend.*

"Visitors?" asked Drcw.

Coleman and at least two other G-positives who are still in New York. They'll be flying out here, so don't pull their helicopter out of the sky. Williamson's cut off the dodecamine supply to everyone who's not here or at Ganzfield. They need boosters, so they have to come to us. I looked across the circle. *Hey, Zack? Zack? ZACK!* He and Ann were encased in the same silvery glow. *Aww.* I'd get the business stuff wrapped up quickly so they could get back to each other. *We have access to the meds here, right?*

"*I* do." His inflection slightly emphasized the "I" part. I bit my lip and swallowed my scowl. I didn't need to be in charge of everything. Really.

Hannah? Will two four-cc vials do it?

"Better get more. You're also due for a booster tomorrow, and Ann needs hers Monday. We're also supposed to restock the Ganzfield infirmary when we go back. With all the extra people there, they've gone through the majority of our supply."

Zack nodded. "No problem."

Ann? Want to check if we have the distance right?

She blushed as she nodded. Tonight, she wanted her mental

privacy as much as I wanted mine—possibly even more.

I walked into the new building, now dark inside except for the tepid light from the rectangle of the door. Ann went in the opposite direction, toward her tent, mimicking the old cell phone ad, *"Can you hear me now?"*

She faded away for about half a minute, and then came back. *Did you hear me?*

I think we're good.

She and Zack retreated to her tent. We planned to shift all the watches forward each night, which meant that Trevor and I were on-duty now, and Zack and Ann would take the last watch of the morning. The first watch of the evening was easy—people were still awake so we could hang out and talk. It wasn't like we were palace guards, standing at attention in little alcoves and wearing furry hats shaped like Q-tips. But after the attack at Ganzfield, we needed to have someone awake and alert at all times—just in case. I felt like I was playing soldier or something in our little tarp fort.

But this was real—a secret war.

I pulled back the edge of a tarp and glanced at the few remaining lit windows in the buildings outside. I hadn't heard any thoughts from the strangers outside our little enclosure today, although the pressure at the edges of my consciousness let me know they were there. In large groups—like in cities—it really built to a roar. Here, at this distance, I could tune it out, like the hum of an air conditioner.

I rejoined the group at the fire. Trevor had just finished checking in with the RVs up at Ganzfield. *Isaiah hasn't moved.* Tendrils of concern flowed through him as he took the cell phone to recharge in one of the trailers.

I frowned. What if this plan didn't work? What if he didn't

come for us here? What would Isaiah do? What were we missing?

"Hannah, you're a healer, so you'll know." Claire leaned forward. "Is it true that Matilda enhanced Isaiah's G-positive abilities?"

Hannah's face became a cool mask, but little yellow spikes of anxiety filled her as she shook her head. "She won't do it again. She refuses."

Claire frowned. "But if someone could become more powerful—stronger—couldn't it be really helpful?"

"Matilda thinks it's dangerous and unethical." Hannah met my eyes. Memories flashed across her mind and I drew in a heavy breath. We'd both been there when we'd found Charlie Fontaine dead—the top of his head cut off. We now knew that'd been part of Isaiah's "research" into stealing abilities, and we'd both seen the tortures Morris had suffered to coerce Matilda's cooperation, although I'd only seen it secondhand through Rachel's visions. I'd been running off to get my brain fried when Hannah and the others had been pulling Morris to safety.

Matilda's been looking for a way to get my speech back, at least partially. But it involves messing with my head again, so I'm kinda freaked out about it. And that's just restoring a basic capacity that billions of people have. If she's against doing dangerous, experimental brain alterations, I'm not going to argue with her. Isaiah was completely unbalanced now, and it could be due to what Matilda had done to him—or what I'd done.

"Her idea for restoring your Broca's area is pretty interesting, though." Hannah avoided looking at Claire as she swung gratefully into the subject change. "She wants to train a series of neurons to re-populate that area of your brain. Once the structure is back in place, she thinks you could re-learn to talk in a year or two of intense speech therapy."

Ugh. A year of intense speech therapy sounded tedious and difficult. *Those trained neurons* — they sounded like performing circus animals. "Ladies and Gentlemen, Maddie Dunn and her Trained Neurons!" — *Don't they already have something to do?*

"She's hopeful that you wouldn't see much of a decline in other functions. The hard part is figuring out how to get the neurons to re-populate the burnt-out area. Neurons can migrate throughout the brain, but we're not sure how to control the process. You even lost the blood supply there. It'd take a lot of energy and finesse to repair it."

And then I would have at least a year of intense speech therapy — and it might not work. Or it might only partially work, and other functions might get messed up. My hope of someday speaking again was pretty weak. I actually *did* know what they were up against. Williamson had made sure I knew a lot about neurology.

Most of the time, I just wanted to move on. My ability to speak was gone, but I was still here and I could still do a lot of other things. *Very glass-half-full.* But the nagging idea kept coming back to me, tickling the back of my mind.

Do it. Fix it. There might be a way to be whole again.

If I didn't have telepathy, I'm sure I'd've been desperate enough for an experimental treatment, but I didn't want to risk more damage on such a dubious option. I frowned at the twitchy, anxious feeling that crawled through me. Had I made a bad decision? Maybe I should let Matilda try. She *had* been able to give Isaiah extra abilities—she could do amazing things. She'd even treated Archer's end-stage cancer. If he'd been younger, he probably would've been okay. And a year of speech therapy might not be too terrible—not if I could actually talk normally again at the end of it.

My gut tightened. But what if the treatment didn't work?

What if I ended up losing more mental functions? I knew Matilda considered that a possible outcome, too, especially with the increased risks I already faced as a rapid-burner. I squeezed my eyes shut. Ugh. I hated the idea of gambling with my brain.

Never bet more than you can afford to lose.

Trevor and I headed into the new building when Drew and Harrison took over guard duty at 10 p.m. Dave, Claire, Hannah, and Jonah drifted away from the circle, but Ellen and Melanie continued to play with the fire with Drew and Harrison. The light cast by the flames changed from a bright yellow to an electric blue, dimming it and throwing dramatic, purple-tinged shadows against the side of the building.

Trevor set up his air mattress in the center of the large, echoing space. The lingering smell of burnt cloth hung in the too-warm air, along with the oily and metallic scents of construction. My battery lantern cast a tepid circle of light as I set my stuff in the corner farthest from Ann's end of the compound. I slid down onto my sleeping bag with a sigh.

Meet you in Aruba?

I felt the smile in his thoughts. *Count on it.*

This isn't Aruba.

A wave of cold passed through me as I realized I was inside a mansion of glass. I stood in the foyer, looking through wide doors at motionless people posed like mannequins. But these weren't hostile strangers. My mom, Rachel, Drew, Sean, Ann, Jon, Hannah, Ellen—their fear screamed out to me. I ran toward them, feeling slow and powerless. My breath caught as tar-black energy flowed across the floor. Sean cried out as the thick, oily substance slid up him and his burning agony seared through me. His shriek cut off as it enveloped his head. I felt my own scream building as his shape dissolved into the ooze, but I couldn't draw enough breath to make a sound. The liquid obscenity spread to the others—their pain burned through me and I crumpled to my knees. I saw something behind the ooze—a golden glow. The shape within became clear as he moved closer.

Isaiah.

The ooze encased Rachel last and her pain and fear stabbed through me. The glow around Isaiah dimmed as her shape dissolved into oily energy—energy that flowed back toward Isaiah. He paused as the wave of death reached his feet. It surrounded him, sliding up his legs and body, but it didn't dissolve him. Instead, Isaiah grew larger as he absorbed the liquid. His giant form loomed over me. There seemed to be flames behind his eyes as his gaze burned into my soul. Horror held me in place, as though I'd grown roots.

You don't stand a chance against me, little girl. You never did.

Monstrous, obsidian hands reached for me. I felt my lungs fight to draw in enough breath to scream—only to have the air knocked out of them as Trevor pushed me out of the way. Isaiah also flew across the room, landing with a thud and sliding across the hardwood floor. His head snapped up, targeting Trevor like a predator.

Trevor grabbed my hand. "C'mon!"

I rolled up off the floor and into his arms. He held me tightly as the dreamscape dissolved around us. I kept my face buried against his chest and tried to stop sobbing. I heard the waves and felt the warm ocean breeze. Trevor's hands stroked my hair. I finally lifted my head.

Aruba. Better late than never.

I sighed, feeling a little stupid for letting a dream get to me like this. Everything was okay now.

The wind picked up, turning icy. A line of charcoal clouds covered the horizon and raced toward us. I felt Trevor's arms tense around me and we gasped at the same moment.

The waves—they'd turned black.

Oily energy flowed with the surf, riding up onto the beach. It kept coming, creeping spider-quick up the sand. Trevor pulled at me, trying to get me to run, but the dark wave touched me, surged through me, both freezing and burning my soul—

I shot up with a cry lodged in my throat.

Dark.

My entire body trembled violently and I felt cold despite the warm summer night.

Just a dream.

I fumbled to turn my camping lantern back on, needing to reconnect with the light. In the middle of the floor, Trevor still slept undisturbed. I rubbed my face with my hands.

Just a stupid dream.

Morning sunlight fell across me from the skylight above, and the beginnings of a caffeine headache stirred behind my eyes. My hair rat-nested around my head and I stifled a groan. I felt more exhausted now than when I'd gone to sleep.

Trevor's dream was...*wow*. Erotic. Hypnotic. Why couldn't I've had *that* kind of dream last night? A rush of red energy raced across my skin as I watched. My breath caught and I yearned to cross the room and simply join in, taking the place of my dream-self. Instead, I lay back and let Trevor's dream fill me with—

Crap! My eyes flew open. I felt Ann's mental presence outside as she tried to focus on *anything* else. I flushed with yet another hot, intense emotion—this time embarrassment—as I jumped up and took Trevor's hand, using the connection to bring up our shared shield. The contact woke him and he pulled me into his arms.

Sorry I woke you. I was enjoying your dream. But Ann's too close.

Trevor frowned. *That's not the only thing bothering you. What's wrong?*

Just a creepy dream.

Why couldn't I shake the feeling that it was more than that?

Trevor took our gear out of the building for the day, stowing it in my tent outside. We didn't want anything singed if the sparks wanted to use the "arena" again.

Now what? After the rush to get down here and put Williamson's plan into motion, we really had nothing to do.

Hurry up and wait.

Trevor called and checked in with Rachel over breakfast.

"He's still there." Her voice sounded brittle. How hard was it on her to watch the man she *hated* for hours? Isaiah'd had her Uncle Charlie killed. His people had shot Sean. It must be hellish. "He hasn't left the house in Phoenix. He spends most of his time on the computer. It looks like he's building a website or something, but I'm not...I can't see things as clearly as I used to these days. The details are kind of a blur."

I felt a scowl pull at my face. Why would Isaiah need a website? Could he use it to recruit a new army, like the Sons of Adam? Did he fund himself through some kind of online company? I doubted he was blogging, although *KillerTelepath.blogspot.com* had an interesting ring to it.

Zack came out of his trailer, his hair still wet from the shower. Ann lit up as she saw him, and then flushed bright red and shielded before looking my way. She hadn't been quick enough on the draw, though—I'd already seen enough to know that Zack had spent the night in her tent. Nothing too racy had occurred—they'd talked and kissed and fallen asleep in each other's arms—but the memories were intense and special to Ann: intimate and private.

I snorted. It could be worse. Actually, it *had* been. While Ann's memories were still in PG, Trevor's dream this morning had been *way* into R-territory. I felt my face grow hot at the memory—and not just from embarrassment.

I flashed her a grin. *Hey, at least it's not your uncle Jon seeing your thoughts.*

Or your mother seeing Trevor's dream.

There was a thought—*ugh*. I rubbed my hands down my face.

On THAT note, I rolled to my feet and went in search of more coffee and a shower.

I'd just finished toweling off my hair when Ann opened the trailer door.

I need to be able to shield better. The idea of Williamson seeing her Zack-related thoughts still made it hard for her to swallow.

Yeah, he does the protective father thing pretty well. How did he handle the other guys you dated?

What other guys? Maddie, I've been a minder since I was fifteen. I went on my very first date last winter, when I was living in Boston. I've never been...they were just casual. This thing with Zack...

Yeah, let's get you shielding, so you can keep this thing with Zack to yourself. A remembered flash of Rachel and Sean's "private time" made me cringe. That'd been awkward and uncomfortable enough. If Rachel had known what I'd accidentally seen…

After several tries, Ann's foggy shield became more substantial and her confidence grew. "You're not getting anything?"

I can feel that you're there, but I'm not sensing any thoughts.

Ann grinned.

You're actually enjoying being a minder now, aren't you?

Her eyebrows shot up as she considered that. "Yeah, I guess I am. I don't feel—last time, telepathy seemed to be—it was like being in a cage or something. I don't feel…trapped by it anymore."

Think you might stay after the Isaiah thing is over?

Ann glanced out the trailer window. Zack leaned against the other trailer as he talked with Dave and Claire. All three of them broke into laughter. The ghost of a smile warmed her face.

The afternoon had grown too hot by the time Zack and Hannah headed over to Building Sixteen. Ann and I both drifted over to the fence as they left. Watching through Hannah's eyes put a filter on what we could see, but conversation came through clearly.

"Dr. Williamson already approved this." Zack scowled at the lab tech. "We have authorization."

These kids don't belong here. They look like they're still in high school. Do they think this stuff will get them high? Tough luck. I've already tried it and it doesn't do squat. "I need to get another approval."

"No, you don't. The existing authorization is sufficient." The resonance in Zack's voice didn't come through the mental connection, but I felt the sudden push in the lab tech's thoughts.

No, I don't. The existing authorization is sufficient.

I suppressed a shudder. *That's so scary.*

At the same moment, Ann shivered with giddy energy. *That's so sexy.*

I rolled my eyes and snorted.

The thup-thup-thup of rotors cut through too-warm air of late morning. I wasn't the only one who got cold shivers, even though we'd been expecting Coleman and the others. Would the terrible connections with that sound ever fade for us?

The copter landed in the same place the other one did—there must be a helipad or something. An Allexor employee drove the three Ganzfield people to our little tarp fortress. Harrison opened the gate to let them in.

Coleman still radiated his usual, sharkish lawyer vibe, even in casual white polo shirt and khakis. His gaze flicked across the assembled group and landed on me. He nodded in recognition and gestured to the slim briefcase in his hand.

We can talk in the trailer. I led him to the one Zack used, feeling Trevor's churning emotions as his eyes followed us. Coleman seemed out of place in our scruffy, makeshift camp. He opened the case and handed a folder of papers to me, moving with the disdainful hesitancy of someone who didn't really want to touch anything.

I read through the papers at the trailer's little built-in table. The first document—signed by the New York judge whom Coleman had charmed yesterday—declared me an emancipated minor. I drew in a ragged breath as I read through it.

I hope my mother never finds out about this.

Setting down the emancipation papers, I skimmed the will. Something near the end tripped my eyes. *Huh?* The final section stated that, if Trevor died within a month of me, the money went to a charity called "Connect" that helped people with aphasia. *Where did that come from?* My frown dissipated and I bit my lip to stifle a laugh. Trevor must've made a call when he'd taken the phone to charge it last night. Coleman would've had no way of knowing I wasn't there beside him.

I turned to the last document—the trust for Rachel's baby. Coleman's eyes flicked to me. "We'll add a codicil once the child is born with his or her full legal name and Social Security number." *Glad she's taking care of this now. If Isaiah catches up with her—well, at least these forms will save me some aggravation in probate.*

Coleman's assumption made a lump fill my throat. I picked up the pen—Coleman would get the notary from his office to "witness" my signature later. *Charm lawyer.* I paused, suddenly realizing the true extent of Coleman's ability. He really was above the law. People would give him anything he asked them to.

Can I trust him?

Williamson did, but he also considered *Belinda* an asset.

I shook myself. Oh well, if Coleman actually wanted a few more millions, he had plenty of options that didn't involve embezzling from me. If the ethical issues didn't deter him, it was a good bet that my ability to fry his brain might. I signed.

As he gathered up the papers, Coleman frowned out the window at the tarp fence. *That won't keep Isaiah out. What are they planning here?*

I answered his unspoken question. *We're here to protect the dodecamine supply. The fence keeps us out of view of the Allexor employees.* That was as much of the plan as Coleman needed to know. *You don't need to worry about Isaiah if you keep in touch with the RVs at Ganzfield. They'll let you know if he's in the area.*

"I have my assistant call them six times a day." He headed out to the other trailer for his booster. I felt a pang of sympathy for the assistant.

My affairs are in order. I'm a seventeen-year-old with "ordered affairs."

"Ordered affairs" sounded more like something Belinda would provide. "Hello? I'd like to order an affair for the night?" *Ick.* I needed to think of something else before *that* mental picture got any clearer. I stepped out into the bright sunshine where our group surrounded the other two new arrivals.

"My patients need me too much for me to evacuate and sit around doing nothing up in New Hampshire." The woman gripped Claire's arm with intense, near-missionary zeal. Claire stared back, wide-eyed, and wondered how she could escape without being rude. "I'm a nurse at a public clinic in the South Bronx. Do you know how many people in this country work full-time but still don't have health insurance or sick leave?" Claire's facial expression didn't waver from polite neutrality as the nurse started in with the statistics.

The other New Yorker looked pretty-boy handsome... and strangely familiar. I suddenly realized I'd seen his face in advertisements for a Broadway show. My eyebrows shot up as his name came to me—*Derrick Downs.*

Derrick Downs was one of *us*?

"Of course I stayed! I couldn't hand over such a *plum* role in a *major* production to that bitch of an understudy." He bubbled as he batted his eyes at his audience. I shook my head slightly. Derrick was a flamboyant stereotype brought to life. I frowned, focused in for a few moments, and then choked back a laugh.

It's an act. He's just playing another role.

Derrick held up his hands in mock horror. "I swear, I think he'd spike my latte with cyanide if he had the opportunity! Oh, if only charming worked through film. I'd love to do movies! This eight-show-a-week schedule is running me *absolutely* ragged!"

I interrupted with a smile. *C'mon. I can tell you love it.*

He gave an exaggerated gasp. "Well, listen to you, all in my head like that! Of *course* I love it, sweetie. I have fame, fortune, and the adoration of my fans! I need to get back to the City soon, though. Thank the *stars* I don't have to go all the way up to *New Hampshire* for a dose of the magic juice. I mean, why did Jon Williamson put that place out in the middle of nowhere?"

Minders don't like crowds. I'd finally gotten the meaning of the name. The original "Ganzfeld" experiment involved sensory deprivation as a way to heighten ESP—the way that people who've lost their sight supposedly have their other senses grow sharper. Apparently, the woods of New Hampshire didn't offer many distractions.

"Well, I don't see why the rest of us have to suffer! I mean, can you even get decent Thai food up there?"

Don't get me started on the bagels or the pizza.

"Oh, sweetie. Don't get *me* started. I can't handle those kinds of carbs!"

I grinned.

Coleman exited the trailer, absentmindedly rubbing the healed spot on his arm and heading toward the gate.

Eager to leave.

The other two quickly fell in behind him—after all, it was his helicopter.

"You all simply *must* come see my show!" Derrick turned back to us for a moment. "Just call me and I'll have tickets waiting for you at the box office."

Thanks. I smiled at him. *Maybe after Isaiah's gone.*

My smile melted away. Would I still be alive at that point? *I guess making out a will at seventeen IS a bit creepy.*

Tell me about it. My smile re-warmed as Trevor came up behind me and put an arm around my waist.

Been listening in? We walked away from the closing gate.

Just to you. I take it you're all done with the stupid document giving me the dirty, dirty money in the unlikely event that I survive your death?

I nodded. *Don't spend it all in one place. Nice addition, by the way.*

You noticed?

Where'd you hear about the aphasia charity?

Found it online weeks ago. You mad?

Nope. I gave him a wicked smile. *I'm just going to have to put the next multimillion-dollar fortune I make in a trust under YOUR name.*

"You *wouldn't!*" He was half-amused, half-horrified at the prospect.

It's only fair. Besides, all that money will be half yours someday, anyway.

I'll get Coleman to write up one of those pre…whatever they're called.

Prenuptial agreement? Score one for the TV legal education.

Yeah, one of those. I don't want a penny.

Too bad. By being far more interesting than any of my classes, you have effectively ruined me for all other occupations. I now have no choice but to amass large fortunes in the stock market and provide you with a lavish lifestyle to which you will reluctantly become accustomed.

More lavish than my current sleeping barn? He gestured dramatically.

Nothing but the best for my man. I wrapped my arms around his waist.

He looked into my eyes with a mischievous twinkle. *I'm going to give it all away to charity.*

Ha! I'll just make more. We can have a race!

Maybe I'll find a way to distract you from all that money-making. He raised his eyebrows as he sent me an image that made me gasp—then melt.

Okay, maybe I'll let you distract me. I leaned into his kiss.

Over the next several days, we started to settle into routines, finding ways to pass the long hours. In the building, Drew and Harrison invented "fire-bowl." Each player used a blowtorch-like effect to knock over pieces of wood from a distance.

Like bowling…with a flamethrower.

When Ann and Zack arrived late for Friday's dinner, Ann seemed to be flying through her exuberant emotions, and Zack's thoughts started coming through erratically—as though his emotions had grown too strong to be contained by his shield and were leaking out through the cracks. She and Zack held hands and stayed close to one another, sending constant little signals of their connection as pulses of silvery light flashed between them.

I smirked. *Love sonar.*

Ann's eyes flashed to mine. *Sorry, I didn't mean to…uh, share.* She tried to pull a shield over the combination of giddiness and embarrassment that danced through her thoughts.

Trust me, I know how you feel.

She glanced down to where Trevor's hand interlaced with mine. A pale glow outlined our twined fingers. *Yeah, I guess you do.*

Her gaze drew Zack's attention to us. He pinked up with a little half-smile. As he looked back at Ann, the swell of affection overwhelmed his shield. *—like winning the frikkin' lottery, the Super Bowl, and an Olympic gold medal all at once.*

Okay. We'd officially reached the too-much-information level for the evening. I mean, *aww*, but still.

Ann and Zack grabbed two cans of soda and a couple of the little white boxes of Chinese food before heading back to her tent. While the waves of emotion from the two of them receded, everyone else's thoughts remained.

Ick.

Most of them had ideas about what Ann and Zack were doing in her tent. Hannah and Jonah both disapproved. Melanie thought it was romantic. Ellen thought it was funny. Dave and Claire entertained slipping away together. I rolled my eyes as a sigh hissed out of me—definitely TMI from *those* two. Drew and Harrison both had thoughts along the lines of *too bad the only girls here are cousins, taken, or WAY too religious.*

Ann and Zack woke us at 4 a.m. for our watch. They were better shielded this morning, but still all incandescent with joy.

Can we talk later? Ann asked me. They headed to her tent, hand in hand.

I nodded and went in search of coffee. The morning was already warm and humid, and it looked like it was only going to get worse. *Ugh.* We didn't have air conditioning, and weather like this made people angrier—more aggressive.

After our shift, I took a cool shower in Hannah's trailer but the hot, enclosed space made me start sweating again before I'd even finished pulling on my shorts and t-shirt.

A few of us slumped in the small patch of shade against the fence near the gate. Drew sprawled back onto the grass. "I wish something would happen already!"

A car pulled up, showing slivers of gleaming white metal between the tarps at the gate. Melanie's brows creased as she gave Drew a funny look. *How'd he do that?*

Trevor turned. *That's not Isaiah, is it?*

I shook my head.

Two men climbed out of the front doors, both thick-necked and dangerous-looking. The thoughts of these professional bodyguards were cold as they assessed the situation for possible threats. One of them yanked open the gate; the clang seemed to travel the perimeter and surround us. I felt their employer's mind inside the car and I gasped as my heart froze in my chest.

Ah, hell.

I jumped to my feet. *Get Ann and Zack!* I ordered Hannah. No time to be polite. She took off quickly, not knowing what'd upset me. I grabbed Trevor's hand. His eyes widened and he sucked in a harsh breath when he saw what I did of the new arrival's thoughts. I gripped his hand harder, determined not to let go of him.

The man in the back of the car was a charm—and he was planning someone's death.

Drew, we've got a hostile charm in that car. Get the other sparks. Where are the earplugs?

The weight in the shoulder holster pressed against the bodyguard as he deferentially opened the car door. "All clear, Mr. Petras." Fear of the person inside made the large man cringe. He had already charmed his way past all of Allexor's security to find us here. Given the nasty feel of his mind, I expected him to look sinister, perhaps dressed all in black.

I hadn't expected the green and yellow Hawaiian shirt, and the black-socks-with-sandals look was scary in an entirely different way. This terror of a person looked like…a pudgy accountant on vacation. Petras's wheat-brown hair receded at the temples and too-large, mirrored sunglasses hid his eyes. "Wait with the car."

He approached the gate with a confident half-smirk twisting his lips.

Ann and Zack ran up to join us and I flashed them a silent update. They both went still as they assessed the new predator on the savannah.

Drew passed out silicone earplugs. The other sparks gathered with us in a loose half-circle around the opening. Petras sized our group up and dismissed us. *Just a bunch of scared kids.*

He pulled the gate closed behind him, leaving the body-guards out of sight. "Is Williamson in there? Tell him Barry Petras is here."

"What do you want?" Ann asked.

"I want the drug," Petras sneered. "Go get it for me. Or tell Williamson I'm here and *he* can tell you to get it for me."

I looked into his mind. Williamson did, indeed, supply this—this *mobster* with dodecamine. I felt a surge of grey anger. How could Jon condone this? He could see this man's thoughts as easily as I could! Barry Petras used his charming ability to extort and terrorize people.

And now he's planning to kill someone. A federal witness, no less.

Actually, Petras planned to charm someone else to pull the trigger—someone with no ties to him or the victim. *Having that stranger kill Telly worked perfectly last time. But I need a boost of the drug, or soon I won't be able to charm for sh—*

My cold eyes stayed on his face as I shook my head. *No way.*

Apparently, people didn't say no to Barry Petras very often. He scowled as his mind darkened into a cloud of steel-grey anger.

His glare shifted to Trevor. "You! Hit the girl. Hit her hard in the face." Powerful charm resonance enveloped each word, but Trevor's hand was still in mine.

Trevor's invisible hands clenched into fists, and a muscle

jumped in the side of his jaw. *"Hell no."*

"That's not going to happen." Ann sounded calm, but her eyes flashed with the anger and indignation I could feel in her mind. She'd seen the same thoughts I had. Supplying this man now would be helping him to commit murder.

Petras' eyes widened. *Hey, the kid didn't hit her.* "What are you—all minders?" His laugh held a sleazy leer. *I know how to handle minders.* His thoughts slid into a pornographic threesome of himself with Ann and me. My gut twisted sickly and I heard Ann gasp. He was taunting us, as though we had no choice but to give him what he wanted and he was going to rub our faces in it.

"Is it true what they say about minder girls?" Petras leered at Trevor and Zack. "Do they give good 'head?'"

He laughed at his sick pun for about half a second until Trevor's invisible fist clutched his larynx. Petras's hands shot up, grabbing at his neck. At the same moment, Zack shouted, "SHUT UP!" with so much charm resonance that even the bodyguards outside the gate fell silent.

I hadn't even gotten around to blasting his Broca's area to silence him.

Zack's shield slipped under the onslaught of crimson fury. *How DARE he talk about Ann like that!*

Trevor's anger mixed with a strangely disconcerted feeling over finding himself on the same side as Zack.

Barry Petras was even less used to *this* kind of treatment. The dirty image fled, replaced by icicles of anger. His mind filled with a new plan—*I'll charm some guy to come here and shoot them all from a distance, sniper-style.*

Ann frowned. *That's not good.* "Um, Zack? He's planning to have us all killed. Would you please tell him not to do that?"

Was that the reason that Williamson gave this guy dodecamine?

Was he afraid that this mobster would target Ganzfield people?

"Forget about having us killed." Zack's lethal tone matched the look in his eyes. His shield snapped back perfectly—mentally invisible.

Why does Jon Williamson supply you? I asked into Petras's head.

Petras wanted me to see the answer. *I'm a powerful charm, minder-girl. People do what I tell them to.* But the real danger was that he could shake off charm commands from others—although it hurt to do so. The only reason that he wasn't speaking now was that Trevor still had a painful grip on his larynx. His eyes narrowed with the venom in his thoughts. *And I'm going to KILL all of you for this.*

I was too pissed off to be scared. *Zack, try charming him again, now that your shield's back up. Charm him like he was a minder.*

Zack frowned and looked from me to Petras. "It didn't take?"

He's got an ability similar to yours. He can shake off other charm's commands.

"Forget about having us killed."

The thoughts melted from Petras's mind.

"So what do we do with him?" asked Ann.

I thought for a moment, and then grinned. *Let's make the world a better place.*

Next to me, Trevor heard the plan forming in my head and started to laugh.

I think you both should try to learn to project. I looked from Ann to Zack.

The four of us sat in the afternoon shade cast by one of the trailers. I had my head pillowed against Trevor's shoulder. He leaned against the skin of the trailer and used his ability to grab two more cans of soda from the fridge inside. The window above us slid open to allow the drinks to escape.

It'd been several hours since Barry Petras and his bodyguards had driven off. We kept meeting each other's gazes and dissolving into the giddy laughter of a shared joke.

"You think I can project?" asked Ann. "I never could before."

You couldn't shield before; now you can. I'm pretty sure they're related skills.

"Why do you think I could project?" asked Zack. "I'm a charm, not a minder."

First off, you can shield, so you're sort of a mix of charm and minder. Second, you two may start sharing abilities at some point. I didn't know everything about how the whole soulmating thing worked. I didn't even know if Zack and Ann were going to have that kind of relationship. But it would've been nice to have the heads-up about a few things, back when Trevor and I had started out together.

"What do you mean?" asked Zack.

I used telekinesis to pick up the empty can in front of Zack, lifting it to his eye-level. Zack looked from Trevor to me, silently questioning us with wide eyes.

Trevor grinned. "She's the one doing it." I smiled at the lack of rancor in his thoughts. Between the confidence that Zack was no longer interested in me and their shared disgust with Barry Petras, Trevor's views of Zack had shifted. I placed the can on the table inside the trailer through the window above us.

"*That's* why you were at the minder meeting." Zack looked at Trevor, reassessing him. "I thought you were just there with Maddie."

"It only works when I'm with Maddie."

"Can you project?" Zack asked.

A little bit.

"Hell, if *he* can do it…" Zack laughed, and Trevor didn't take offense. I grinned—the vibe had completely changed between them. They were allies now, rather than rivals.

And all it took was death-threats from a Jersey mobster.

I showed Ann exactly what it felt like to project, the same way I'd showed her shielding. *Practice with Zack, or maybe with some of the others. I won't be able to tell when you're doing it, since I hear your thoughts anyway. And if you figure out how to project while shielding, you can be the one to show me.*

Deal. She nodded. *Hey, Maddie. Can we have that talk now?*

We moved to the far end of the enclosure, near her tent. We sat across from one another and she dished in super-fast minder communication. *Oh, my gosh. I've never felt like this before. I feel like I'm about to…explode with happiness! I feel like I can tell you, since you know and I'm not always shielding and…I just feel like I have to tell someone to…I don't know…make it real. Does that make sense?*

I nodded. A quick little thud of concern gripped my heart. *I know what it's like, but I'm worried you might distract one another. Zack's shielding's pretty erratic when his emotions for you overwhelm him.*

Ann's eyes brimmed with dismay. *I…I don't want to put him in danger. What should I—what can I do to help him?*

Help him keep that shield in place. You might eventually be able to shield together. How funny was it that I was now the minder love-life expert?

"Speaking of protection, do you have…?" Ann trailed off as her face turned crimson. She and Zack hadn't reached that point yet, but she was pretty sure they were headed that way.

Um, well…we don't have a need for it. A burst of pink colored my thoughts and I bit my lip.

Her eyebrows shot up. *Oh. In eight months?* Apparently, with us living together and all, the physical relationship was just assumed.

Nope. Not really a priority, you know? With the other stuff?

And now the thing with Rachel.

I cringed. *You know about that?* Did I accidentally leak something about the pregnancy to her?

Uncle Jon told me. When he was warning me about Zack. She laughed at the thought of being warned away from someone so incredible, so perfect. *That's why I was asking about protection.* She trailed off into blissful daydreams that I really didn't want a front row seat for.

But Jon still let you come with us.

I think he wanted another shielding minder more than he wanted his nearly twenty-year-old niece to remain celibate.

He seems to have his own agenda sometimes.

At least it doesn't involve a minder breeding program.

Yet, I added.

We both cracked up.

Dave and Claire volunteered to pick up dinner again. I realized that neither Trevor nor I had been out of the enclosure since we arrived. As "bait," it made sense for us to stay close. Isaiah could RV us at any time. Ah, hell—he could be watching us right now. I glanced around as though I'd somehow sense his mental presence. The dream with the oily black energy hadn't faded. What if Isaiah could enter our dreams like Ann had?

"WHAT?" The blood drained from Trevor's face.

Just a thought. A creepy, horror-movie-inspired thought. *If it makes you feel better, I'm pretty sure that if he were that close, he'd just kill us rather than get into our dreams.*

Trevor shook his head and frowned. *Strange, but that actually DOES make me feel better.*

"He'd have to be asleep for it to work, too." Ann leaned around Zack and shrugged. "Sorry. You thought my name so I've been eavesdropping. There's no place here where Isaiah could hide."

Zack stopped chewing. His eyes flashed to our faces in turn as he picked up the thread of the hushed conversation.

I chewed on my lip as I nodded. *You and I would sense him and the RVs would know where he was.*

"He knows about RVs. Hell, he *is* one now." Zack's agitation came through for a moment before his shield swept it from our senses. "So, how could someone fool an RV?"

You can't.

"So Isaiah could be watching us right now?"

Yup.

Zack scowled.

I inhaled sharply. *The plan didn't count on him being able to RV everyone, did it?*

Zack met my eyes and I could see the fear in his. "How do we fool an RV?" he repeated.

"Distract him," said Trevor. "He won't use his ability if he has to deal with something else."

I nodded in agreement. *Or strong emotion. It'll upset his concentration and interfere with his ability...probably.* What was Zack planning?

"Rachel's not...is she watching us here? Has she told you—" He cut off as his gaze darted to Claire.

I'm not using the phone much these days. Why did he care what Rachel saw? *Is there something I'm not supposed to know about?*

"Actually, there's some stuff you *do* need to see. Outside the compound."

So, field trip after dinner?

You've been outside the compound?" Trevor frowned. "More than the time for the meds?"

"Yeah. Several times. I needed to make some...preparations."

He has? Oh. I fought the urge to pout. I was still sidelined. I looked at Trevor. *Nobody tells me anything!*

You're telepathic. We never think we need to.

"Actually, going out after dinner is a good idea. I can show you what Jon thinks we should do."

Zack? How out of the loop am I?

He considered that for a moment. "There are a few things I've been told to shield around you. Logistical stuff that Isaiah shouldn't know—stuff we don't want him to pick from your mind. You've got the big picture stuff."

Are you going to try to charm him?

Zack frowned. "I'm not sure I should answer that."

I felt a sudden chill for Ann—for what she might lose if this went badly. I looked Zack in the eye. *If you do, keep your shield up. Isaiah's the strongest I've ever seen. I was able to get past your shield when you charmed. He'll be able to do the same. No matter what happens, keep your shield up.*

"No problem." His mind was invisible to me, just like it usually was, and I couldn't read anything in his face.

He's worried, Trevor told me.

I met his eyes. *So am I.*

After we finished eating, the four of us walked out the gate of the enclosure. I felt strangely vulnerable, as though the thin fence of metal chain-link and blue tarp had somehow been a magical ward, keeping us invisible and safe from our enemy.

But that was just silly. Superstitious.

I wondered if Rachel was watching us right now. I kind of hoped she was. Having an RV watching our backs gave me a guardian angel vibe. And she'd find envisioning us hanging out in New Jersey less stressful than RVing Isaiah. I'd gathered from her last few conversations with Trevor that her ability was fading—she hadn't been able to read the computer screen to find out what Isaiah kept doing online. My brow furrowed. What was he up to? Maybe we should send a team out to Phoenix to get Isaiah. It'd be dangerous, but probably not much more so than sitting on top of the drug supply he was willing to kill for.

The thin road lay ruler-straight between the lines of blocky buildings. The last of the sunlight faded to our left, so we must be facing north. Somewhere in that direction, the people at Ganzfield were finishing their day, as well.

My thumb brushed against Trevor's knuckles. He frowned as anxiety scraped across his mind. *Isaiah stopped at the security barricade in Detroit because he calculated his odds of success were too low. What will he do to increase his odds here?*

I sighed. *I still haven't ruled out the tank.*

The road turned in front of the yellow, manor-like administrative building, which looked even more Gone-With-The-Wind in the glowing light of early evening. A few lost-looking cars remained scattered throughout the parking areas, but nearly all of the Allexor employees had cleared out for the weekend.

The endless, excessively-groomed lawn sloped slightly down from the manor house to the fence, the gate, and the road beyond. The guardhouse sat between two striped, hinged barriers that blocked the ways in and out. Metal teeth pointed up from the roadbeds on both sides, ready to inflict severe tire damage on drivers who couldn't resist driving the wrong way across them.

Trevor chuckled at my itch to test their efficacy. *You're never one for doing things the easy way, are you?*

I just don't like being forced in a particular direction.

Forced. I looked back at the spikes. Isaiah would try to force us to give him the dodecamine. How would he do it? Would he kidnap people we knew, hold them hostage until we met his demands? What about innocent people? If he showed up with a gun to a stranger's head, would we give in to his demands? What if he was holding a gun to a child? I drew a shaky breath. Isaiah didn't need a gun. He could simply *think* a hostage dead. If he threatened an innocent person, or many innocent people, what would we do? What could we do? What should we do?

Ann looked back at me with concern. *Are you okay? You just turned stress-grey all over.* "You know, the gun thing is easy. The sparks can stop guns."

I'm the only one who might be able to stop him when he's using his mind, though.

Ah, hell. It was the same problem we'd faced in Peapack. How did I get close enough to blast him without him blasting me first?

Zack stopped walking. "Maddie, what's your effective killing range?"

The question once would've left me feeling sick, but I'd habituated to its emotional punch. I was a killer. I'd killed five people.

Not huge. Maybe twenty feet—more if I have a good focus. Like the lethal blast of energy that Isaiah'd probably be directing at one of us.

Trevor squeezed my hand. *It's okay. You really are a good person.*

I bit my lip. *What a terrible judge of character you are.*

Trevor suppressed a laugh, but his wave of reassurance and love warmed me.

Another thought made my eyes widen. *Isaiah probably thinks my range is bigger than it is.*

"So…" Zack gestured at the scene in front of us, "if you wanted him to stop just inside that guard station, where would you stand?"

The sudden "a-ha!" lit me from within. *Where would I stand so that, say, someone hiding in the guard station, shielding his thoughts to invisibility, could pop up and charm him into not frying anyone with his mind?*

"Exactly." He gave me a lopsided grin.

I eyed the scene again. *Probably about sixty feet in from the guardhouse.*

Zack pulled a tape measure and a piece of chalk out of his pocket. He made a long line across the pavement at the sixty foot mark. Trevor and I stood there, staring at the chalk-mark—*the battle line.* This was where we'd stand down Isaiah.

I looked at Zack. *When you're up against him, you'll need to keep the charming going so he doesn't have time to shake it off. Say it over and over. I can shake off your charm commands, so count on Isaiah being able to. Use his name so you don't accidentally whammy me. Otherwise, I won't be able to fry him. I'll need time to get in close enough.*

He looked at each of us. "There's only one way in. The other gates are blocked off. We know we can get him to this place when he comes."

I felt the waves of concern flowing off of Ann. *I don't want Zack to be in danger. But it's so SEXY how cool and in-charge he is.*

I rolled my eyes skyward for a moment, and then looked back to Zack. *It's a good plan. Just keep your shield up, no matter what.* As usual, the empty shell he presented was mentally invisible to me.

I still felt that nagging twinge that we were missing something. Was it simply because I couldn't read Zack?

Trevor tingled with nervous orange splashes—but he was onboard. *It's going to work.*

It has to.

The next few days passed, slow and hot. Drew arranged a Fireball tournament, but the other sparks quit after the metal building got furnacelike by mid-morning. I wrote more emails to Rachel. Her spirits had faded with the last of her RV abilities and the pregnancy had stolen her energy.

I'm a bad friend. She needed someone and I wasn't there.

From my mom's emails, I understood that this breathless, anxious waiting also gripped Ganzfield. I realized that I hadn't communicated with Williamson since our arrival, although Ann updated him daily by phone. Again, I felt the tinge of marginalization from my disability.

We'd been here nearly two weeks and the waiting wore on us. So, in a strange way, it was almost a relief when we got the call after lunch on Tuesday from one of the RVs at Ganzfield.

"Isaiah's in the air and he's flying east."

CHAPTER 12

Electric excitement raced through our group, tinged with fear and anxiety. We still had several more hours of waiting, but things were finally happening. Rick, the RV, filled in the details. "He's moving at several hundred miles an hour toward you guys. He'll land in late afternoon."

That meant that most of the Allexor employees would be gone before he landed.

Good.

We intended to chase out any late-night stragglers with something like a radon scare. It'd frighten people to think there was carcinogenic gas in the building's air, but it wouldn't be enough of an emergency to get the police or firefighters onto the property.

I speed-dialed Coleman then handed my cell phone to Trevor. *I promised we'd give him a heads-up when Isaiah was on the move toward us.*

After a simple, "Isaiah's coming," Trevor hung up. I put the phone in my pocket, wondering yet again why I was the one carrying it.

Zack came up to us, his face set and serious. "Maddie. Trevor. Do you two trust me?" His voice was low and his gaze darted back and forth between us, as though he didn't know what the answer would be.

Trevor met my eyes. *Do we trust him?*

I bit my lip, hesitant. *I'd rather know how the plan worked.*

Trevor emotions swirled around one question. *How can I keep Maddie safe?*

I gave his hand a squeeze. *We'll keep each other safe. Williamson trusts Zack. Ann trusts Zack. I think we can, too.*

We nodded to Zack.

"I have to do some things now that you can't see. You'll have to stay away from the compound for a few hours. You also need to stay away from the front gate."

This is the "logistical stuff" you mentioned before, isn't it?

"Yeah."

Trevor's jaw worked as he processed that. "Okay. Where do you want us to go?"

"There's a place on the other side of the administrative building. Building Four. Half the offices in there are empty right now. If you go there to wait, Ann can get you when...when it's time."

Ann would find us—the only other person who could shield. Zack certainly seemed to know a lot about the layout of the Allexor campus. *How do you know all of this?*

Zack shrugged. "I scouted it all out in the first few days we were here." I suddenly realized that I'd had no way of knowing when he'd left the compound—his shielding made him mentally invisible. *Out of sight, out of mind.* It made me queasy, realizing that I had no idea what he'd been doing.

Anxiety crackled through the people staying behind as we headed to the gate.

Where are Trevor and Maddie going? Are they bugging out now that Isaiah's on his way?

Are they leading him away from us? That's either really brave or really stupid.

Is Zack in charge now that he's banging Williamson's niece?

Hell, what's Zack going to do to us after Maddie's gone? Isn't she the only one who can keep him in line?

Ann followed us.

I gave her a nervous smile. *Testing to see when we're out of range?*

"Exactly."

You don't know—

"Zack'll tell me the plan when you can't overhear. I'll shield when I come get you."

The afternoon sun was too hot on our heads and shoulders. We passed the yellow manor house, and then counted to Building Four. *You really think we can trust Zack on this?* Trevor's steps slowed as his doubts increased.

He's not going to put anyone else in unnecessary danger. Isaiah's going to focus on us. I felt something tighten in my chest as I flashed back to how Isaiah had stabbed through my shield—and seen images of Trevor. *If we know what Zack's planning, we might put others at risk.* I hated being out of the loop, but being responsible for putting the others on Isaiah's radar would be worse.

The door to Building Four remained locked for the two seconds it took Trevor to pop the inside handle. The air-conditioning hit us like a cold wave—we'd become acclimated to the outdoor heat. A long hallway with light grey walls and granite-colored industrial carpeting spanned the entire building. The faint scent of cleaning chemicals hung in the air.

I felt out with my mind. Four people worked in rooms at the far end. Their thoughts focused on the tables of data on their computer screens and charts of dosage efficacies from clinical trials.

Trevor opened the nearest office and we locked the door behind us. Muted light fell through the slats of the blinds at the window and a layer of dust coated the desktop. The roller feet of an upside-down chair splayed in the air like the legs of a dead insect. We dragged the covering sheet off the burnt-orange couch against the far wall.

Trevor pulled me into his lap as he sat. *Alone at last.*

I smiled. *Now what can the two of us possibly do for the next few hours, all alone in a dark room?*

He kissed me. *I have a few ideas.*

You read my mind. Normally, soulmating was something we did—excuse the greeting card sentiment—as an expression of our love. Today, I intended to make my connection to Trevor as strong as possible. I wanted to be able to shield and protect him as much as I could. A smile pulled at the corners of my mouth. If rocking his world as pure energy was the way to keep him safe, so much the better.

He nuzzled my neck. *Ah, the sacrifices we make.*

The thought *one last time* seemed to float between us. Neither of us knew who'd put it out there. It added a tender sadness. If anything went wrong—

Trevor captured my eyes with his own. *If anything goes wrong, I'll meet you on the other side.*

I remembered something that might've been from the Bible, a story of a widow who'd remarried several times, and the question of whose wife she'd be in heaven. There was something about how, when we die, we become like the angels—that the connections between people were not based on a sexual bond. That story resonated with me right now. Between Trevor and me, it wasn't about the *physical* connection. We connected as *souls*. I could believe fully in souls now—I'd felt Trevor's with mine. If we didn't survive this physically, I knew we'd still go on somehow—and we'd still be together.

The dusty office fell into the darkness as the energy swelled between us, bright and iridescent, pulling us into a single, pulsing entity. We were one, a shimmering, cascading intensity that shattered softly and lowered us back into each other's physical embrace, content and whole and warmed with inner light.

My head lay against Trevor's chest. I felt his heartbeat drop slowly back to normal. The outside light slanted through the slats of the blinds. Neither of us moved. We didn't want to disturb the beautiful peace of this moment. We both knew it wouldn't last forever, but right now we felt no fear, no tension-filled waiting. Finally, a rumble from Trevor's stomach reminded us both of our hunger.

He moved his head slightly and checked his watch. It was nearly 6 p.m. *Maddie? Maybe we should try to grab some food before facing down our mortal nemesis.*

Yeah, dinner and a show. We could make it a full evening!

The workers had left the building and only the mechanical hum of moving air in the vent system broke the stillness. I wondered if Ann was within range. *Ann? Can you hear me? Ann?*

A few seconds later, my phone rang. I recognized the number; this was one call I could answer myself.

"I'm shielding now," Ann said, "but it's probably better that I stay out of your range."

But you can hear me. Really, I had the tiniest telepathic range compared to every other minder! It was almost enough to give me a complex.

"Sure can. Don't get a complex. Everything's just about set. Claire's RVing Isaiah now that he's so close. He landed in Newark a little while ago. It looks like he's heading to Peapack again, but the rush-hour traffic is slowing him down. We've cleared out the remaining Allexor employees, too."

Do we have an E.T.A. for him? How much longer?

"Not sure."

Any way we can get something to eat before this showdown?

"I'll ask Claire or Hannah to take something over to you. They're in the administrative building with me."

Thanks.

"No problem," she said, imitating Zack.

I laughed, but the sound carried more anxiety than amusement. A few minutes later, Trevor unlocked the doors for Claire, without leaving the sofa.

"Sorry for the meager pickings." She dropped a small stack of energy bars and a couple of sodas on the desk. We winced at the sudden brightness when she flipped the light switch. "This is the best we could do from the vending machines over there."

She seemed cheerful and relaxed—*too* cheerful and relaxed— and her eyes seemed overly bright and extra blue, for some reason.

Is everything on track?

"Everything's fine. Dave's going to be safe."

She's been charmed, Trevor and I thought in-synch. We both sat up straighter on the couch.

Why would Zack—? I thought to Trevor.

Was she upset before?

Oh. Rachel's ability shorted out with intense emotion. Perhaps

Zack'd just charmed Claire to calm her down. Something seemed…
off about that, though. Trickles of yellow anxiety squirmed up the
back of my neck and I felt Trevor tense next to me.

"Claire, where's Isaiah now?"

She focused for a moment; the reflective tubes shot out
from her mind. She slipped her consciousness into the one that
connected to Isaiah. "He just finished loading the gun. Now he's
checking something on his cell phone." Her casual tone creeped
me out. I saw Isaiah in her thoughts, and sick dread squeezed
my gut into a cold fist. He was in the Peapack house again—the
mansion of glass. An open wall safe spewed its contents across
a cluttered upstairs room. The gun rested on one of his thighs
as he sat on a bare mattress and fiddled with the functions on a
fancy smartphone. Wait. Why did *he* have a phone? Weren't they
as useless to him as they were to me? A wave of ice shuddered
through me—had we missed something? Oh, God. Did Isaiah
have his voice back? Could he charm again?

Claire's vision suddenly cut off, flicking me back into the little
office and leaving me dizzy. Trevor shook his head like a wet
dog—he'd been along for the mental ride.

Claire gave us a cheerful little wave as she headed for the
door. "Okay, I've got to go now. Isaiah will be here soon so you
should finish eating. Ann'll tell you when to get into position."

We finished off the food in a few minutes, but my stomach
felt like it was churning the meager dinner into cement. I kept
clenching and unclenching my hands, so I sat on them to force
them into stillness. Trevor slid an invisible arm around my
shoulders, as though practicing to protect me. Not a bad idea. I
touched his hand and pulled a mental shield up around us both.

The cell phone rang and we both jumped. My breathing
stopped as I flipped it open. I already knew what I was about to

hear.

"He's coming," Ann said. "About ten minutes out."

Trevor and I clasped hands as we walked outside. The setting sun laced the bottoms of the drifting clouds with a vibrant pink.

It's too pretty right now for someone to die.

We got to the chalk line and lined our toes up behind it, like children playing a playground game. The guard station seemed deserted. I knew that Zack must be crouched down within it already, shielding strongly.

Shielding.

I pulled up the strongest shield I could around our minds, feeling the steely intensity of it. I'd protect Trevor with my life. Invisible arms wrapped me in a wall of solid sunlight. His chest pressed against my back with each of his rapid breaths. My senses seemed to be in overdrive—every detail around us seemed distinct and too-sharp, as though each piece of the world had been outlined in razor cuts. I felt like I could smell the approaching confrontation.

Where was everyone else? I glanced back at the yellow manor house but didn't see any signs of life in the dark windows. No cars drove on the road outside the gate. Had Zack set up some kind of roadblock or detour to keep others away?

I looked across the overly-perfect lawn, with its mowing-pattern stripes of slightly lighter and darker green. Trevor's thoughts were the only ones I could feel, although I vaguely sensed the little rustling thoughts of some burrowing moles beneath the grass. I smiled weakly—the groundskeeper had more to worry about than the damage we'd been doing to the area behind Building Sixteen. *Don't worry about that now. Focus.*

Trevor and I drew closer to each other. I sent him a wave of adoration, silvery and glowing. *I love you.* Just in case I didn't have another chance to say it.

I love you, too. He turned me in his arms and gave me a toe-curling kiss. *And I'm going to tell you that again later tonight, once all this is over and we're both safe.*

Promise?

I promise. And you know how important it is to me that I keep my word.

I do. That actually made me feel better—more confident—that this was going to be okay. It would end tonight. Isaiah would be gone and Trevor and I and everyone else would be safe again.

I felt the cold, oily-black touch of a familiar mind at the edge of my range. My heartbeat thudded in the lump in my throat as I turned to face the guardhouse. A golden glow flared to life around me.

Isaiah knew I was here.

The navy blue rental sedan turned off the otherwise deserted road.

CHAPTER 13

My stomach tried to flutter into a different time zone. I pushed more energy into our shared mental shield, making sure we were protected from Isaiah. Trevor's invisible embrace tightened around us. Both of our faces slid into cold masks—our game faces.

He can't hurt us. He can't hurt us.

Isaiah's thoughts were so loud! I exhaled in sudden relief— he hadn't brought a hostage. I could see his lone silhouette in the driver's seat. His headlights illuminated the place where we stood, cut by the dark bar of the security barrier. *I can't read any thoughts off of either of them—just like last time. How am I supposed to deal with them if I can't get a good fix on their thoughts to kill them? I could ram the gate and try to run them both down. But I still need the drug.*

TELEPATH!

The power behind his mental voice made me gasp. He'd never framed a thought to me before. Hatred speared out through the windshield to where Trevor and I stood in the middle of the road like High Noon sheriffs. Isaiah and I were outside each other's killing ranges, and we both knew it.

He wanted to talk.

No, he wanted to threaten.

Zack? Any time now! I couldn't send it to the invisible mind inside the little structure because I was still shielding.

TELEPATH! Isaiah repeated. *Can you hear me?*

I nodded slowly and deliberately. I wasn't going to drop the shared shield to communicate with him.

Give me 60ccs of dodecamine or I send links to THIS to the government and the news media. Isaiah played a series of images across the screen of his smartphone, knowing I would see them though his eyes.

Oh. My. God.

The world seemed to spin, and I couldn't get enough air into my lungs. Lists of people's names, addresses, and abilities flashed across the screen. Jon Williamson. Trevor Laurence. Nina Dunn. More names. *Remote Viewing. Pyrokinesis. Mind-Control.* Hi-res scans of the basal ganglion of Charles Fontaine—Rachel's Uncle Charlie.

Video clips showed the sparks playing Fireball, pulling helicopters from the sky, and practicing the flamethrower technique. Another set showed healers laying hands on people in the infirmary. The angle in all the medical clips was the same, as though the camera sat in the ceiling above the exam table. Heather McFee cut into Archer's chest, extracted some tissue, and then touched either side of the wound. It bubbled blood then sealed closed without a scar. The next clip showed a lifeless Archer as Matilda tried to revive him. Trevor's heart lurched at the sight and he choked back a sob-tinged breath. The final video showed me floating mid-air, twenty feet off the ground. Trevor flitted in and out of the bottom of the frame beneath me, with Archer briefly in view walking beside him. I remembered when it'd happened, the day before Archer's surgery.

Oh, God. How had Isaiah gotten all this information—and this footage—from *inside* Ganzfield?

Isaiah has hostages, after all. WE'RE his hostages.

I could feel the desperation in his mind—he wasn't bluffing. If he couldn't get dodecamine—if he couldn't keep his own abilities—he knew it was only a matter of time before we'd track him down and destroy him. His plan was to blackmail us—or expose us and take us all down with him.

I used to be in politics. Isaiah's glee at the dismay written on our faces painted him in pale-green light. *I know EXACTLY the right people to send this to.*

"Where did you get all that?" Trevor couldn't keep the tremor out of his voice.

Wouldn't you like to know?

Someone had helped him. Someone inside Ganzfield had sent these clips to him. Isaiah didn't have a face or a name in his memories—and that was completely intentional.

Ah, hell. Ganzfield had a—a *traitor*. Maybe more than one. The word didn't seem overly-dramatic, given the situation. Who would risk exposing all of us by giving information to this sociopath? And how had they stayed off the minders' radar? We should've heard someone shooting blackmail video, thinking, *Gee, I can't wait to send this to Isaiah!*

Telepath, do you know what a dead-man switch is?

I nodded. I'd seen enough movies to know that it activated when the holder let go of the trigger—if he was killed, the bomb would still explode, or whatever.

Isaiah held up his cell phone. His hand was on a button on the front. He grinned in smug satisfaction. *I wrote my own app.*

Oh, crap. I understood. If he released that button, or if the phone suddenly died, the link to all of those files and videos would go out to dozens of people in the government, the military, and the media.

His smile twisted into a cold sneer. *Sorry I missed you two in Detroit. I've been watching you.* Memories flashed to me, sledgehammer-blunt. I felt my jaw start to shake, so I clenched my teeth tightly. He'd been remote viewing us *a lot*—sleeping, eating, and… *oh, ick.* This creepy old guy's been watching me in the *shower.* The golden RV glow flared around me again and I saw us mirrored in his thoughts. My face looked death-pale. *Crap. He's trying to psych us out. I need to focus.*

My hand tightened on Trevor's arm. *Trevor, whatever you do, keep his finger on that button.*

Someone at Ganzfield betrayed us to Isaiah. Dismay and anger tornadoed through him; it took a moment for my words to register. *Okay, I can do it, but I'll need to be closer.*

We took a first, slow step forward.

Isaiah slid out of the car. He glanced in through the glass door of the security station, and my heart seemed to lurch to a stop. *He's going to see Zack!*

The cold shock came to me in a sudden flash of knowing. The security building was empty.

Zack wasn't there.

Trevor's invisible arms tightened as the near-panic bounced between us. *Is this a trap—for us?*

He's not there. Did Zack set us up to die?

Did ZACK send that stuff to Isaiah?

Oh, God—he can shield. He could've shielded his intentions.

Why would Zack do this? Is there a connection between him and Isaiah?

Has he been playing us all along? What other things has he sabotaged?

What's he done to Drew and the other sparks?

Was he able to charm Ann, too?

Are they okay?

Oh, my God in Heaven.

Oh, no, no, no, no.

Isaiah sidestepped the security barrier. His shadow reached for us in the still-illuminated headlights. Holding the smartphone up at shoulder height, he approached with the stalking gait I remembered with horror from the last time I'd been this close to him.

When he'd nearly killed me.

Oh, God. What should we do? Everything had gone horribly wrong. We'd been—*betrayed*. Terrible things could happen if G-positives were exposed: forcible conscription, confinement, experimentation. Groups like the Sons of Adam would swell to overwhelming numbers, fed by people's fear of our abilities. We'd be targeted and hunted. Gah—most of the witch trials and burnings in history may well have started when families or groups of G-positives were discovered. Were we about to experience it firsthand? Hell, were Trevor and I going to live through the next few minutes?

Should we give in to his demands? Did we have any choice? If we did what he wanted, he'd be supplied with dodecamine for another year. Was this going to be an annual event, coming to Jersey to be blackmailed by this monster? My God, was that the *best case scenario* in this mess?

Maddie, we have another choice, but we need to be closer. I'll grab the phone, and then you blast him.

He's gauging the distance between us right now—I can feel him doing it. You'd have to be fast. He won't let us get too close. I couldn't seem to get enough air in my lungs.

This was it.

I knew Isaiah would blast me back, using the energy burst from my mind to channel his killing force into me. It was like going over the fence at Peapack all over again. I was screwed either way, but there was a chance I could save the others.

Wait! With our connection, would that killing blast spread through to Trevor? I had no way of knowing, but at that moment, I knew I couldn't risk it. Endangering Trevor like that...*NO!* I couldn't. I knew we'd discussed how far we'd go to stop Isaiah but now, with reality slapping me across the face, I just *couldn't.* Trevor was the hostage here, ensuring my compliance. It was as though Isaiah knew about our special connection. If Zack was Isaiah's inside man, he probably *did* know.

Trevor swallowed hard. *We could still try it, but if I died, the dead-man switch would be released.*

I felt a completely inappropriate sense of relief at that thought. We couldn't attack Isaiah, even if I could somehow stomach the risk to Trevor.

Ah, hell. We really don't have a choice.

Isaiah couldn't read our thoughts behind the shield, but he seemed to sense the defeat that suddenly filled me. His cold smile widened as he stepped closer, confident now that he was in no danger from us.

"GIRAFFE!"

The world seemed to explode. Painful bursts of thought slammed into me—many minds at once. The lawn erupted as several grass-covered hatches flew backward. I startled back against Trevor with a cry.

What the HELL?

"Isaiah, freeze!" I couldn't hear the charm resonance in Zack's voice—he was completely shielding.

Six sparks had popped up through manholes that'd been hidden in the lawn by thick circles of turf. Burning energy surged within them as they focused on Isaiah.

Isaiah froze. Pain spiked though his forehead as he fought off the charm command.

Trevor and I started to move. *We have to get that phone!*

I felt the charm lifting from Isaiah's mind and I flashed that thought to Trevor.

"Zack! Again! Freeze him again!"

Isaiah pushed the compulsion out of his mind and took a step backward. His face reflected his anger and surprise.

Did that kid—?

"I said FREEZE! Don't move!"

The sparks became statues.

—can't move! How are we supposed to—

—Oh, God, Isaiah's RIGHT HERE and I'm stuck—

—we're all gonna die, and I never even got a chance to—

Pain ripped through my head as I tried to push the command from my own thoughts. Zack was stronger now than he'd been at Ganzfield. I wasn't able to fight it off! *No, Zack! Not OUR people!* Gah—I couldn't tell him without dropping the shield!

He gasped and whipped his head around as the horrible realization hit him. "Sparks—move!"

I let out a strangled whine.

"Maddie and Trevor, unfreeze!"

The pain dropped away and we staggered forward again. Geez, Zack didn't even say "Mother May I," or "Red Rover, Red

Rover, let—" *Dammit, focus!*

Trevor's vision narrowed. *I've got to get that phone.*

Pain lanced through Isaiah's temples as he fought the charm command. His feet moved as though sunk into clay.

I shot a thought to Trevor. *Zack needs to hit him again!*

"Zack! Again! Hit him again!"

"Isaiah, freeze!"

Isaiah's feet stuck to the pavement. He still gripped the smartphone with reaper-white fingers.

"Now!" Dave's voice cut through the clamor of thoughts.

The sparks let loose, and Isaiah screamed as searing agony poured across him. It whipped into me and then into Trevor like we were being branded from within.

No! Trevor fell to one knee, and my vision swam with little white flashes as I staggered against him.

You did this. Isaiah lashed out with his mind, targeting Zack. Lava-thick killing energy flashed from him, hot with pain and hate.

Zack's shield cracked under the sudden attack. His surprise and fear burst through to us, flowing around the pain. —*need to… keep the shield up…or he's gonna*—

Dammit! I have to do it NOW! A pulse of killing energy exploded from inside my skull. I tried to launch it at Isaiah, but I felt it dissolve. He was still out of my range! I needed to be closer! *Closer!*

Trevor lurched forward and reached for the phone with one invisible arm. Liquid-fire pain from Isaiah seared through us. His shirt was now ablaze. Smoke rose from different parts of him, and we caught the sick sound of sizzling meat. We were too slow!

"Isaiah, freeze!" The power was gone from Zack's words.

An invisible burst of white-hot lightning shot from between

my eyebrows. Isaiah turned away from Zack, whose thoughts drained away as he fell forward, sprawling facedown and unmoving on the grass.

Isaiah's face contorted in a mask of pain. *I'm surrounded! I'm going to die!* His vicious eyes locked with mine as he threw the phone to the ground. *You're going to die, too.* I felt him target my mind, determined to take me down with him. *You're the girl who ruined everything.*

I frantically blasted his mind again with as much killing energy as I could. A low, incoherent cry ripped from my throat. My mind was on fire! Could I only destroy Isaiah if I destroyed myself in the process? Burning agony enveloped me from within.

Isaiah's own killing burst fizzled against his pain. He was frying inside and out. His body crumpled, engulfed in oily smoke and flames, but his silent, excruciating shriek stabbed through me before he faded into oblivion.

I went ragdoll limp against Trevor. The edges of the world blackened, threatening to close over me. *No!* I forced myself to pull back toward the world with each breath, as though inching back up a lifeline.

The others swam through my vision in a distant fog. Their thoughts and voices didn't register—as though I'd gone deaf on several levels. Trevor'd caught the phone with his ability just before it would've hit the pavement. He frantically tried to figure out which button to press to make it stop—to take it all back.

I started to shake my head, but the motion made me want to hurl.

We're too late.

Isaiah had set up his dead-man switch to work just this way. His surety had permeated his thoughts. The email had flown out to all of those people.

Email.

"Maddie? Are you okay?" Trevor's concern washed through me. He lowered us both down to the grass as he scanned my face. *She's hurt! I can feel it! Isaiah did something to her and—*

Trevor. Coleman. Call Coleman. I fumbled for my own phone, handing it to Trevor with weak and shaking fingers. I couldn't make my brain work. I felt floaty and dizzy and queasy. *Something about Coleman and email.* I focused back on my breathing, using the rise and fall of my lungs to anchor me to reality. At some point, Trevor and I had lost our shared shield, but that didn't matter anymore.

Breathing.

I'd managed to keep breathing. The blackness threatening my vision receded slowly, although it still felt like someone had driven a spike between my eyebrows.

Only a few feet away, Isaiah's body continued to burn, casting greasy light and foul-smelling smoke into the evening air. Zack lay unmoving in the grass, caught in the light from the flames and the blue-white glare from the headlights of the rental car. I couldn't feel anything from him. Was he alive?

Drew rolled Zack over with hesitant hands. *Is he dead? Oh, man, I think he's dead.*

Behind us, Ann's silent scream hit me like a pillar of pain. She ran toward us from the administrative building, with Hannah and Claire trailing behind her. I knew that panicked feeling from personal experience, knew that the run from the main building felt never-ending to her, like the slow-motion movement in a nightmare. Another wave of sick-and-shaky hit me and I wasn't sure if it was from taking down Isaiah or feeling Ann's emotional anguish.

Probably both.

Trevor's arm tightened around my shoulders. "Coleman. Trevor Laurence. We have a problem."

"Does it have to do with the 'big problem' you were dealing with?" Tonight, I didn't find Coleman's coded talk as amusing as I usually did. I watched Zack's still, pale face. His jaw hung slack and his eyes showed only white through his half-closed lids.

"The big problem is…solved, but…the man in question created another one. He put…um, proprietary information on a website, and then sent an email to the media and…others. Government people. He wants to make it public…make *us* public. Names, addresses, and…uh, skills. And it's all documented by video. Any way we can get that website down?"

"Give me the web address. I'll go back to New York now and see what I can do."

Trevor read off the information from the email on Isaiah's phone. Once they'd hung up, Trevor called Williamson. "It's over, Jon. But Maddie's—" His eyes met mine.

I'm okay.

You're NOT okay.

I will be.

We'll get Hannah to check you out. Worry painted him dove-grey, and he kept running his hand up and down my arm.

"Maddie's conscious, but she…Isaiah tried to kill her. And Zack—we don't know how badly he's hurt. But right now, you need to know that someone there at Ganzfield's been shooting videos and sending them to Isaiah. They're up on a website with a lot of information about us…and a bunch of people just got an email with a link to them."

Tell him about the camera in the infirmary ceiling. That's probably the first one he can find.

"Infirmary ceiling, probably right above the exam table." A

fresh burst of anguish hit Trevor as he recalled the images of Archer. "Fireball and other spark stuff, some of my ability, and the healers. No charms or minders, at least that we saw. No RVs."

Did that mean that the traitor was a charm or an RV? Maybe it was simply that minder, charm, and RV abilities were harder to document on video.

It wasn't Zack.

Trevor solemnly met my eyes. *No, it wasn't.* "Jon, I just talked to Coleman. He's trying to get the website down, but I think we have a major problem."

Maybe it was Belinda.

"Maddie thinks it might've been Belinda."

The frown in Williamson's voice came through. "I've known her for nearly a decade, and she's always been on our side. I know Maddie has cause to dislike her, but that's not a valid reason to accuse her of something like this."

My stomach heaved, and got a nasty retaste of the energy bars I'd eaten for dinner as they came back up. I twisted to the side to avoid splattering myself.

Trevor held my hair back with invisible fingers. Boulders of concern piled up in his gut. *You're not okay.*

I'm breathing. I'm conscious. I'm not bleeding. I wasn't bleeding, was I? Isaiah hadn't given me another stroke, right? I started running some basic neurological tests, wiggling my toes and sticking out my tongue to see if it went straight out. Could I remember today's date? The president's name?

Trevor looked over to where Hannah had her hands on Zack's temples. In his head he understood Zack probably needed her attention more, but a big, emotional part of him wanted to yank her over to my side and make her take care of me.

I took Isaiah's phone from Trevor's other hand. After spending a minute figuring it out and getting my hands steady enough to hit the right buttons, I forwarded the dead-man-switch email to my own account, along with all of the addresses. The list included a sickening combination of news-dot-com, dot-gov, and dot-mil accounts. The media, government, and military would soon know about G-positives. Some might already know, if they'd checked their email in the past few minutes.

The text of Isaiah's last message read like Sons of Adam propaganda:

People with dangerous abilities live among you. They can manipulate you, deceive you, and kill you with a touch. I don't know if the evidence I have compiled will convince you, but I hope that you will conduct your own investigation. If this message has reached you, then they have murdered me.

He'd signed it with his real name.

I took a breath. Okay. This was bad, but it wasn't beyond hope. First off, Isaiah had faked his own death years ago, so signing his own name wasn't going to give him great credibility. Dead men don't send a lot of email, and the message made him sound like a ranting loon. But all of what he'd written must've seemed reasonable to him—probably because it was all basically true.

Maybe we could discount the videos by claiming that an amateur special-effects club at the Ganzfield "school" had made them. YouTube had more than a few clips featuring special-effects fakery. It wasn't even that hard to do anymore. But what would happen if people did as he suggested and launched their own investigations?

I looked back at the group clustered around Zack's still-prone body. Hannah had her hands on his head, feeling for injuries. Zack was still alive. Pent-up breath released from my chest.

Alive.

But how much damage had Isaiah done to him?

The effort of isolating Hannah's thoughts from the jumble of other anxious minds made me start shaking again. Ann's minder-loud, keening panic drowned out most of the others' thoughts.

—ZACK HAS TO BE OKAY—

—another brain bleed—

—PLEASE, PLEASE, PLEASE, GOD DON'T—

—repair the damage to the—

—NEVER GOT A CHANCE TO TELL HIM—

Hannah's calm, professional focus was at odds with her erratically pounding heart. She knew what she was doing, but she worried she was missing something. Zack wasn't regaining consciousness.

Not again.

I started to roll my eyes but stopped because it hurt. *What good are frikkin' SUPERPOWERS if we keep overloading our fancy brains and ending up in these stupid comas?* I knew most people lost consciousness if intense pain overloaded their brains. Did dodecamine make G-positives conk out when our abilities were pushed too far? *They never put THAT warning label on the bottle.*

Just...SHUT UP! Ann flashed wordless anger at me from where she knelt by Zack's head, holding his hand. Her mind jangled with unspoken fears and tear-tracks streaked her cheeks. When our eyes met, another wave of dizziness hit me and the lawn tilted as though trying to spill me off. I tried to shield my mind, but that made the sick, whirling feeling even stronger.

It's okay. I've got you. Trevor lifted me from the grass and walked back toward the fenced compound. The intensity of the others' emotions faded with his every step.

"Where are you going?" Dave McFee followed us. His agitation made a spot on his shirt smolder before he thought it out. *Are they leaving the rest of us to clean up this mess?*

"I've got to get Maddie away from…there are too many people here. Ask Hannah to come find us when…when she's done with Zack."

"What about the car?" Dave fiddled with some kind of earpiece; I guessed they must've used them to communicate among the different hidey-holes.

But how had they shielded their thoughts? I hadn't known they were there—and neither had Isaiah.

Get gloves from one of the labs. If the paperwork's in the car, take it back to the rental drop-off up at the airport. Someone else can follow in the van and bring you back. No missing car; no ties to us. I'd have to get rid of Isaiah's phone later, but we still might need some information from it.

Dave nodded. "Good idea. Hey, Drew! Get the van."

Jonah moved in to finish with Isaiah's remains. As he focused, the still-burning corpse lifted suddenly—like a horror-movie monster that refused to die—and slid into one of the open manholes in the lawn. Flames flitted out of the hole for a moment, and then the circle flared bright white as Jonah poured power into reducing our former enemy to ash. The other sparks replaced the covers on the other holes, and I felt them weld the metal in place as we moved out of range.

This is far enough. I couldn't hear Ann anymore.

Trevor dropped us down onto the grass at the edge of the driveway. He took my face in his hands and examined me in the fading evening light. *What did Isaiah do to you? Are you all right?*

My fingers encircled his wrists. *Pretty sure I will be. Give me a few minutes.* With just Trevor's thoughts in my head, I might even be telling the truth. The other minds felt like they'd been picking at my mental scabs. I lowered myself down until I lay on the ground with my head resting against Trevor's leg. Invisible fingers stroked my hair as I watched the others in the distance. Their movements threw wild shadows in the headlights of the rental car.

With the sod-covered lids in place, the holes were nearly undetectable. The trampled grass should be unnoticeable after a day or two, but there was nothing we could do about the black scorch marks on the driveway where the body had burned.

Drew drove the van past us. Dave fiddled with the gatehouse controls until the barriers lifted, and then got into Isaiah's car. The evening seemed to close in as the headlights rolled away, leaving a line of yellow-gold on the western horizon as the only light. The others moved through the gloom as blue-tinted silhouettes until my eyes adjusted.

Hannah stood up slowly, dusting off the knees of her jeans. The others picked up Zack and started carrying him back up the driveway toward us—a funereal procession with a living body. Their thoughts grew louder as they approached. I pulled myself up to sit, and the world settled back without too much tilting this time.

Ann met my eyes and her pain-filled thoughts hit me like bullets. *He wasn't supposed to be targeted! He was supposed to be safe! Isaiah was supposed to—* She stopped her mental voice, but I'd heard the thought behind it. *Isaiah was supposed to come after you.*

I shielded—at least I could do that again. So, it was okay with Ann if Trevor and I were attacked? Why hadn't Zack been where he'd told us he'd be? Why hadn't anyone thought about how Isaiah's physical pain from the spark attack would slow Trevor and me down?

She's hurting. Don't say those things.

I met Trevor's eyes and took a deep breath. *I'm shielding so I don't say them.*

I know. I'm proud of you.

Trevor kept one arm around my waist as we trailed behind the ragged group. I leaned against him. I still felt so weak! A hot ache pressed against the inside of my forehead. Hannah approached with concern and put her hands on my temples, but her assessment only confirmed what I'd suspected—my problems weren't from physical injuries.

"We need to pack up and get back to Ganzfield." Trevor's voice cut through the silent group.

"What's the rush?" Ellen helped carry Zack, and she glanced down at his pale, vulnerable face. *Should we really be moving him?*

"Our secret might be out." He explained how the rest of the world might wake up tomorrow to cable news shows featuring video clips of Fireball, instant healing, and flying teenagers.

Holy crap seemed to be the dominant reaction.

We got our gear together as we waited for Dave and Drew to return with the van.

The cell phone rang and I passed it to Trevor. "The website's down," Coleman told him. "I know a judge who has issued an injunction. The web hosting company pulled it for us a few minutes ago."

"Over the phone?" Trevor's brows crinkled in confusion.

"I've had previous discussions with this judge, and…um… prepared him for telephone requests from me."

Oh.

I was so glad Coleman was on our side. He was one terrifying charm lawyer.

"I just got back to the city a few minutes ago. The bad news is that eight people had already viewed the site, and some of them have downloaded the material. It's out there."

My legs threatened to give out.

"We're tracking the URLs. Four of them are here in New York. Media people. I'm on my way to visit those four people tonight."

Trevor gripped the phone harder. "And the other four?"

"One is in Los Angeles. We have…someone like me out there on the way now. She's going to have a short chat with him."

Three left.

"I was one of the viewers…but the other two were classified military users. We can't get additional information about them."

Oh, God. I'd had nightmares about things like this.

"A ch—another person like me currently works at the Pentagon. He's going to see what he can do, but there may be a problem with these last two. Given the special security protocols, we might not be able to trace them, so there's a chance we've been exposed to some very powerful people. I'm not sure who they are or what they could do to us."

Even dead, Isaiah still threatened us.

It was after 10 p.m. by the time we got on the road. I'd recovered a bit, but I still felt weak and achy, like I'd had the flu. Dave drove with Claire beside him, RVing for speed traps…and the U.S. Army. A visceral, protective pull had me by the gut—we had to get everyone back to Ganzfield as quickly as possible. *Circle the wagons.* We planned to drive through the night. The media might not be a problem after Coleman and his L.A. counterpart got through with them, but what about the military people who now had those files? What would they do with them? We needed to get our people to a safe place.

If there even WAS a safe place for people like us anymore.

Zack lay across the middle bench of the van. Ann cradled his head in her lap and gently touched his unconscious mind.

My brows shot up. How was she doing that? He was doubly invisible to me—both unconscious and a natural shielder. Was it part of their connection, or was she simply a more sensitive telepath than I was? She ached to feel him respond to her, but he was simply…there. An empty vessel. No response.

With Zack lying across the bench, we didn't even have enough seats. The rest of us squeezed onto the other benches, and the air in the packed vehicle seemed stale and over-breathed, even with the AC vents drawing in the cool of the surrounding night. The gear in the back added a slightly funky camping smell, as well. I sat on Trevor's lap, my back against the side of the van. The seatbelt Trevor had pulled around both of us tugged against my side. I kept my mind shielded with Trevor's—I didn't want to draw any more of Ann's desperate anger. Exhaustion simmered through the assembled minds and I felt a small stab of jealousy that most of the others could sleep. Jonah was taking the first watch among the sparks, keeping his mind alert for flare-ups from the sleepers.

Next to us, Drew started snoring. On his other side, Ellen's head hung loosely down to her chest in a way I thought might give her a sore neck when she woke up. Despite the exhaustion that pulled at my mind, I didn't want to share nightmares.

Trevor pulled me close. *Do you want to get some sleep? I'll shield your dreams. I have to stay awake, anyway.*

I tucked my head against his neck, feeling his warmth against me, strong and comforting. *Thanks. If you wake me in a little while, I'll take a turn and keep you from ripping the van apart.*

He kissed my hair. *Deal.*

I tried to settle in to sleep, but Ann's anguish from the next bench plucked at me, keeping me awake. Her thoughts were so close—loud, raw, and painful.

Trevor felt my distress. *Need me to send you calming thoughts?*

My tired smile didn't reach my eyes. *Thanks, but it's no use.*

"Ann? Can you shield, please?" Trevor asked her quietly.

I felt the single tear slide down her cheek. Her turbulent emotions crystallized in crimson shards. *Maddie, it's YOUR fault! You didn't take down Isaiah fast enough! You should be the one lying here, not Zack! Not my Zack!*

Trevor's thoughts hardened and he dropped the shield he'd been keeping around our minds. *You don't know what you're talking about, Ann. I know you're upset right now, but do NOT take it out on Maddie. Do you know why Zack is still alive at all?*

The sparks burned Isaiah.

I popped the shield back around Trevor and me. *It's okay, Trevor. She doesn't need to know.*

She does. He pulled down the shield. My jaw dropped—since when could Trevor control a shield that *I* had put up around us? Trevor sent Ann the mental play-by-play of the seconds in which I distracted and then fried Isaiah before he could finish delivering the killing blast to Zack's brain.

Ugh. I didn't want to re-live it. I didn't want Ann's shock rolling through my mind. I was so tired of death. I'd killed six people now. *Maybe after the tenth I'd get a free pizza.* I had a heck of a body count for someone who was still too young to even buy beer.

I closed my eyes. I didn't feel guilty about Isaiah's death. He'd harmed so many people, and he'd been about to kill Zack. I think the military or the police had a term for something like that—a "clean kill."

I don't really feel clean, though.

Ann churned with confusion. She didn't know how to respond

to the images Trevor had sent her. She'd been thinking some pretty cold things at me, but I knew how she felt—both from experience and from her overflowing thoughts. And it wasn't as though I was the poster child for anger management, after all. When Zack woke up, she'd feel better and she'd probably apologize.

If he woke up.

The thought chilled my gut. We still didn't know what was causing this coma-state in G-positives. Trevor's had occurred when he'd stopped bullets while half-drugged. Mine had happened when I had been attacked by Isaiah—like Zack—and I'd been unconscious for nine days.

Zack might be out for a while.

What if the damage he'd suffered was worse than what I'd experienced? Why did this happen to G-positives?

Now Ann felt even worse—we'd added guilt into the mix. If anything, her emotions were even stronger now, making it even harder for her to concentrate on shielding.

So much for sleeping.

At this moment, I just wanted to be somewhere peaceful and quiet with Trevor, possibly sitting lakeside and feeding each other grapes, or lying on a beach in Aruba. Maybe we needed to take a vacation.

Trevor gave me a tender smile as he pulled a shield around us. *A vacation sounds great. Something like this?* He pictured us under the grass umbrella in our dream-spot, floating grapes to one another. It didn't block out the thoughts coming from Ann, but it helped. I closed my eyes and snuggled closer to Trevor.

Yeah, that seems perfect. Two sets of arms tightened around me. In Trevor's double-embrace, I felt so safe, like everything would work out in the end. Coleman and the other charms would get the videos suppressed. Zack would wake up. We'd find the person who'd been leaking intel to Isaiah. Everything would go back to normal—normal by Ganzfield standards, at least.

With Isaiah gone, all the new arrivals could return home. Trevor and I could go to college next fall. Maybe we'd even stay at that creepy house over in Hanover and go to Dartmouth.

Freedom. Choices. Home.

Real beds—no sleeping bags. A real shower, not that pathetic little trickly one in the trailer we'd been using for the past few weeks. I drifted to sleep in the anticipation of simple pleasures.

"You weren't kidding about how strong he was." Zack rubbed his forehead with a shaky hand.

I laughed. "Are you actually here, or is this a dream?" The fact that I was speaking out loud was a pretty big tip-off, though. We sat in Williamson's office at Ganzfield. I was behind his desk—in Williamson's chair—a place I *never* sat when Williamson himself was on the property.

Zack shrugged. It was irrelevant to him. "So, what's wrong with my brain?"

I shrugged back. "We don't know. You seem okay now, though."

"Yeah, but you're able to talk here."

"Fair point."

"Remember how you blasted my speech in your backyard?"

"I try not to." It burned in my memory with brightly-colored shame.

"Did the speech-place you fried feel the way my mind feels now?"

I frowned. "Your mind doesn't feel like anything now."

His eyebrows shot up. "Like I'm dead?"

"You're not dead."

"So I've got to have some brain activity, right?"

I thought about it. "Yeah, but not consciousness. I can only hear conscious minds. Ann can feel your mind right now, but it's not responding to anything."

"So, where is my consciousness?"

"It's not a 'thing' that comes and goes from your head. It's an activity level. Certain areas of the brain generate energy, and I sense it."

"So, is something blocking or overloading those areas in my brain right now? Is that why I'm out?"

"It would have to be a part of the brain that was connected to both conscious brain activity *and* reacted to dodecamine. Oh. OH!"

I snapped my head up as I popped awake from the dream. Cool air hit the dampness on my face from where my forehead had rested against Trevor's neck.

Striatum! I thought, feeling my energy return with the thought, waking me like a jolt of caffeine.

Sounds like the name of an indie band. Dormant feelings of jealousy stirred at the edges of Trevor's mind. He didn't like that I was dreaming about Zack.

My lips twitched at that. *Please! When I dream about Zack, we discuss neurology. When I dream about you—* I flashed a rather steamy image to him, one that involved satin sheets and far less clothing.

Trevor pinked up and closed his eyes with sigh. *Good answer. That wasn't the real Zack, right? Ann was in our dream once.*

I frowned and focused back to feel Zack's mind. *No, he's still out...I think.* I tilted my head over the edge of the seat to double-check. After all, with his shielding ability, Zack could've been wide-awake and considering charm-plans for world domination or something and I wouldn't have been able to tell.

The dream remained clear in my memory. Maybe it was my subconscious mind figuring things out. Maybe it was a little push from a Higher Power. Heck, maybe it was Zack—unconscious and communicating through a strange new channel now open to him. The basal ganglion was the part of the brain affected by dodecamine. It was the "seat" of our special abilities, the way that speech was localized in Broca's area. A part of the basal ganglion—the striatum—played a role in conscious thought, even in G-negatives. I seemed to remember that it was strongly affected by intense stimuli, too.

Ah, neurology. Maybe all those hours that I'd spent reading Williamson's books hadn't been wasted.

Perhaps the problem was in the striatum. Something in that structure might be keeping Zack from regaining consciousness. Could it be some kind of seizure? Wouldn't the healers feel it?

Hannah's thoughts came to me from the back row; she wasn't asleep. Instead, she was going over and over what she'd done with Zack, trying to figure out what she was missing.

Hannah? I startled her. Some people never seemed to get used to me being in their heads.

After a recovering pause, Hannah framed a thought back to me. *Yes?*

Did you notice anything out of order with Zack's basal ganglia? Maybe in the striatum?

Ann's attention pricked up at the mention of Zack's name.

Hannah frowned in concentration, her thoughts methodically running through the assessments and healing she'd done with Zack. *I didn't feel anything wrong in the striatum.*

Can you check again?

"Why?" Her defensive hackles rose at the thought she might've missed something.

Would you believe I had a weird dream?

Grey skepticism filled her. *I guess there's no harm in checking.* She climbed awkwardly around to the middle seat. Momentary lights from a passing car illuminated her and she turned her face away from the glare.

Ann watched with guarded desperation as Hannah placed her hands on either side of Zack's head. She said a quick prayer before sliding deep into Zack's brain, locating the part of the basal ganglia known as the striatum.

I frowned. *It's too big.* I shielded my immature, size-doesn't-matter comments before Ann could catch a whiff of them and get mad at me again.

"That's normal in enhanced G-positives. It's one of the effects of dodecamine." Hannah's voice was quiet, so as not to wake the sleeping people around us. She suddenly frowned and focused more intensely. *That's strange.*

"What's strange?" Ann asked before I could even get the thought out.

"It feels...I don't know. Wrong. Like there's something there...I can't really get..."

I tried to make mental contact with Zack, like I had when I'd gotten through his shield. I couldn't feel anything, even when I attempted to use Hannah's ability to guide me in. *Pathetic.* Why was I the only minder who couldn't sense unconscious minds? Well, my mom couldn't either, but she didn't really count. *Ann?*

What? She still wasn't sure how she felt toward me.

Can you focus in on the striatum?

Huh?

Like this. I showed her the memory of focusing in when I

zapped a charm's Broca's area.

I don't know much about neurology. Apparently, Williamson had reserved his special course of study for the brain-frying girl.

Gee, I felt so special.

Okay, but can you follow in on Hannah's focus?

What are you trying to do? Trevor frowned.

Wake Zack up.

Won't he wake up again on his own?

I looked at Trevor. *I don't know. Maybe. He might be wired differently from you and me, or the damage might be more severe. But if you could've had me awake for those nine days—*

A rush of sympathetic understanding washed through our shared connection as he glanced at Ann. *Try it. Those were the worst days of my life.*

Ann looked lost. *Just follow in to where Hannah's looking,* I told her. *You ended up in one of our dreams. I think you might be able to do this, too.*

I looked at Hannah. *Keep visualizing the striatum. We're going to try something.*

I felt Ann's mind shift as she focused in. She seemed to flow into the parts of Zack's mind, feeling tentatively through different sections. I'd never felt an unconscious mind before—it was like a dark cavern in which strange shadows flitted along the walls, only to vanish when I turned to look at them. There was no emotional texture, no sense of person-hood.

Weird.

Ann closed her eyes, concentrating more fully. The worst of her anxiety seemed to fall away as she felt the energy of Zack's mind with her own.

There!

I sensed her connect to the striatum. I zoomed in more closely with her, feeling the exact place that seemed wrong. An electric, twitchy energy, like the killing energy that'd pulsed through me—and had pulsed through Isaiah—was contained within the structure of the striatum.

Hannah vaguely sensed that something wasn't "normal," but she had no idea what it was or how to fix it. Healers could call up the body's own healing mechanisms, but this coma-like response to ability overload wasn't normal. Did that make it something that the body didn't know how to repair?

I frowned. *If I can pulse energy into someone's mind, can it be drawn out the same way?*

In response to that thought, Ann gave a sudden, mental "push" to the overloaded place we could sense in Zack's brain.

And the world went purple-white with pain.

CHAPTER 14

I gripped my head and screamed but no sound came out.

Trevor's arms tightened around me as the pain shot through his mind, as well. The van lurched as it bounced off the guard-rail and back across the two lanes of the highway. It scraped against the side of the overpass bridge and tipped sickeningly as we ran off the road. The seatbelt brutalized my side as Trevor fell against me. One of his invisible arms held me—he'd flung the other across Drew and Ellen, soccer-mom style. An agonizing crack in my chest competed with the molten-lava that poured through my head.

The van finally stopped in a ditch close to the tree line. The engine cut off.

What the hell was THAT?

—is Claire okay?

—ARE WE BEING ATTACKED?

What happened? Did—

—an accident?

—something's on fire!

—my head hurts.

The pain still bounced around within my skull, and Trevor and I weren't the only ones feeling it. Whatever'd happened, it'd hit all of us.

Jonah focused on killing the three blazes the sparks had started in the upholstery during the chaos. Unexpected bursts of mental energy? Running the van off the road? Sudden fires this close to a gas tank? Hell, we were lucky we weren't all *dead*.

"Maddie? Are you okay?" Trevor's voice came to me as though from far away, even though he was speaking into my ear.

I might've whimpered, but I really couldn't hear it over the sound of my brain exploding—or whatever it was doing. Each heartbeat made something pound against the inside of my skull, and pain in my side stabbed me with each breath.

"Maddie? What's wrong? Where are you hurt?" Trevor's mind focused into mine, so he answered his own question.

Ann and Hannah had tumbled off the seat behind us. Zack had landed on top of them. The two of them worked to disentangle themselves when Zack suddenly screamed. Blind terror thrashed through him. Oh, God. Had we injured him somehow? After a few seconds, Zack went still.

"I'm not dead?" He sounded surprised.

ZACK! Ann's mental voice sledgehammered into my already overloaded mind as relief erupted from her. *OH, ZACK!*

I cringed, noticing Trevor doing the same.

Everyone else seemed to react, too. *Huh?* Something was off about that.

"Hey, keep it down, minder. Some of us were trying to sleep." Drew took stock of the situation. *No witnesses—good.* Traffic on Route 84 after midnight in this part of Connecticut was almost non-existent.

Harrison shook his head like a wet dog, trying to clear the pain out. He'd slid off of his seat in the back row as the van had jolted off the road.

Ann's emotions for Zack firehosed into all of us. If I hadn't already had pain-tears running down my face, I would've started crying from the waves of joy and love—emotional concentrate, minder-to-minder, caustically strong.

"Hannah, Maddie's injured." Trevor's concern wrapped dusky-rose energy around me.

Tears of joyful relief ran down Hannah's face, but they weren't from her own emotions. Ann was projecting, and not just to me—to everyone. Big time. We all heard her every thought and felt her every emotion.

What the *hell* had happened when she'd released the energy in Zack's head? It was like a mental explosion had hit us all.

Trevor unbuckled the seatbelt from around us, trying not to move physically as he did. I winced as my obviously-broken rib stabbed me again. Someone rolled open the side door, letting the cool air into the vehicle.

Hannah gently pulled up the hem of my shirt and placed her hands on either side of my ribcage. "Maddie, hold still."

Yeah, like I was planning on moving anytime soon. I gritted my teeth and moaned as she pressed the shard-ends of my broken rib together. The pins and needles of her healing poured through me and, finally, the pain melted away. I drew a cautious breath, and then exhaled with relief. *Thanks, Hannah.*

She acknowledged that with a small smile and nod as she moved on to mend Ellen's broken fingers.

"Um, Ann?" Trevor wrapped long fingers around my shoulder. "You know you're projecting, right?"

Ann's horrified realization hit us all. *I'm—? Oh, my God. I can't stop!* Her most private thoughts were on display. She jumped from the van and ran into the night.

"What's going on?" asked Zack.

"The short version? Ann just pulled you out of a coma," said Trevor. "And whatever was keeping you under just blasted through her and into everyone's mind. Now Ann's projecting her thoughts to the rest of us and can't bring up a shield to stop."

"*That's* what that was?" asked Drew. "It felt like something exploded in my head. That *sucked*."

I humphed. *Welcome to my world.*

Drew grinned back at me.

"Hey, when you minders want to do that again, why don't you *not* do it in a moving car, okay?" Dave couldn't stop shaking. "Especially one that *I'm* driving." *Oh, God, if Claire and I hadn't had seatbelts on, we would've gone through the windshield.*

Zack made a move for the van door. Hannah put a hand on his arm. "I need to assess you before you go anywhere."

Zack narrowed his eyes and cleared his throat.

Wait! Don't charm Hannah. I'll go talk to Ann. Having me hear her thoughts is no big deal. Get checked out first then come find us.

Harrison walked around the vehicle, examining the damage. "I'll go back and see if I can find our fender."

"We lost a fender?" Drew sounded almost impressed.

"Yeah, and scraped and dented both sides. The van's a mess. I hope it'll still run." Harrison and Drew had worked on cars with their dad before he'd died. I moved past them into the darkness as they went to take a look under the hood.

"Even if the engine's still running, how're we gonna get the van out of this ditch?"

Drew humphed. "Hey, Trev. We've got a job for ya."

The chirping of thousands of crickets grew louder as I stepped away from the others. The three-quarters moon cast a pale light onto the highway, but left the shoulder in the shadow of the trees. A car whished by, the sound dopplering lower as it receded.

I picked up Ann's sobbing distress and stepped a few paces closer to her.

Hey.

What do you want, Maddie?

Can we talk for a minute?

Talk? I can't shut up! I'm projecting everything! I can hear my thoughts coming back to me from everyone else!

Ann, you'll be able to shield when you calm down.

How do you know? How do you know I still can?

I drew a heavy breath. *Well, you just blasted everyone. That's what I do. If I can shield, you can.* I had no idea if the logic of this assumption would hold up, but it might be enough to end her freak-out.

Somehow, Ann had pulled the energy from Zack's brain—energy that'd felt like the blasts that Isaiah and I did—and she'd funneled it through to the rest of us. Had the number of people somehow diluted the effects? Could it've killed Ann if she'd tried to reach Zack like that when she was all alone?

I felt the edge of her hysteria seeping away as my words sank in. *Ann, I throw nightmares. I know what this is like. Once you calm down, you'll be able to shield again.*

Is Zack okay?

Zack's fine. Hannah's checking him over now. He's worried about you.

I don't want him to hear all of the stuff running through my head. I—I have mental diarrhea right now!

I gave a laugh at that. *Okay. They're trying to find the pieces of the van that fell off, so you've got a little time.*

Pieces of the van fell off? Guilt pinged from her.

Yeah. And we had a few broken bones and some bruises, but Hannah's fixed them already.

Is everyone all right?

Everyone's fine. Now we just have to get you shielding and we'll be all set.

"Where's Ann?" Zack's voice came out of the dark behind me.

Gah! Don't sneak up on me like that! I'd jumped like I'd been pulled up on a wire.

Behind him, the headlights silhouetted the people reattaching the front fender. Trevor held the piece in place while Drew and Jonah focused mental blowtorches and welded the metal back onto the vehicle.

Zack, hold on a minute. Ann's projecting private thoughts. She doesn't want anyone to hear.

"I need to talk to her."

Zack's with you? Ann couldn't hear him when he was shielding, either.

Yeah. He wants to talk to you.

I don't want him to see me like this! I'm a mess!

She doesn't want— I began.

"I heard her." He gave me a calculating look. "Maddie, I *need* to see her."

I crossed my arms and scowled. *Not if she doesn't want you to.*

"Don't make me charm you."

Don't make me blast you, Zack. You just got out of a minder-induced coma. Another zap probably wouldn't be good for you right now.

We squared off in the moonlight, each wondering if the other really meant the threat.

Zack dropped his shield. *I think I'm in love with her. I...I need to be with her.* His sincerity made his thoughts like glass—clear, sharp, and fragile.

I took a step back. *Ann, are you hearing this?*

Zack? You…you think you're in love with me?

Zack inhaled sharply as he felt the tenderness in her mental touch. His mind seemed to light up.

My lips twitched. *Okay, guess I don't need to be here anymore.*

Zack and I stepped around each other. I made my way back to the van.

How's Ann? Trevor asked as my arms wrapped around his waist.

Zack's talking to her. She's pretty upset.

Are you all right?

Tired. I grimaced. *This has been one long, weird day. How are you holding up?*

Terribly. I broke my word.

What? When?

I promised to tell you something—when it was all over and we were safe.

I smiled, remembering. *The night's not over yet.*

Maddie?

Um-hmm?

I love you. I love you with every fiber of my soul.

My response flashed from words into a silver glow as Trevor kissed me.

We'd needed to unload the gear to get the van up the steep grade, even with Trevor's ability doing the brunt of the pushing. Ann and Zack returned—shielding and smiling—as we finished re-loading at the side of the road.

Drew drove the next shift. He and Harrison sat up front and talked about working on cars in hushed tones. Trevor leaned slack-jawed against the side of the van and slept deeply. I kept his hand in mine and listened for the start of a dream.

With Zack no longer out cold and taking up a whole bench, the van felt less crowded. *Hey, Zack?* I twisted on the seat, careful to keep contact with Trevor's hand. *I've been wondering. What was that thing with the giraffe?*

He gave a quick laugh and kept his voice low. "I needed a trigger word that Trevor wouldn't use in your conversation with Isaiah. I wanted to use something cool, but once I had 'giraffe' in my head, I couldn't think of anything more impressive."

Trigger word? Did you charm them? I remembered the plan he'd proposed months ago for getting the non-shielders into Isaiah's home in Peapack. I leaned forward as the thought hit me. *Wait, were THE SPARKS the moles we felt? That's just...bizarre.*

"I couldn't make them completely invisible and keep them conscious, so I had to command them to believe they were animals. Ann said she couldn't feel human thoughts from them. We were pretty sure Isaiah wouldn't sense there were people there, either. I worried that he might RV them, but I hoped you'd keep his concentration on you."

You charmed people into thinking like moles. I tried to wrap my brain around it. I had to admit—it was outside-the-box thinking. *And the sparks—they were okay with this?*

I filled them all in after you two left. Full disclosure. His thoughts popped into my consciousness like a jack-in-the-box as his shield dropped. I saw how he'd explained it to them—*"mental camouflage."* He'd tested it on a volunteer—Drew—while the others watched. His memories flashed through the dark to me.

"Drew. I'm going to count down from ten. When I finish,

the human part of you will go to sleep until you hear the word 'giraffe.'"

"If I wake up as part of your stage act in Vegas, man, I'm setting your hair on fire."

"You'll be a mole—a rodent happy to be in its burrow. When you hear the word 'giraffe,' you'll wake up, instantly alert and ready to attack Isaiah."

He counted down, and Ann gasped. "You did it! His mind doesn't sound human at all!"

"Giraffe!"

Human awareness flashed back into Drew's eyes.

Not bad, Zack. I had to give him credit. *I gotta admit, I couldn't tell they were anything but moles. The pain slowed us down, though.*

"Pain?" Zack frowned. *What pain?*

"Minders feel the pain of the people around them." Ann's voice was hoarse. She'd had been following along, still shielding strongly. I didn't know what she and Zack had done to get her shielding again, but it was effective. She wasn't talking mentally, though.

And I have no way to block it from Trevor when we're shielding together.

Zack looked from Trevor's sleeping profile to me. "So you two felt the—the *burning* when the sparks attacked Isaiah?" *They felt what it's like to be...burned alive?* Guilt seemed to slap him from the inside. The plan had been his idea, after he'd heard about Isaiah's attack on us at my mom's house.

Yeah, it hurt back then, too.

I was half-tempted to share full-sensation memories of the experience with him, but I restrained myself. I felt hollowed out. At the very least, I needed that vacation.

Something else occurred to me. *When did you get those holes put in?*

When the crew was setting up the building. Williamson arranged it—made the work crew look like they were servicing underground electrical conduits. I just had to stop by at the end and make them forget what they'd actually been doing.

We had no clue. And you scared the HELL out of us when Isaiah looked into the guardhouse and it was empty.

Sorry about that. You weren't kidding about how strong he was. Ambivalence wormed through Zack's thoughts. His plan had worked—but he felt weak for not being able to hold off Isaiah. I could tell that Ann had filled him in on what'd happened after he'd blacked out, including what Trevor had shown her. He pulled something up from deep within—a reluctant, yet genuine emotion. *Maddie?*

Yeah?

Thanks.

I smiled. *No problem.*

An hour later, Trevor began to dream. I pulled him awake quickly, but he still managed to thunk a dent into the van roof above him.

"Oops." Chagrin blossomed within him—both for the damage and the noise that woke everyone else up. "Sorry."

It was just before 3 a.m. and we were still only halfway home. We pulled into a 24-hour gas station in Massachusetts and refueled. Claire took the next driving shift and everyone resettled.

Do you want to get some more sleep? Trevor asked me.

In a little while, maybe. I tried to snuggle against him and he wrapped an arm around my shoulders. It was harder to get close to him now—with the seatbelts and all. Everyone in the van buckled up now—running off the road had turned us into the safety patrol.

I had too much on my mind to sleep, anyway.

"Yeah, we still have a big problem up at Ganzfield," Ann responded to my thoughts.

I nodded, projecting to Trevor and Zack as well. *Someone took those videos for Isaiah.* Ooh, a minder mini-meeting—how... alliterative. *Whoever it was did all that AT GANZFIELD, and we didn't hear their intentions. None of the minders did. I thought it might be Belinda, but—*

"I took care of Belinda. She can't set foot outside that area behind Ann's cabin."

I nodded. *And Jon's pretty sure she's...* I couldn't even think the word "trustworthy" in relation to her.

"Is there someone else who can block minders?" asked Zack.

I felt a pang of guilt for even thinking that he might've betrayed us. *The four of us—and Williamson. I missed your shield when you first arrived at Ganzfield, but Jon didn't. If someone's shielding up there, Jon would probably know it.*

Zack nodded. "Then the person passing the information on doesn't know they're doing it."

I frowned. *How is that possible?*

Zack hesitated. "The stuff charms learn in practicals—it's usually about getting people to think they're acting on their own ideas. It's not like we ever practice trying to fool minders."

I had a few memories of charms trying exactly that. Fortunately, they'd sucked at it.

"So, one of the charms sent someone else—someone whose thoughts were innocent—to take the videos and gather information." Trevor felt twisting nausea at the thought of such manipulation. "The real traitor stayed out of the minders' ranges."

Ann shook her head. "That'd be tough. Seth's range is huge. Maybe someone who didn't come to Ganzfield charmed one of the new arrivals to do it. Could they've sent someone in as a spy without them knowing it?"

But why would they? Why would any charm want Isaiah to have dirt on us? Wouldn't they know that Isaiah wanted them dead, too?

"It just doesn't make any sense." Trevor's words filled with a bleak sense of hurt.

We drifted into separate contemplations. Zack's mind disappeared as he began to doze. Ann kept stifling yawns, but I knew she wasn't planning to sleep. She didn't want to share her dreams any more than she wanted to share her thoughts.

Dawn broke as we made our way off the highway and onto the smaller road that took us into our little corner of New Hampshire. Rosy light flashed across the pearl-grey sky, glinting off of Lake Winnepesaukee as we skirted along the shore. Things grew darker again after leaving the water and entering the endless gauntlet of trees that lined the winding road to North Conway. Trevor drove this last leg and I kept him company, riding shotgun and mentally scanning for danger as we came closer to Ganzfield. Yellow reflective tags stuck up from the median line, flashing hypnotically past. Diamond-shaped signs warned of moose crossing points, but in all of my months in New Hampshire, I had yet to sense the mental presence of a moose.

We pulled in through the front gate of Ganzfield a little after 7 a.m. A shadowy figure flickered in my peripheral vision, moving behind the trees.

So, you actually did it.

Yeah, we did it, Seth. I sent him an image of the sparks burning

Isaiah but his mental wince made me wish that I hadn't. He already had enough nasty stuff haunting his memories. *Sorry.*

Williamson wants to see you right away.

Any clue as to who's been passing info to Isaiah?

Not yet. His frustration flashed orange and tasted like bile. Seth took pride in how much mental data he gathered from the people at Ganzfield. Missing this traitor made him question his value as a minder.

We parked the van in the barn. Ann, Zack, Trevor, and I grabbed our packs and headed to the main building. Everyone else trooped off to get a few more hours of sleep. I mentally checked in as we thudded up the wooden stairs to the third floor. Williamson was waiting for us. The additional chairs in his office made it seem smaller and too crowded. I let out a silent groan—the "silent" part being pretty much useless in present company.

Looks like we gonna be here a while. So much for a quick debriefing and getting some sleep. I should've grabbed some coffee on the way up. Williamson's eyes fixed on mine as I slumped into the chair next to Trevor.

Show me.

I knew what he needed to see. I put as much of the detail into my memories as I could—all the way to the point when Isaiah's remains had flared to ash.

Williamson felt oddly let down. *I thought I'd feel more closure at Isaiah's death.*

I know what you mean. I also felt the same...ambivalence. *Incomplete victory.* We hadn't stopped Isaiah from exposing our secrets. Dangerous people might now know all about us—and we didn't even know who they were. But the recipients were high up in the military, and Isaiah'd thought they'd want to hurt us.

Not good.

I set Isaiah's smart-phone on Williamson's desk. I didn't want to deal with it anymore. Williamson picked it up like he was handling a poisonous snake. He keyed up the email message and read it twice. *We need to figure out our next move.*

That's easy. Find out who's been sending stuff to Isaiah. Someone here's probably been charmed to gather information and videos and they don't even realize they're doing it. We'll need to figure out which charms didn't come to Ganzfield, but had contact with people who did.

Ann? Why are you shielding? Williamson had noticed as soon as we'd arrived.

Ann sighed. "Because if I don't, I'll project my thoughts to everyone in the building."

Williamson's brow furrowed. "What?"

We gave Williamson the recap of the whole getting-Zack-out-of-the-coma thing.

Ann fiddled with a stray strand of hair by her ear. "Sorry about the van."

"Interesting." Williamson didn't care about the van being trashed. "You're all okay?"

Cracked rib, some broken fingers, a bunch of bruises, and killer headaches, but we're good now. Just tired.

"With Isaiah gone, a lot of people are planning to leave today," said Williamson. "But if someone's being charmed to spy here at Ganzfield, we'll need to…um, interview everyone before they go."

Ann and I both groaned.

Ugh! That'll take most of the day. Minder interrogations. I hated "thought-police" duty.

"Seth, Nina, and I will handle the people who want to leave this morning. Why don't you both grab a few hours of sleep now?" Williamson shifted. "Zack, please stay a moment. We need to discuss how you've been using your ability."

Zack frowned. "Is this about Barry Petras?"

The blood drained from Williamson's face. *"Barry Petras found you? What did he do?"*

The four of us glanced at each other. Ann's lip twitched and I put a hand over my mouth. We tried and failed to hold back our laughter. A giddy second wind filled us with quivery energy.

Williamson didn't share our amusement. He locked his gaze on me. *Start from the beginning—and tell me everything.*

I took a deep breath. *Okay, Barry Petras charmed his way past Allexor security and came and threatened us. Did you know he was plotting the murder of a federal witness? Then he told Trevor to hit me in the face, and—*

"Trevor hit you in the face?" Williamson interrupted.

Of course not. Trevor's not vulnerable to charms when we're together. So, Barry Petras then thought up some porn and made some rude comments about us, and Trevor grabbed him with that throat thing he can do to charms, and—

"Throat thing?" Williamson interrupted again. I flashed him an image of Trevor grabbing Barry Petras's larynx with an invisible hand.

Then Zack charmed him, and—

"Barry Petras is immune to charm commands," said Williamson.

"Zack is no ordinary charm." Ann flushed pink as her eyes met Zack's.

Williamson gave Zack a long look. Zack shrugged, as though to say, "Who am I to argue?"

Do you want me to tell the story or not, Jon? I asked.

"What did you tell him to do?"

"Well, first we had to stop him from killing us," said Zack.

"He was planning to have us shot by a sniper at that point."

"Then we took that one step further and got him to stop killing *anyone*," Trevor said.

And I got to thinking about the whole hit-me-in-the-face thing and decided that Barry Petras was going to start...giving back to the community.

Williamson's eyes widened. "You didn't."

We started laughing again.

Yup. He's writing ten-thousand-dollar checks to the regional battered women's shelter every time he even THINKS of hurting someone.

"Or telling someone else to hurt another person," added Trevor.

It's like a compulsion, Jon. He can't help himself.

"But it makes him feel really good inside when he gives something to the community," Zack grinned. "Barry's *much* happier now."

"And Zack made sure he couldn't hurt someone else or try to take off the charm commands," Ann said.

If and when he shakes off that charm command, he's going to come after you. Williamson's glare—a mix of anger and concern— deflated our shared manic bubble.

I frowned back at him. *If that charm command ever wears off, he's going to be out of dodecamine, so he won't be a threat. Honestly, Jon. Why were you supplying that guy?*

Williamson exhaled. "Because he knows where we live and he *is* a threat. He doesn't need dodecamine or charm ability to have people killed."

Our security is much better now. And really, do you think Barry Petras'll start a war with us when he no longer has his ability? Besides, he was a BAD guy! I think it's worth taking a little risk on ourselves to stop people like him from doing terrible things.

Trevor nodded. "Jon, we need to be using these abilities to help people. And part of that is making sure that G-positives don't harm others. Like what Belinda did to me to hurt Maddie—that sort of thing shouldn't be tolerated."

My jaw tightened at the memory. *Where's Belinda now?*

"She's right where I told her to stay." Zack's chin came up. "No way she shook off my charming."

I turned to Williamson. *Jon, think about it. A charm who wanted to hurt us; a charm who could send unwitting agents to gather information and take video clips; a charm who was out of our mental range; a charm from Washington, D.C. with inside information on exactly who in the government and military would be most dangerous to us.*

Williamson frowned as he considered my words. This time he didn't dismiss them.

Does Belinda have an internet connection out where she is?

He nodded.

I'd been filled with fury when Belinda had charmed Trevor. The intensity had been hot and red in my head. I'd wanted to kill her. This current feeling was cold, but just as intense. If Belinda had done this—had given this information to our mortal enemy so he could blackmail or expose us...

I felt the killing energy surge within me. I didn't want to *murder* her, but part of me wanted to *execute* her. Not a big part—I was *so* sick of killing. If I didn't have to use deadly force, I wasn't going to. A soundproofed cell in a basement wouldn't have stopped Isaiah—but it *would* stop Belinda.

Williamson's jaw muscles jumped as he processed my train of thought. He looked at me through narrowed eyes. *You're in control of yourself?*

I nodded. *As long as no one's hurting Trevor.*

"Go to her trailer. All four of you. Check her mind. If she's the one behind the leak, keep her quiet and bring her to Blake House." Williamson's thoughts twisted through his mind. He genuinely liked Belinda, but if she'd put people—*his* people—in danger, he'd be merciless. He didn't want to believe that she would've betrayed us, but he knew Belinda was resourceful... and also could be vindictive. He framed a thought as we trooped out. *Seth, see what you can do about tracing Belinda's internet use and contacts.*

I felt his distant response. *I'm on it.*

I guess Seth had been putting all that time spent alone into developing some skills.

The walk to the far side of the lake took less time than getting a car and driving the long way around on the unpaved access road. We reached Ann's cabin, and then followed the electric and internet lines that led several hundred feet into the woods beyond. The path seemed well worn; Belinda must've had a lot of company over the past few weeks.

Plastic strips of orange hunter's tape marked the edges of the clearing in which Zack had charmed Belinda to stay. The track we'd been following led further into the woods where it joined the access road that ran along this edge of the property to the back gate. It didn't look wide enough for a trailer to've made it through, but a trailer was here, so I guess it was.

I tightened my grip on Trevor's hand, determined to keep him immune to Belinda's ability. I met Ann's eyes and she shook her head—neither of us could feel Belinda's mind inside the trailer. Trevor opened the trailer door while we were still a dozen feet away. A quick look inside confirmed what we already knew—Belinda was gone.

Zack's dismay flared red and orange, like a bonfire. "I thought

I had it!" He kept muttering to himself—going over the charm commands he'd given her. Suddenly he let out a very loud version of a very bad word. Birds startled into flight from nearby trees.

"I told her not to set foot anywhere at Ganzfield outside the circle. NOT TO SET FOOT." He clenched his fists to his temples in uncharacteristic frustration. "Arrrgh! She could've worked around that. Crawled...or gotten someone to carry her."

"Or drive her." Trevor looked at the tire tracks in the soft ground.

I pulled out my cell phone. No bars. *We need to get the RVs on this. We need to find her.*

The tracks continued on the dirt access road and led toward the back gate. Katie Underwood and Jim McFee were ready to end their watch.

"Hey! When did you get back?"

"Did anyone come through here last night?" Trevor asked them.

Jim shook his head. "No. No one. Quiet shift. Nothing unusual."

Zack frowned. "Stop doing what Belinda told you to." Charm resonance permeated each word.

"Did anyone come through here last night?" Trevor asked again.

"Yeah. Grant was with the hot blonde with the fancy red car." Jim frowned. *That's weird. I thought I just said I hadn't seen anyone.* "They came through just after we started our shift."

I hissed out a sigh through my teeth. Dammit. She had a big head start.

Zack repeated his loud profanity.

"We need to use the phone." Trevor called Williamson. "Belinda's gone, Jon, and she took Grant McFee with her. She's got a night's lead on us. We'll need the RVs to locate her. We're coming back there now."

Williamson scowled as he met us at the front door of the main building. "I asked Rick to find Belinda. He said she was in her trailer on the far side of the lake. But you were just there. And…it also looks like the infirmary's been cleaned out of dodecamine."

Urgh. At least Hannah had brought some back with us from Allexor. *Did Rick have any "overly affectionate" memories of Belinda, by any chance?*

He nodded. *You think she charmed him?*

She charmed the watch at the back gate last night to forget that they'd seen her when she and Grant McFee drove out in her car. But Jon, she left BEFORE the thing with Isaiah went down last night. I think she's running. I think she knew when to run.

Williamson's mind filled with a phrase he'd never utter aloud.

We found Rick in the front room across from the library, packing up the search materials that he and the other RVs had used for tracking Isaiah. By now, we knew the drill.

"Rick," said Zack. "Stop doing what Belinda told you to do."

"Who?"

My jaw dropped. Rick wasn't joking. His mind was completely blank of any thoughts or images of Belinda.

"How did she do *that*?" Ann met my eyes.

Oh, crap. What was that—a mental booby trap? Had Belinda somehow given a charm command that would clear Rick's mind of any concept of her if another charm tried to undo her work?

Yikes. If I wasn't so ready to lock the woman away in a

makeshift basement dungeon forever, I might've admired her skills.

"Rick," said Trevor. "Do you know Grant McFee?"

"Sure."

"Where is he?"

Rick's mind seemed to expand as that cool, 3-D model of the earth played across his thoughts like a video game world. He frowned and tried to re-focus. There was no spark of energy marking Grant McFee in his mind.

My gut twisted. Did that mean there was no Grant McFee anymore? We needed an RV who hadn't been influenced by Belinda.

Claire.

We found her with Dave in one of the cinderblock buildings down with the sparks.

"Claire, where's Grant?" Trevor's voice didn't convey his anxiety. "We need to find him immediately."

The image formed in her mind. I gasped and felt my stomach lurch. Grant's lifeless body—blackened and burned—lay on the shoulder of an isolated back road. Belinda must've needed him to get her out of Ganzfield. Once they were clear of the gates, had she tested her ability to "set foot" outside, and then decided she no longer needed Grant?

Oh, God. Had she actually charmed him into—*burning himself alive?*

That's what it looked like. I covered my mouth with my hand.

Tears ran down Claire's face. Dave put his arm around her. Her vision collapsed and she turned into his shoulder and sobbed.

Dammit! What was the frikkin' point? I rubbed my face with both hands. We'd removed one enemy from the picture, but now we had Belinda trying to bring us down, and we had no reliable way to track her. Scary military types might descend on us with a battalion or two at any time and possibly put us in camps and experiment on us or God knows what else. And there was always the chance that Barry-the-mobster would snap out of it and come after us again.

The walk back up to the main building seemed to take decades. I flashed enough images to Williamson to let him know where to send people to find Grant's body. Trevor silently picked up our gear from where we'd dropped it on the porch and we headed to the church.

At some point later today, I'd seek out my mom. I'd see how Rachel was doing. I might even hunt down a sociopathic, bottle-blonde charm and lock her in a soundproof basement dungeon. But right now, I was going to sleep. I dragged myself up the ladder to my loft and threw myself on my bed. And when I'd finished all of that, perhaps Trevor and I would feed each other grapes on the rock down by the lake.

Why wait? Trevor levered up on his elbows and met my eyes with a sweet, tired smile. *Meet you lakeside in our first dream.*

I sent him a wave of adoration. *You bring the lake. I'll bring the grapes.*

THE END OF BOOK THREE

Keep reading for a sneak preview of:

ACCUSED

THE FOURTH GANZFIELD NOVEL BY

KATE

KAYNAK

Coming in August 2011 from Spencer Hill Press

CHAPTER 1

"We're going to Aruba."

Trevor leaned one elbow on the check-in counter as he handed the airline employee our passports. His eyes met mine, sharing a secret meaning behind the words. I grinned back, holding my thoughts behind a mental shield. Boston's Logan airport was crowded and hundreds of minds stomped across mine. I needed to keep from sharing them with Trevor, who'd pick them up through our special connection, so at least one of us would be able to concentrate.

— *passports here someplace —*

— *so stupid we have to take off our shoes—*

— *remember when the blood-sucking airlines didn't charge us to check a bag—*

— *already want to go home. This trip is going to—*

—*forgets to feed the fish while I'm gone, they're all gonna die and the apartment will smell like—*

—*can't pack lightly to save her life. What's in this bag? Rocks? Is she bringing designer rocks to—*

—put the carry-on in front of me and wear the backpack, maybe they won't notice the extra—

In about eight hours, Trevor and I would be in Aruba together. The two of us were renting a house for a week—with its own private beach. Giddy little amber sparkles passed through me at the thought. This trip took the phrase "dream come true" to a whole new level.

The desk agent handed back our passports, gave us boarding passes, and directed us to the security line. Trevor took me by the hand and led the way through the crowds. He knew how hard it was for me to focus with this many people's thoughts pressing down on me. Sometimes being telepathic sucked.

It didn't help that I was also functionally mute, thanks to that fight with Isaiah last spring. At least I could project my thoughts to others so I could still communicate. We tried to keep all that G-positive mental ability stuff low profile, though, so the whole getting-part-of-my-brain-burned-away thing kinda limited my social life these days.

We'd only been in the security line for a few seconds when I felt a cool prick of mental recognition. *Madeline Elizabeth Dunn.* Goosebumps prickled along my arms. Everyone who knew me called me Maddie. I didn't recognize the mind.

I twisted to look behind me, trying to make the move look casual. At the second flash of recognition, icy yellow tendrils of fear shot through me.

Hunted.

Maddie, what's wrong? Trevor wrapped a protective invisible arm around me. I dropped my mental shield, wincing with him as my too-loud thoughts suddenly body-slammed his.

Someone's targeting me. At least two of them.

Trevor's grip tightened on my hand and his face hardened as

he glanced around us. Four more people with my face in their thoughts approached, joining the first two.

They're cops.

The uniformed transit police approached us cautiously. "Madeline Elizabeth Dunn?" One of the officers asked. Ah, hell. The repeated use of my middle name couldn't mean anything good.

What do they want? Trevor's thoughts flashed to us making a break for it. Trevor could stop bullets with his telekinetic ability. He could also use it to move really fast.

I think...they're going to arrest me. I tightened my grip on his hand. There were too many witnesses here, too many security cameras for him to try anything.

Maybe taking a vacation right now hadn't been such a good idea.

* * *

Acknowledgements

The Ganzfield series exists because a bunch of people enabled my writing addiction. I'd like to single out several for interventions: My incredible editor, Deborah Britt-Hay, and everyone at Spencer Hill Press. Jack Noon, who hasn't seen this manuscript as of this writing, but I suspect he'll find at least half-a-dozen typos before we go to press—he always does. Cassandra Hogle, Tyler Hussey, Rosa Burtt, and Kathy Mihachik, for making sure my kids didn't play in traffic or die of linoleum-borne illnesses while I was writing. Olin, who successfully lobbied for a brief stay-of-execution for a favorite character (now you're wondering who was going to be killed off, aren't you?). Early readers Laura Jennings (a.k.a., Mom), Mitch and Alison Ross, Heather Tessier and "Aunt Nancy" Schoeller. A special mention to Rich Storrs and Jessica Porteous, who not only caught typos like pros but also filled their copy of the manuscript with comments that cracked me up. Nick Kessler, whose previous home outside D.C. inspired the sparks' "stadium seating." Taner, Aliya, and Logan, who still make me smile every time they shout, "Mommy's book!" when they see one of the Ganzfield novels. Finally, Osman, who's not only the partial inspiration for Trevor, he also made it possible for me to find enough time to write and bring all of Ganzfield to life. Çok teşekkür ederim, canım.

About Kate Kaynak

I was born and raised in New Jersey, but I managed to escape. My degree from Yale says I was a psych major, but I had *way* too much fun to have paid much attention in class.

After serving a five-year sentence in graduate school, I started teaching psychology around the world for the University of Maryland's Overseas Program.

While in Izmir, Turkey, I started up a conversation with a handsome stranger in an airport. I ended up marrying him. We now live in New Hampshire with our three preschool and kindergarten-aged kids, where I enjoy reading, writing, and fighting crime with my amazing superpowers.

Come find out more about *Minder, Adversary, Legacy,* and the other books of the *Ganzfield* series at **www.Ganzfield.com**.